# Beyond Broken Colors

Dev Hahn

FOX ARROW PUBLISHING

eBook Edition ISBN-13: 979-8-9896823-2-4

Paperback ISBN-13: 979-8-9896823-3-1

Cover design by Dee Garcia, Black Widow Designs.

Editing services by Dee Houpt of Dee's Notes.
https://www.deesnoteseditingservices.com/

# Also By Dev Hahn

**<u>Standalones</u>**
Beyond Broken Colors


**<u>Bellwood Lady Baller Series</u>**
Coming Out on the Sidelines
Catching Feelings in the End Zone, *Coming November 2024*

To every person who has survived a traumatic
experience caused by the hands of another
person.

# Author's Note

B eyond *Broken Colors* is a complete standalone that takes place about three weeks after the ending of *Coming Out on the Sidelines*. You do not have to read my previous book, but it will help you understand certain events and side characters in this book.

Some scenes in this book may be upsetting; therefore reader discretion is advised. Please check copyright page for content warnings.

Due to it's sexual content, bad language, triggers, domestic violence/sexual assault scenes, this book is suitable for readers age 16+.

———*ele*———

Chapter 12 was such a difficult scene to write, taking me almost a week to get through, but I needed to write it. It was necessary for me to show that we can consent but we also have the power to change our minds. That decision should be respected and if the other person doesn't listen to us, then we become a victim of sexual assault. We all have the basic idea of what rape is, but rape can look different to each victim and in many cases, they never seek justice because in most cases, the victim is casted as the one *in the wrong*. Not the assailant.

So, in case anyone needed a reminder ...

-**<u>NO</u>** is a complete sentence.
-You are allowed to change your mind.
-What you wear does not mean you're "asking for it."
-If you say no, even just once, and they don't stop? It's rape.
-If you don't think anyone will believe you, just know there is *always* someone who will, including me.

#MeToo

# Contents


Chapter 1 — Jenna ... 1

Chapter 2 — Nathan ... 13

Chapter 3 — Jenna ... 23

Chapter 4 — Nathan ... 31

Chapter 5 — Jenna ... 41

Chapter 6 — Jenna ... 53

Chapter 7 — Nathan ... 69

Chapter 8          81
    Nathan

Chapter 9          89
    Jenna

Chapter 10          101
    Nathan

Chapter 11          117
    Jenna

Chapter 12          129
    Jenna

Chapter 13          141
    Nathan

Chapter 14          151
    Jenna

Chapter 15          163
    Nathan

Chapter 16          177
    Jenna

Chapter 17          191
    Nathan

Chapter 18          205
    Jenna
    Nathan

Chapter 19          217
    Nathan

Chapter 20                                     231
  Jenna

Chapter 21                                     245
  Jenna

Chapter 22                                     255
  Jenna

Chapter 23                                     263
  Nathan

Chapter 24                                     271
  Jenna
  Nathan

Chapter 25                                     279
  Jenna

Chapter 26                                     289
  Jenna

Chapter 27                                     299
  Nathan

Chapter 28                                     305
  Jenna

Epilogue                                       313
Seven Months Later
  Nathan

Acknowledgements                               319

About the Author                               323

Connect With Me                                325

# Chapter 1

## Jenna

"**A**re you sure you guys don't want to tag along? It would be a lot of fuunnn," I singsong. Sadie chills on my bed as I stand in front of my full-length mirror looking over my Catwoman costume to make sure everything is perfect.

"No thanks. Chad's hosting this Halloween party, so where there is Chad, there's also Nathan and Brady. The last thing we want is to be in the same breathing space as them," Sadie says. "Besides, I'd much rather be snuggled up next to my girlfriend, watching a movie and sucking her face off."

"Mm-hm, I bet that isn't the only thing you'll be sucking off." I give her a knowing look, teasing her, and she throws one of my pillows at me. "Hey! Don't mess up my makeup. I need to look impeccable for Felix." I flip my hair dramatically over my shoulder.

"Jen, you look incredible. He's going to *die* when he sees you!" my bestie says.

I take another good look at my reflection. The black leather suit hugs my body like a glove, showcasing my curves just right. My smokey eyeshadow is on point and my lips are the perfect shade of crimson red. Sadie helped me add the extensions, giving my sleek black ponytail a little extra length.

"He better not! Because I need his dick to make this kitty purr tonight."

"Okay. I'm out! That was way more information than I needed to hear," she says as she stands from my bed and crosses the room. She wraps her arms around me and gives me a hug. "Have fun, but also, please be safe. Text me when you get there and when you leave."

"Okay, *mom*." I roll my eyes. Then a honk comes from outside. "There's Felix. You and Pace have fun, and I will see you later tonight! Love you!" We do a little air kiss before I grab my phone and secure it into the cute black leather crossbody bag that complements my costume. I double-check I have everything before I head downstairs to meet Felix.

"Love you too, bestie!" Sadie yells as she heads for her room across the hall to get ready for her date. I dart down the stairs and out to the driveway to find my hunky boyfriend decked out as a Roman gladiator standing by his blue Dodge Ram. Damn if he doesn't look good showcasing those thick thighs and Herculean arms.

"Damn, babe. You look smoking hot," Felix says as his blue-hazel eyes roam my body from head to toe. "I think we should just skip the party and head to my place instead. We would have way more fun there."

"As fun as that would be, I promised a few friends we would be making an appearance, and I keep to my word. A few drinks, some dancing, then we can leave and you can do whatever it is you please to me." I lean up on the tip of my black stiletto boots to give him a kiss. His luscious lips pull mine in, but I cut him off. "Mm, babe. Easy there. I need my makeup to look good when we show up." Felix rolls his eyes before releasing his hands from my waist and opening the passenger door for me.

We make our way across town to the bigger homes that sit on the outskirts of Bellwood. It's on the countryside, with wider lawns and longer driveways, rather than the suburban part where Sadie and I live. We spot the massive rows of cars lining the driveway when we get closer to the address attached to the text invitation sent out earlier this week. Some cars are parked on the lawn and others along the main road.

"God, did he invite all of Bellwood?" I ask as I take in all the people heading toward the party. "No way this is just kids from school."

"It's a party, babe. Where there is a party, there is alcohol and a good time, and teens flock to a good time," Felix says. He manages to find a place to park his truck closer to the house. Thank God because my feet are already hurting. I probably should have rethought my costume choice and footwear.

The music blares, causing the windows to vibrate to the beat. People are everywhere, dressed in various costumes, dancing or talking among each other.

I follow Felix through the house, holding tightly onto his hand as he makes a path through the throng of people toward the kitchen for drinks. As the linebacker for Greystone Academy, his massive size helps to deter people.

Felix and I met at a bonfire party a few weeks back. The moment my eyes latched onto him, I knew I needed to introduce myself. A beast of a man with muscles exposed and an ass I could take a bite out of. Mm! After I introduced myself, we exchanged numbers and started texting each other daily. He kept asking me to go on a date with him, but I would politely decline. I didn't want the attachment of a boyfriend, especially in my last year of high school. I offered a friends-with-benefits option, but he was dead set on wanting me to be his girl more than anything. When Payson broke up with Sadie, we figured out Sadie's ex-boyfriend, Brady, and Lydia, the skank he cheated on Sadie with, were the ones behind it. Neither of them wanted Payson to play the homecoming game since it was taking away from Brady's playing time, especially when it was discovered a college scout would be in attendance. Despite how heartbroken she was, Sadie knew Payson deserved to be seen by those scouts. That's when an idea came to me.

With our homecoming game being against Greystone, I knew Felix would be the perfect person to help ensure Payson got her opportunity. Since Felix is a defensive player, I told him which play call to listen for from Brady and then our number eighty-two would subtly create an opening for Felix to run through to get to Brady. I promised him if he could take out Brady and injure him enough he wouldn't be able to play for the rest of the game, I would go on a date with him. And my man came through! Didn't expect him to ruin the rest of Brady's season, but the asshole deserved it, in my opinion. Felix and I have been dating ever since, and I couldn't be happier. I think I'm slowly falling in love with him. Granted, that wasn't in my plans.

When we finally make it to the kitchen, Felix heads toward the keg sitting on a marble-top island. Stacks of red Solo cups are nearby, along with bottles upon bottles of liquor spread about. Felix offers me a Solo cup, but I decline.

"I just want a bottle of water."

"Suit yourself." He shrugs, then fills a cup with beer and chugs it while I look in the fridge for water. I'm disappointed to find none. I tap Felix's shoulder so he can lean down. The man is a whole foot taller to my five-foot-four-inch self.

"I'm going to check the garage for some water. I'll be back." Felix nods, then I squeeze through the sea of bodies to find the garage door.

Opening the door, I flick on the light, spotting the fridge along a wall and hoping like hell there is bottled water inside.

"Bingo," I whisper as I snatch two bottles from the garage fridge. I want to make sure Felix stays hydrated since he's drinking, especially for what I have planned later. As I turn around, I nearly collide with someone. "I'm so sorry. I didn't hear anyone come in after me."

"Are you with Felix Martin?" the girl dressed up like a fairy asks. There is a big purple butterfly painted on her face. I wonder if she did it herself? It's symmetrical and the detailing is breathtaking.

"Come again?" I ask. The artist in me got a little lost in her face paint.

"Are you dating Felix Martin? The big guy dressed like a gladiator?"

"Um ... yeah. Who's asking—"

"You need to be careful with him. You seem like too nice of a girl to be caught up with that guy."

"What is that supposed to mean?" I scoff. I don't know who she is or what business she has asking about Felix, but it's really none of her concern. Is she one of those clingy ex-girlfriends?

"Take it from someone who knows him. Just ... *please* be careful. He starts out sweet and charming, but that's how he lures you in before he shows you who he really is. I can only pray you don't come face-to-face with that side of him. Just thought you should know."

Before I can ask her anything else, she rushes back into the party. I try to follow and catch up with her, but she's disappeared into the crowd. My eyes roam the sea of bodies, looking for any glimpse of the blonde-haired fairy with purple wings, but I don't see her.

I make my way to the kitchen to ask Felix about any clingy former girlfriends, but he isn't where I left him. I search around the first floor of the house, maneuvering my way around my classmates and strangers. When I don't find him, I decide to head to the backyard where the overflow of partygoers has spilled out. Lanterns float in the inground pool. Fog machines are set up around the yard to give it that eerie feel. People are spread out in clusters, talking among each other. Some couples are making out on the lounge chairs, whereas one couple looks like they may actually be having sex, with no care of hiding it. I mean, if they are into that sort of thing, by all means, good for them. I'm not one to ick someone's yum.

"Jenna!" someone yells my name. I look around until I spot a familiar face. Or more like half of a familiar face. I'd recognize that wavy brown hair anywhere.

"Marcus! Loving the Phantom of the Opera look you got going on. Nicely done." He did a phenomenal job.

"Thanks!" He gives me a big smile. "Jenna, I want you to meet someone. This is my girlfriend, Kasey. Kasey, this is Jenna." He points to the girl dressed up in an olive-green renaissance dress standing next to him. Her blonde hair hangs in loose waves around a white floral crown on top of her head. She's adorable, and seeing them together, they are quite the cute couple.

I extend my hand and give her a warm smile. "It's a pleasure to finally meet you, Kasey. Marcus here never shuts up about you. It's nice to finally put a face to the name of the girl who clearly has stolen his heart."

"Happy to meet you too. It's nice to finally meet some of the people Marcus hangs out with."

"Sadie and I have been bugging him to give us your number so we can get together, have a girls day, but he refuses to give up the digits."

"Yeah, I don't trust that," Marcus retorts.

I feign shock. "What!? You don't trust your girlfriend with Sadie and me?"

"No. Sadie I trust. You? Nah. You would absolutely tell her something embarrassing about me from grade school, and I can't have that."

I give him my best sad, puppy-dog eyes. "I'm hurt that you think I would do such a thing." I turn to his girlfriend and whisper, "I have the best stories I could tell you. Like this one time in second grade—"

"Mmm, nope. Not happening!" Marcus interrupts, shaking his head. "Kasey, let's go meet some of my other friends who won't *embarrass* me."

"I'm just pulling your leg, Marcus. Chill." I lightly punch his shoulder and laugh.

Marcus looks around. "Did Sadie and Payson come with you? I want to introduce them to Kasey."

"Nah. They are having their own little date night. They didn't feel comfortable being here because of who was hosting." I nod toward Chad who is dressed like a wannabe Hugh Hefner, talking to some of his football buddies. Nathan and Brady are among the little group with that leech Lydia attached to Brady's arm.

"Oh ... right. I didn't think about that," he says as if he just remembered what happened two weeks ago at homecoming. "I'm surprised you came, then. You and Sadie always had a united stance when it came to certain things."

"We do, but Sadie practically pushed for me to come. Said she didn't want me to be alone on a Saturday night. Plus, she knows I can handle that bunch if worst comes to worst. Like I have any intention of crossing their paths tonight." I roll my eyes. I really am going to avoid Chad and his posse like the plague.

"Did you come alone?" Marcus asks.

I give the smile I get whenever I think of Felix. "Actually, I came with my boyfriend, Felix. He's from Greystone Academy." Kasey's gaze darts away from the crowd to me, and she shifts from foot to foot, biting her lip, her brows drawn together. "I would like to introduce you to him, but I have to find him first." I glance around to see if I can spot him. *Where did that man run off to?*

"D-did you say Felix ... from Greystone?" Kasey asks.

"Yeah. Do you know him? Sorry, I mean, you probably do. You go to Greystone too, right?" I am certain that's where Marcus said she attends school, because she doesn't go to Bellwood High.

She licks her lips. "I do. But out of respect, I hope you won't dislike me too much when I tell you, you should stay away from him."

I let out a soft chuckle. "What?" *She can't be for real. Right?* "Not you too."

"You too? Like someone else said the same thing?" Marcus asks, his eyebrow quirked.

I give him a nod. "Yeah, some girl said something similar to me when I went to grab some water from the garage. I have no clue who she was. I'm assuming an ex-girlfriend of Felix's." I give a shrug.

Marcus looks from me to his girlfriend. "Kasey, why would you say something like that to Jenna?"

Her eyes dart around, like she's making sure nobody is around to hear her, before leaning in close to us and whispering, "Because he's scary and dangerous!"

At that moment, strong arms wrap around my waist, pulling me back against a hard chest, and a familiar tribal wolf tattoo comes into view.

"Who's scary and dangerous?" Felix asks our small group.

For a moment, no one says anything. Kasey stares like a deer in headlights, and Marcus's attention goes to Felix, then to me and back to Kasey.

"Marcus!" Kasey exclaims, breaking the silence. "Why don't we go get refills? I definitely could use another drink!" Kasey grabs a hold of Marcus's hand and pulls him away from us.

"Later Jen!" Marcus says as he goes with Kasey toward the house.

"Who's the guy?" Felix asks, his eyes following Marcus and Kasey as they head through the sliding patio doors.

"That is Marcus, a friend from school. We grew up together, along with Sadie. He's also on the—"

"Is he going to be a problem?" Felix snarls.

I pull away to look at him. "He's a friend, Felix. Nothing more than that." His hands are in fists, clenching a little bit. "Not to mention, he was with his *girlfriend*, or did you not see her standing beside him?" *What is his deal?*

"Just because a guy has a girlfriend, doesn't mean shit. Especially if the girl goes to a different school. How can I trust he isn't putting the moves on you since I'm not around?"

"First of all, Marcus is not the player type. Okay? He has done nothing but talk about Kasey and how happy she makes him ever since they started dating. He was the one who got me to come to this party because he wanted to introduce her to me and my friends. Only reason Sadie didn't come tonight is because the jackass who is hosting this party is best friends with the guy who cheated on her with multiple girls. So yeah, I know guys can cheat, but that isn't Marcus. And you can say you don't trust him, but really what you're saying is you don't trust me. Right?"

His stormy hazel eyes stare into my chocolate-brown ones, yet he doesn't say a word.

I stand with my arms crossed in front of my chest, waiting for a response, but I guess there isn't one.

"Wow. Message received." I go to storm past him, but he snatches my arm in a firm grip, stopping me in my tracks.

"Where the hell do you think you're going?" His tone is harsh and unnerving.

"I'm going to find Marcus and have him take me home. You kind of ruined the night for me," I grit back. His grip tightens on my arm as he drags me toward the side of the house where it's dark and no one is around.

"Felix, let go. *Ow.* You're hurting my arm!" I try to pull my arm loose, but his hand squeezes even tighter. I'm sure there will be bruises tomorrow from how tight he is gripping me. When we reach the shadowed corner, Felix slams my back against the brick, and a sharp gasp escapes me. He latches onto my arms, holding me in place. His eyes darken a little as they stare intensely into me.

"Like hell you're going to go search out another dude. How would that look for me? Huh? My girlfriend leaving with another man?"

"Marcus is just a fr—" He releases my arms and clutches my jaw in his big hand.

"I don't give a fuck if he is an acquaintence. You will not embarrass me by leaving this party with another man. Got it?"

When I don't answer him, his fingers squeeze harder, so I claw at his hands, trying to get him to loosen his grip.

"Is there a problem over here?" a voice asks from behind Felix. I'm not sure who it is, but I am grateful for the distraction, as Felix releases my jaw and faces them. I rub my fingers into my jawline, massaging the ache left behind from his grasp. When I finally look to see who came over, I stare at the guy dressed in a black and white race car driver suit. His hair is perfectly tousled on top of his head, with his hands clenching and unclenching as he glares at Felix. The darkness makes his eyes look like they are glowing, and even though I can't see him, I know exactly who it is.

Of course, of all the people at this party who would come to my aid, it's none other than Brady's best friend, Nathan Ward.

# Chapter 2

## Nathan

I don't do these kinds of parties. I honestly hate them, hate being around my peers from school and being the center of their attention. Which says a lot coming from a guy who leads the record for most sacks in the state of South Carolina and one of the top 100 high school linebackers in the country. Not only am I a great defensive player, but my best friend is also the star quarterback for our school and the son of a former NFL quarterback.

Well, I guess he's now the *former* star quarterback. When Payson Moore moved here over the summer, she kind of stole his thunder. Have to say, she impressed me, and if I had been honest with my best friend, I would have told him the better QB won. After Brady got injured, she led our team to an undefeated season; something Brady has come close to but never accomplished in the last two years of him being the quarterback. Thanks to Payson, we are heading to the state championship after beating the Ryattville Raptors in the playoffs last weekend. We have three weeks to rest up and train for the biggest game our small town has ever faced.

Hence why Chad felt the need to throw this ridiculous Halloween party tonight. His parents went out of town for the weekend, so he was compelled to invite the entire school and the surrounding schools to celebrate our win. Not sure why he invited people from our rival schools, but then again, this is Chad. He has this need to gloat about his victories, and I have a feeling that's what this party is about. Plus, he's already claiming we will win. He has high hopes for us. As for me, I want to play the game I love and take my frustrations out on the opposing team.

Being one of the country's top linebackers makes me a shoo-in for scouts, and I need the football scholarships to help pay my way through school. Especially if I'm going to get away from my overbearing father and his incessant dream that I will follow in his footsteps. I have no desire to join the police force and one day be the chief of police. I want to go to college to get my business degree to take over my uncle's car shop. Possibly expand the business across the country. It was once my brother's dream and has now become mine.

Before he left for work, Dad had the audacity to insist I stop working at the garage with Uncle Dean so I can put more focus into preparing for the police academy. He is pushing for me to take the practice tests he brings home with him so come graduation, I can ace it, securing my spot in the academy. Instead of speaking up and arguing with him about it, I nodded to let him know I heard him. However, he took it as me being compliant, then left to head into the station to busy himself with work like he always does.

I'm not quitting the garage though. That would be unfair to my uncle. Especially since he's showing me the ropes of the shop to prepare for taking over the family business. If my father asks where I'm at, I'll just use football practice as a guise. He knows our school is heading to the championship game for the first time in years and doesn't need to know my actual schedule. It's not like he's home, so I may be able to get away with it. I just don't know what I'll do once football is over.

Normally, I would find solace being at home, but I couldn't take the quiet of the house after Dad's lecture to prioritize my future to be the next officer of the law. Especially since there is no football game to help release the frustration I'm feeling. So I ended up here, at this party.

When I showed up in my regular clothes, Chad was unhappy. He made me follow him to his massive walk-in closet, then tossed me a race car driver costume. He said being one of his boys meant I needed to partake in the full Halloween spirit, so I had to wear the silly costume. Not that it wasn't totally ridiculous, but with bro code and all, I agreed.

We are hanging inside the house until it becomes overcrowded, so we move to the backyard and find a group of our teammates talking.

We are talking about the upcoming championship game when my gaze lands on the most stunning woman I've ever seen. The conversations surrounding me become muffled and nothing else matters as my attention zeros in on her.

Her Catwoman costume hugs her curves in all the right places. The pointed black boots make her legs look long and lean, causing her hips to sway when she walks. Her raven-black hair pulled high in a ponytail makes me want to wrap it around my hand and give it a gentle tug so I can kiss those plump lips painted in a sultry crimson red. Her dark eyeshadow fills her cat mask to complete the full look, bringing every comic nerd's Catwoman fantasy come to life.

Jenna Altwood has been the one girl to always capture my attention. No matter who approached me, no girl ever really drew me in the way she does. She's loyal to the people she cares about, fiery and outspoken, and doesn't take shit from anyone. A true spitfire of a woman, and Jenna is all woman.

"Brady, I'm really not feeling good. Can we please head out now?" Lydia's whiny voice breaks through my Jenna tunnel vision and back to the conversations with my teammates.

Brady rolls his eyes. "I told you to stay home. A high school Halloween party is no place for someone in your condition."

"Excuse me? That *condition* is our baby!" Lydia pulls her arm from his and shoves him, then crosses her arms over her chest. "Besides, I wanted to come. I have to get all the fun in before she gets here."

"You guys already know the gender?" Benjamin Pitman, our center, asks.

"Not yet. We find out in a few weeks," Lydia says as she rubs her belly. There isn't a bump yet, but she's only like two months along. "Just call it mother's intuition."

"Nah. If it's Brady's kid, it's got to be a boy," DeAndre says.

"What do you mean *if* it's Brady's kid?" Lydia snarls. Her eyes are murderous as she glares at our cornerback, and the group goes silent. The last thing you want to do is be on Lydia's bad side. She has a mean streak and is known for doing some horrible things to people who cross her.

"I meant it as ... well ... ya know ..." He looks around the circle, panic in his eyes. "Guys? Help me out here?"

Dominic pats him on the shoulder. "What the idiot was trying to say is *knowing* it's Brady's kid, it's got to be a boy. Got those strong Thomas football genes to pass on to the next generation. Now apologize to Ms. Johnson, DeAndre."

"Sorry, Lydia. It just came out wrong. I wasn't insinuating anything. Really! I should have said it how Dom did. He's right in the fact that I'm an idiot."

Lydia rolls her eyes. "Well, we shall see in a few weeks. Now, won't we?" She turns her attention back to Brady. "I'm going to find Christina and have her take me home. Hang with your boys. I don't care. But if you want to get laid, I'd really think about it." She walks off in search of her friend, and the guys all take a deep breath.

"What's it going to be, Brady?" I chuckle. "Clearly, the ball is now in your court."

He tilts his head back, face to the sky, and groans. "I'll catch you guys at school on Monday." Then he heads off after Lydia.

Chad makes a whipping sound, and all the guys laugh. "Dude is so pussy whipped." He shakes his head. "So, do you think we will have a parade when we take state champions?"

The conversations go back to football, and thank God they do. I hate dealing with Lydia and Brady drama. I'm glad Brady went after her because if he would have stayed, then shit would have only gotten worse, and we would have had to deal with the aftermath of it come Monday.

My eyes wander around the party scene until they land on Jenna. Only, instead of being enchanted by her beauty, I'm seeing red. Some big ass dude has his hands on her, dragging her to the darkest part of the yard. I don't know who the hell this guy is, but it's clear she is trying to get away from him. She attempts to pull her arm free from his grasp but isn't having any luck. I glance around but no one else seems to notice what is happening. They are all too engrossed in talking and drinking. As soon as the duo walk into the shadows, I move in their direction.

"Nate, man, where are you going?" Dom asks, but I don't answer. I need to go check on Jenna and make sure whoever this asshole is doesn't harm a single hair on her body. The thought alone boils my blood and has me quickening my steps.

As soon as I turn the corner and my eyes adjust to the darkness, the fucker shoves her against the side of the house and grabs her face. My jaw tightens, my hands balling into fists.

"Is there a problem over here?" I snarl. The douchebag releases Jenna's face and turns toward me. I keep my eyes on this prick, wanting his attention on me and not her.

"Nah, bro. No problems. Just my girl and I having a nice little talk. Ain't that right, babe?" He grabs Jenna and pulls her into his side, draping his huge arm across her shoulder, then giving it a tight squeeze, and Jenna winces. "Tell him, babe."

"Y-yeah, yeah. W-we just had a little disagreement is all." It's not her usual strong, confident tone, and I'm two seconds away from ripping her away from his side.

"See? All good here, bro." He smirks. "Now, if you'll excuse us." He starts to leave, pulling Jenna along with him, but I stand in front of them, blocking their path.

I ignore the giant ogre glaring daggers at me and keep my eyes trained on Jenna. "Are you okay? Did he hurt you?" I ask gently.

"Un-fucking-believable!" the ogre shouts. "You have some balls." He releases Jenna and stands chest to chest with me. He's only slightly taller than me, probably by an inch, but I stand tall and firm. His nostrils flare, our noses so close together, but I'm not intimidated. If this asshole wants to go rounds, we will go rounds. Plus, my teammates are here, and they will have my back if I need it.

"Felix, let it go! It's not worth it," Jenna says as she's trying to pull him away from me. He doesn't budge, though. The fucker continues to hold my stare. "Felix! His dad is the chief of police. If you hit him, you could get in serious trouble."

At the mention of my father, the ogre snarls and backs off but not before he whispers in my ear. "This is a warning. Get in my way again and I'll make you pay. I know people, and I will make sure it doesn't come back on me." He shoulder-checks me as he passes, Jenna right behind him. I hold my arm out, stopping her.

"You don't need to go anywhere with him. I can take you home or get you an Uber. Maybe call Sadie to come get you?" I have a bad feeling about this guy, and I don't want her going anywhere with him. She isn't safe.

At the mention of her best friend's name, her eyes snap to mine, anger written on her face.

"Sadie is busy, on a date with her girlfriend who treats her a million times better than your manwhore best friend ever did. I will not interrupt her night, and I sure as hell won't get in the same car as you. I don't need you putting yourself in my relationship. Like I said, it was just a disagreement between us, and he didn't hurt me. Now, mind your own business, Ward, and stay out of mine."

Moving around me, she catches up with her boyfriend who didn't even realize she wasn't behind him. She glances over her shoulder, eyes narrowed in my direction, before lacing her delicate fingers into his big, grubby hands.

"You good, man?" Dom appears by my side, glancing from me to Jenna as she heads into the house.

"Yeah, man. I'm good." We bump fists, and he heads back to our group of friends.

Standing there, I contemplate going after Jenna. I could try to convince her to stay, or maybe just keep a watchful eye on her. Better yet, I'll just throw her over my shoulder and lock her in a room upstairs—anything to keep her away from that guy.

I hate that I lied to Dom, but I couldn't be honest with him either. Despite what I'm feeling, I don't need to worry my friend. I'm angry. Worried. How could she lie to my face about him not hurting her? I know what I saw. Even worse, how could she just leave with him? This guy is bad news, and she needs to get as far away from him as possible.

# Chapter 3

## Jenna

The weekend flew by, and before I know it, I'm rushing out the door to get to school on time. Had Sadie not knocked on my bedroom door to wake me up on her way out, I would have overslept and missed my first class.

After making my way across town to the red brick building that is Bellwood High, I manage to arrive at school with five minutes to spare.

I stop by my locker to grab my sketch pad and art supplies before speed walking to Mrs. Wailing's classroom. Nothing can make a bad morning better than starting with my favorite hobby in the world—painting and sketching.

I live and breathe art, loving the way colors can be blended into beautiful creations. How the graphite of a pencil glides across a smooth piece of paper when you sketch out whatever is in your mind. An escape from reality, the same way a bookworm gets lost in a good book, according to my best friend. I love losing myself in a sea of colors and endless strokes whenever a spark of creativity takes a hold of me. Bringing all my wildest visions to life on paper or canvas. Art soothes my soul and allows me to relax.

It's why I also took a part-time job at Beyond Broken Colors, a local art therapy studio that helps people heal from their traumas through the process of creating art. I couldn't have applied fast enough when there was an ad looking for an assistant.

The late bell rings as I sit at my desk. Breathing a sigh of relief, I couldn't have timed that better.

"That was a close one, Altwood," Rebecca says from beside me. We are both seniors and have been in the same art classes since freshman year.

"Tell me about it, Chang," I respond, trying to catch my breath since I hauled ass to get here. "How was your weekend? Get into anything crazy?"

"Not unless you call staying home and working through endless hours of calculus homework crazy," she huffs, leaning back in her chair. "How about you?"

"It was … okay." I wish it was better. Instead of the weekend I had in mind, it turned into a complete dumpster fire. Felix and I left the Halloween party after the little showdown with Nathan, and I made him take me home. At first he refused, driving me to an unknown area, but when I faked feeling unwell, claiming food poisoning, he got me to my house quickly. He said he didn't want me ruining the interior of his truck if I vomited in it before proceeding to go on about how the smell would be a pain in the ass to get rid of.

*Such a gentleman.*

"Really? I thought you said you were going to Chad's Halloween party?" she asks.

"I did for a little bit, but then left. It was way too overcrowded, and I felt guilty for going because of Sadie." A small part of me did feel like I was betraying my best friend by attending it, even though she reassured me a thousand times it was fine.

"Oh ..." She sounds disappointed. "I was hoping for some juicy gossip or crazy drama to account for my lame ass weekend. You know, considering I live vicariously through your stories since my parents are overprotective, helicopter parents who don't trust I'll make smart choices for myself."

"They just love you and want what's best for you." I reach across our table and grab her hand, giving it a gentle squeeze.

Rebecca's eyes widen. "Oh my god! What happened to your arm?"

I glance to where she's looking and pull back. "Oh ... it's nothing."

*Liar.*

"Jenna, that doesn't look like *nothing*. It looks like someone grabbed you hard enough to leave an imprint of their hand. I can practically make out the fingertips."

"I tripped on one of those lounge chair legs and almost fell into Chad's pool when some big guy caught me before I fell in. Clumsy me," I say with a soft chuckle. "Seriously, it's nothing."

*I hope that's believable.*

"What—"

Mrs. Wailing stands in front of the class, effectively ending our conversation. "Good morning, class. I hope you guys were able to enjoy your weekend."

Some students groan, either from a case of the Mondays or an uneventful weekend.

Glancing over at Rebecca, she rolls her eyes, and we laugh softly. I feel for the girl. I wish other teens had parents like mine. Ones who know they can't control what I do but trust me enough in how they raised me to make smart decisions. Rebecca wouldn't do anything too crazy or be irresponsible. She has big dreams of being some architectural engineer and wouldn't dare do anything to derail her journey to achieve her dream.

"I have some exciting news to share with you all. The state of South Carolina has just sent me information in regards to their statewide art competition, and this year Bellwood was chosen to be this year's hosts!"

The state holds an annual art competition every year for high schoolers to enter for a chance to win prizes. The grand prize? A fifty-thousand-dollar scholarship toward their tuition at the college they get accepted to. Each year, it's hosted in a different city or town in our state. I considered entering last year, but the competition was held hours away, falling on the one weekend both of my parents had to travel out of town for work related business. Without a car, I had no way of being able to go so I had to miss out. The fact our town is getting to host it this year, meaning I can actually participate and showcase my craft, makes me even more excited to enter.

Plus, that money will help cover my college education so my parents won't have to fork out a single penny for me. They have done so much for me, I want to lessen that burden for them. It's my education and it should be my financial responsibility to make.

"This year's theme is about identity and self-expression. Who are you as an artist? Who are you as a person? You must be able to express yourself by communicating your personal thoughts and feelings through art. I must warn you, though, this theme may expose you. You may even feel a bit vulnerable, but isn't that the beauty of art? To feel? To release those feelings within us and into our work?"

There are murmurs of agreement around the classroom. Well, the ones who take art seriously. The rest of the kids in here are only taking it for an easy credit.

"If you would like to register for the competition, please see me after class and I will be happy to give you the information. You have one week to register. The deadline for your artwork is November nineteenth so it is ready for the art show on November twentieth. Now that we got that out of the way, why don't you guys grab your art projects from last week and continue working on those for the remainder of class."

We retrieve our projects and retreat to our seats to work on them some more. I'm really enjoying this one. You take a character of your choosing and divide it into four equal sections. One section is the original character. The other three sections you pick what effect you want to give to the character. You could make the image have a glitch effect, using red, white, and blue markers to give the illusion the image is distorted. You could give it a drip effect, making it appear as if it's melting, adding depth and texture to the drawing. There are so many creative ways you can go about it, but the finished product is an insanely badass picture. I've seen these on TikTok before and love how they turn out.

I chose to do Stitch for my character, and not to toot my own horn, but it's the best piece of art I've done in my life. Well ... so far.

"Dude, yours looks amazing! Way better than mine," Rebecca whines. She is using Sailor Moon's face for hers.

"What are you talking about? Yours looks really good!" Rebecca is very artistic. Anyone with eyes can see that. "Stop doubting your beautiful artwork. You're a badass artist!"

She gives me a small smile. "Thanks, Jen. But still, I like yours a million times better than mine." She sticks her tongue out at me before getting back to work.

Before long, the bell rings to dismiss us to our next class. I stop by Mrs. Wailing's desk to get the information for the competition so I can register for it during lunch. The sooner I do it, the better.

Stopping by my locker, I drop off my art supplies and grab my chemistry notebook for my next class. As I close the door to my locker, I jump. Someone is standing right there in front of me.

A six-foot-three someone.

"Holy shit, you scared the hell out of me!" My heart is racing, and I'm trying to calm myself before I look up into his green eyes. "What the hell do you want, Nathan?"

"I just came to check on you," he says. "Was going to before school, but I didn't see your Beetle in the parking lot."

"And why the hell would you want to do that?" I'm being snarky, but I have my own personal reasons for that.

"You lied to me on Saturday."

"Exactly how did I lie to you?"

"You told me to my face that he didn't hurt you."

"I wasn't lying. He didn't hurt me."

"Cut the bullshit, Jenna. I saw what he did to you right before I got his attention." His gaze darts to my arms, and his jaw clenches. Why the hell I didn't think to put on a long-sleeve shirt today is beyond me.

*Because your dumbass overslept and you were rushing to get to school on time.*

He grabs my hand and lifts my arm, revealing the bluish-purple marks on my tawny brown skin. "If he didn't hurt you, then why do you have bruises on your arm from where he grabbed you?" he snarls, like a wolf ready to attack its prey.

I pull my arm away. "Would you calm down? No need to be animalistic about it. They are just bruises. It's not a big deal."

"Not a big deal? You're kidding me, right?" He shakes his head and bites his lower lip before releasing it. "If a man puts his hands on a woman hard enough that it leaves a mark, then yeah, Jenna, that's a big deal. It's a fucking red flag!" He gets loud, drawing attention from a few people passing us in the hall.

"You know what, Nathan? I don't have time for whatever antics you're trying to pull. So why don't you go find your little playboy clique or whatever hoe of the week you got. I've got a chemistry class to get to."

I shoulder-check him as I rush past to get to Mr. Feeser's class before the bell rings. The last thing I need is for the six-foot-three Adonis footballer to make me late for my second-favorite class. I may struggle with chemistry a little bit, but Mr. Feeser always creates a fun and entertaining atmosphere which makes me work extra hard to pass his class. Plus, I have a three-point-eight GPA to maintain.

I mean, I can admit Nathan is handsome. Green eyes that stand out against his sun-kissed skin. Chestnut-brown hair tousled on top of his head. An athletic body that shows he works out to stay fit for football. I'm not blind ... or dead. I may have had a crush on him when his family moved here sophomore year, but that was before he became friends with Brady and Chad and became a part of their playboy posse. I don't think I've ever seen him with the same girl for more than a week. Not that it matters.

Nope. Nathan is one hundred percent on the no-date list. I despise him as much as I despise the people he surrounds himself with. Why he is so concerned about my relationship with Felix is beyond me. I can take care of myself. I can handle Felix. Besides, it was a one-time thing. It's not like he intentionally set out to hurt me.

Right?

# Chapter 4

## Nathan

Sitting at lunch, I glance over at the table where Jenna sits with Payson, Sadie, and some of the junior guys on the football team when someone bumps my shoulder.

"You good, man?" Dom asks as he sits next to me with his lunch.

"Yeah. I'm fine."

Jenna sits across the lunchroom laughing with her friends, seeming happy. She's so beautiful when her face is lit up like that.

"Something going on between you two that I don't know about?"

I break away and look at Dom. "What?"

"Don't think I haven't noticed your lingering stares on a certain raven-haired girl." He tilts his head in Jenna's direction before a smile spreads across his face.

"Nah, man. It's not like that. She doesn't even like me for some reason." She seems to have ill will toward me, and I have no clue why. "Just concerned about her. Saw something happen between that guy and her at the party. I didn't like it and was trying to check on her, make sure she was okay, but she just brushed me off."

"You talking about Felix? The guy dressed as some gladiator?" he asks.

"Wait, you know him?" I'm kind of surprised. I have been trying to figure out who the guy is all weekend long. I checked Jenna's social media accounts, but I'm not able to see anything since we aren't friends and her pages are set to private.

"I don't know him, but I know of him. He's the linebacker who plays for Greystone Academy.  One of their best players. I recognized his wolf tattoo on his forearm. Not to mention the dude is a beast on the field. He's the one who fucked up Brady's arm in our game against them."

"Do you know his last name?" My interest is piqued.

"Starts with an M, I think? Can't be entirely sure. You think he hurt her?" He nods his head in Jenna's direction.

"Let's just say she has some bruising caused by him. I tried to check on her before second period, but she told me to mind my business and shoved past me. I just get a bad vibe about the guy."

"Your dad's chief of police. Maybe ask him if he can find any information on the guy for you."

He makes a valid point, but I don't want to involve my dad. I didn't forget that ogre's little threat toward me either, and the last thing I want to do is cause any harm to Jenna. However, I do know of someone who could help me get some information, so I pull out my cell phone and send a text.

NATHAN

Hey, can you look up someone for me?

CASSIDY

I might be able to. But you know I have to ask. Does your father need to know?

NATHAN

No. He doesn't need to be involved. Just need info on a certain person. It's for a friend.

CASSIDY

Who am I looking into?

NATHAN

Someone who goes to Greystone Academy. First name Felix. Last name unsure but may start with an M? Also has a wolf tattoo on his forearm. Plays on defense for their football team.

CASSIDY

Is this your way of scoping out your competition?

I pocket my cell phone and eat my lunch, talking with Dom and the rest of the guys who joined us. Cassidy and I used to hook up on occasion when she was a senior and I was a sophomore. We were both in a dark place at the time, so the occasional hook up was how we escaped. The moment she graduated, she went into the academy, and now she's working as an officer for the Bellwood Police Department. We've maintained somewhat of a friendship, and I have only ever asked her for a handful of favors when I needed to know something without my father's knowledge.

I hope she can pull information for me about Felix. The more information I have on the guy, the more I know who Jenna is dating, and maybe I can convince her to get away from him, especially if it's bad. Seeing those bruises on her arm set off the need to hunt him down and beat the shit out of him myself. Her cheek also had some discoloration, most likely from when he grabbed her face. It makes me wonder how long they have been together and how long he has been leaving marks on her body. And if he has, where?

After school, I pull my cobalt-blue Subaru WRX into the parking lot of Wesley's Auto Repair and Detailing. Once I'm parked, I place my school stuff in the trunk. Grabbing my coveralls, I pull them up over my clothes and switch out my white Jordans for my brown Timbs before I head into the garage in search of my uncle.

"There's my nephew!" My uncle greets me. "How was school today, kid?"

"Not bad. Same old school, different day. Learning and shit."

"School's important! Your education is important. Especially if I'm going to be handing you the keys to this place after you get your certs and that business degree you're always talking about."

"It's the dream, Uncle. You know how much I enjoy working with you, working here." I smile at him. "I want to make this place the best of the best. Possibly expanding so there is a Wesley's in every state."

He's owned the shop ever since I can remember. It used to belong to my grandfather, Oliver Wesley, until he passed away some odd years ago. Then Dean took it over after there were rumors of someone wanting to buy it out and replace it with some fast-food joint. He fought tooth and nail to come out the victor in the end. It mattered to him to keep the garage a family-owned business in honor of his dad and the Wesley family name. Not to mention, the nearest garage is like a half hour away from Bellwood and their prices are absurd.

Wesley was my mother's maiden name. She was the oldest child of Oliver and Catherine Wesley, five years older than Dean. Sadly, my mother passed away when I was five years old due to cancer. Every day I feel like I'm slowly losing the few memories I have of her, but I do my best to hold onto them. Working with my uncle makes me feel closer to her. He loves to tell me stories about her while we work, and it helps to dull the pain of missing her.

"What's on the schedule for this evening?" I ask. I'm ready to get my hands dirty and do what I love to do—fix up cars.

"I've got a Honda Odyssey in need of an oil change, and a Volkswagen Jetta needing a tire rotation. You pick," he says.

"Jetta it is," I respond, and put myself to work. During the week, we are busy with the usual car maintenance stuff, but the weekends are my favorite. That's when I get to do the fun stuff, like restoring my uncle's 1969 Chevelle. It was my grandfather's car that got passed down to my uncle after he died. Dean's always so busy with the shop though, so it's done nothing but sit in that garage, in need of repair. My uncle made me a deal. If I can get her running and looking new, he'll give me the car. Says it would be great practice for when I'm a certified mechanic. So that's what I do every weekend.

My uncle and I work through our shifts, and before I know it, we are locking up shop and heading out to our vehicles.

"How is your old man holding up?" Dean asks, always checking in on my dad's well-being. My mom, dad, and uncle were close, so he's been worried about Dad since the loss of my mom, Sarah. Even more so since …

"Working," I say. "Always working."

Dean just shakes his head, unsurprised. "So like Gregory. Working himself hard to work through the grief instead of seeking help. If he doesn't start taking care of himself, he's going to work himself into an early grave."

Silence encases us for a few moments.

"Sorry, kid. I shouldn't have said that. That word has been like a curse on this family."

"It's fine, Uncle. You're not wrong, though. I worry about him, his health. I want to tell him to cut back on his hours, spend more time at home …"

"It's not that hard. Just tell your old man the truth. I'm sure he will understand, especially since he should be cherishing every moment with you."

"Not that simple, ever since Ryan …" I pause, swallowing the knot forming in my throat and taking a moment for myself. "Ever since then, he has really been prioritizing work like he's trying to put some distance between us." I sigh. "We don't have the father-son bond like we used to."

Dean places a hand on my shoulder. "Don't you think it's time to speak up? Tell him how it makes you feel?"

"I hear what you're saying, but I don't know how to approach him. Especially since when he's at home, I'm either at school, at football, or here." Dad isn't a big fan of expressing emotions, not anymore at least. It's like with all the loss our family has endured, he's closed up. Afraid to show an ounce of emotion. Kind of like me, I guess.

"Don't lose hope yet, kid. Just find the time to sit with him and open up. Tell him how you're feeling. Check in on him. Even if you have to show up at his job to do it. If you got to cause a little trouble where you get arrested and he has to interrogate you, take your shot." Dean shrugs. "Now, I'm not telling you to steal cars or commit arson, but if there is one thing your father will understand, it's compassion. Sarah was one of the most compassionate people I knew, and I think you're a lot more like your mother than you know. I just wish you would have gotten to have more time with her to see it ..." He looks off into the dark. Losing my mother really hurt him. I know siblings don't usually get along, and I'm sure my uncle and mother had their fair share of disagreements, but it's clear as day they were close.

"Yeah ... I guess." I don't agree, but I don't tell him that.

"Well, you better get home. Wouldn't want your dad to have a heart attack if you're not home yet." He pats my shoulder before heading to his moss-green 1972 GMC 2500 truck. He has a weakness for the classics. "Let me know when you make it home, kid. Love ya!"

"Love you too. And I will!" I say before getting in my car to head home. My uncle isn't wrong though. I should tell my father my true feelings. The late hours, the distance between us. How I wish he would be home more, be more active in my life. I mean, I'm one of his only family members left. How could he not want for us to be closer? Why push me away like he has? If I bring up how I'm planning on taking over for Uncle Dean instead of taking my father's lead like everyone else assumes, that could end in disaster. Not only does it have the potential to ruin the relationship between my father and uncle, but what if it leads to something terrible happening to my dad? Like he gets shot in the line of duty or there's an accident and he doesn't make it? Death—it's happened too many times before and look how I'm handling my life. My uncle wasn't wrong when he said death is a curse in our family.

# Chapter 5

## Jenna

"Hey." Sadie nudges my foot with hers, trying to get my attention. "I've noticed a certain linebacker has been looking your way recently. Quite a lot, frankly."

My bestie nods toward the playboy posse's table—my nickname for the footballers who sit with Brady and Chad. I don't have to glance over to know which one she's talking about.

"Yeah, not sure what his deal is," I quip. "He, for some reason, has been a thorn in my side as of late." I know why. Ever since the incident at Chad's party last weekend, he has seeked me out between classes to check up on me. I've been lucky enough to avoid him as best I can, but the few instances I have had to force my way past him, his green eyes have perused my exposed skin, probably seeking for any marks Felix may have caused. Fortunately for Nathan, there are no new marks and the ones that were there are almost gone.

Felix has apologized numerous times for what happened, stating the alcohol got the best of him and he lost his temper. He said he would never harm a beautiful hair on my body, and I accepted his apology. Things between Felix and me are going great, so Nathan needs to back off.

"Maybe he's got a secret crush on you," Sadie says, wiggling her eyebrows.

"Ha! Please. Does he even know the meaning of a crush? Or better yet, the definition of a girlfriend? The guy has never gone steady with one girl since he moved here back in tenth grade. And besides, it doesn't even matter. I'm with Felix, and I'm happy with him."

"But if you weren't, would you?" Marcus asks, tilting his head to the side. I get the feeling the way he's asking has to do with what his girlfriend said about Felix. Like Nathan, he seems concerned with who I'm dating. Marcus is a good friend, and the last thing I need is for him to be concerned about me too.

Before homecoming, it used to be just Sadie and me at our lunch table, with the occasional appearances from Brady when he was posing as Sadie's boyfriend. But since the drama of homecoming, we have added a few new members to sit with us. Marcus sits with us now that Sadie and Brady are broken up. Brady had an issue with any guy near Sadie, so Marcus stayed away for his own safety. Payson joined us since she is now dating Sadie. Colton is Payson's cousin and the two of them are close like siblings. He joined along with his group of friends from football: Zealand, Rhett, and Jeremiah. This group of guys had Payson's back the moment she showed up for the first day of football camp. She didn't get a warm welcome from the team because she was a girl. They didn't want to take her seriously, but she allowed her skills to do all the talking. The guys took her in as if she was a sister, and they make sure nobody fucks with her. Not that I think she couldn't handle her own.

"Ooohhh, this ought to be good," Jeremiah says, crossing his arms over his broad chest. Jeremiah is also a linebacker and is slated to take over Nathan's position next football season since he graduates this year.

Everyone at our table is staring at me, and I have no idea why.

"I'm sorry, what was the question again?" I'm trying to play it off as a question not worth answering. In all honesty, it's not.

"Would you date Nathan if you weren't with Felix?" Zealand says. "It's just a question, Jenna. A hypothetical one."

I glance around, everyone waiting with bated breath for my answer, and I'm not sure why this seems to be a topic of discussion.

"To put it simply, if Nathan and I were the only two human beings on this planet responsible for recreating life, I would cut off his dick and let him bleed to death before allowing him anywhere close to me. There's your answer."

The guys wince at the mention of cutting off Nathan's dick, some reaching for their own junk under the table as if the vision caused them actual pain.

"What have I ever done to you to hate me so much, Spitfire?" a deep voice says from behind me.

I turn around to find the tall wall of man before me. Narrowing my eyes, I glare at him for standing so close to me and butting into our conversation. He stares back, as if he's curious what my answer will be.

*How long has he been standing there?*

"For your information, it's rude to be eavesdropping on conversations that don't pertain to you."

He leans down so his face is close to mine. "On the contrary, I believe my name was mentioned, therefore I think it does pertain to me." He then has the audacity to smirk in my face.

I'd do anything to slap it off if I wasn't worried about getting detention and ruining my image. The last thing I need is a mark on my record, especially since I don't plan to stick around Bellwood after graduation. My dreams are to attend a college in California, and if I plan to win that scholarship money to pay for my own college education, then I can't jeopardize my chances with the art competition because of a single slap.

"Why are you over here, Ward? Trying to get a peek at something?" I question. "Because I can guarantee you, there is *nothing* you are going to see."

Nathan's eyes dart from mine to my arms, then back, like he's wanting to check me for bruises but not stare for too long. Being the nice person I am, I move my arms up slowly to cross in front of my chest. I'm wearing a T-shirt today, so he will be able to see that the bruises have faded.

The moment his eyes drop to my arms again, I stand up, forcing him to take a step back. "Do us both a favor and leave me the hell alone. I'm not any of your concern," I grit out. I face my friends, some of whose mouths are gaping, then snatch up what is left of my lunch. "Sorry guys. I've suddenly lost my appetite." Shoving past Nathan, I head to the nearest trash can to dump what I couldn't eat of my lunch. After exiting the cafeteria, I make my way to the nearest girls bathroom. As I stand at the sink, splashing cool water on my face, I hear the door open and shut. Glancing in the mirror, I spot a curly-haired blonde with steel-blue eyes staring back at me.

"What happened back there, Jen?" Sadie asks softly. "What's going on between you and Nathan?"

"*Nothing* is going on between us. He's ... he's just being a nuisance because he saw something and won't let it go."

Sadie tilts her head, her brows furrowing. "What do you mean by that?"

Sighing, I turn and face my friend. "It's nothing for you to worry your pretty little head about." I never told Sadie what happened. She was having a wonderful evening with her girlfriend, and I wasn't going to dampen her good mood about a petty argument with my boyfriend. Besides, it was a one-and-done incident.

"Jenna, we have been best friends since we were in preschool. I know you better than anyone, and vice versa. Whatever that was in the cafeteria, something happened. I mean, Nathan was just about to chase after you before I asked him to let me talk to you instead. He seems to be concerned about you, and not going to lie, I find it ... endearing."

"Endearing? The guy who is best friends with the school man-hoe is endearing?"

Sadie gives me a pointed look, not backing down from this. Can't blame the girl, because I have done the same for her on numerous occasions, pushing her to step outside of her comfort zones. Had I not, she wouldn't be happy with someone who treats her the way she deserves to be treated. Payson worships the ground Sadie walks on, and I have never been happier to see the gorgeous smile she puts on my bestie's face.

"Okay, okay. Fine. But you have to promise me you won't overreact." I hold out my pinky. We have done this since we were little. Whenever we make a pinky promise, we know it's serious and we can't break that promise. If we break it, then the person who broke it has to do whatever the other person says for a week. No questions and no arguments. It's a part of our friendship pinky-promise pact.

Sadie hesitates for a slight moment before reaching her hand out and twisting our pinkies together. "You have my promise. Now spill."

"Something happened at Chad's party. Felix had some alcohol in his system and got kind of upset with me because I was talking to Marcus, who introduced me to Kasey. It was just something petty like him not trusting Marcus around me. I told him where his lack of trust fell more on me than Marcus, which pissed me off, so I went to walk away. He grabbed my arm when I went by him, and basically, Nathan caught it all and felt the need to disrupt. He put himself in the middle of our dispute and now he keeps checking in on me." It's not entirely the truth, but she doesn't need to know the full details. If she did, she would probably be on my case about Felix, or worse, take it to my parents. The last thing I want or need is to put any burdens on them.

"Did Felix hurt you? Were the marks from him?"

*Shit.* She must have noticed them when I forgot to cover them up on my dash out the door on Monday.

I avoid eye contact when I answer her question. "He just grabbed a little too hard. It was a drunken error, though, and he didn't realize he had a tight grip on me."

"Drunken error or not, Jenna, he shouldn't have placed a single finger on you if he was angry. Those were some serious bruises, and honestly, I don't fault Nathan for being worried."

She can't seriously be siding with Nathan on this.

"Well, he doesn't need to be. Felix apologized for it, and I have forgiven him. All is good."

"Nothing else happened at that party?" Sadie asks. She doesn't seem one hundred percent sold. I will just have to make her believe it though.

"Nothing else happened. I *promise* you." I reassure her.

At that moment, the bell rings, dismissing seniors from lunch to head to their next class. We both walk out of the bathrooms in time for Payson to meet up with us.

"Everything good?" Payson asks, looking between Sadie and me. "Or do I have to teach Nathan a lesson?"

"Everything is peachy, QB," Sadie says before giving Payson a quick kiss. They lace their fingers together as we walk the halls. Sadie and I tend to walk to our classes together after lunch since we are next to each other, and Payson loves walking Sadie to her classes every chance she gets. They are the cutest couple and so in love with each other.

"So, what's the plan for the weekend?" I ask Sadie and Payson. "You two got something special going on?"

"I actually want to get the guys together this weekend and work on some plays for the championship game. I hate having this last week off. I don't want anything to jeopardize our chance at winning."

"Coach wants you guys to be healthy and not risk any injuries. Plus, you earned the rest," Sadie says.

"I know, Cherry Pop, but still. I just don't want the team to lose its chemistry. I mean, the way we have connected these last few weeks to be in the championship game has me in awe, considering how tough it was since I joined. I want this win for them just as much or even more than myself. These guys busted their asses all season, they deserve to be the winners I know them to be."

"Wow, Payson. That's so admirable of you," I say. "I have no doubt the team is going to be just fine, though. You all are going to kick ass and come out on top."

"Being on top is what I do best." Payson smirks at Sadie before she leans in and nuzzles her neck.

"Okay, TMI for me." I let out a soft chuckle. "And I'm a little jealous because I'm not getting any action."

"Wait, you didn't seal the deal with Felix after the party?" Sadie asks.

"Uh, no. I wasn't feeling up to it after our argument and had him drop me off at home."

"Jen, why didn't you tell me?"

"And ruin your night? What kind of friend would I be? No. Nuh-uh. You two need your time and not me ruining it. I will not be held responsible for that. Besides, I had a nice evening to myself. I did a facial and some sketching." I shrug, but Sadie's body shifts, and her eyes lower to the ground.

"Please stop with the sad puppy face. I was fine. But if you feel like you need to make it up to me, you can go with me to the outlet mall tomorrow night. Help me find a cute outfit to wear that will make Felix drool at the sight of me?"

"She'll go," Payson answers for Sadie.

"Jeez, QB. I didn't know I was incapable of answering for myself."

"I know you can answer for yourself, Cherry Pop. But I also happen to know you are going to hesitate and think about me and if we have plans. Truth is, Colt and I have some plans with the family. We're taking Judson to Wreck-It-Rage for some therapy and to hopefully get him to open up and tell us what's going on."

"The rage room? That's your therapy?" I ask. I have never been to Wreck-It-Rage, but I know of it.

"Yes, because according to Payson and her uncle, the best way to release pent-up emotions is to smash the crap out of things. Legally, of course."

"Oh, the absolute best way! Not to mention, it's also where this cutie and I shared our first kiss," Payson says. She lifts their linked hands and kisses Sadie's fingers, making Sadie blush.

"Yeah, I definitely need to make some plans with Felix soon," I say as we reach the doors of our classes, then tell them bye before heading into calculus.

The rest of the day goes by slowly, and when I'm heading to my car, my phone vibrates with an incoming text.

HELENA

Hey, sorry to bother you. Is there any chance you can come in sooner this evening? My mother was rushed to the hospital.

JENNA

Yeah no problem. Are you at the studio? I can come there now.

HELENA

Yeah. I was about to lock up and meet you somewhere to give you the key and alarm code.

JENNA

I'll be there in like 10 min.

HELENA

Ok. Thank you so much Jenna!

No trouble!

I send a text to my parents to let them know I'll be going into work early before heading to the art studio.

Helena lets me in and goes over how to close the studio and set the alarm when I lock up tonight. She isn't sure what's happening with her mom or how long she will be, so I told her if she showed me what to do, I'd close up, that way she can be with her mom for as long as she needs to be. Family is so important, and I adore my mother so much. I don't know what I would do if anything ever happened to mine, and knowing Helena, she would have allowed me time to be with mine if the roles were reversed. It was only right for me to do the same for her. Time is so precious and every minute with your loved ones should be treasured.

# Chapter 6

## Jenna

After Helena leaves for the hospital, I gather everything I will need to set up for the 4:00 p.m. session. Easels, paints, clean paintbrushes and water to rinse them off, along with paper towels and freshly sharpened pencils. I place primed canvases onto the easels before going over what Helena has planned for the clients to paint. As I'm getting the music ready to play in the background, my phone vibrates in my apron pocket, and I smile when I see Felix's name on the screen.

I'm about to respond to his texts when the bell above the door chimes and a pretty girl walks in. She has shoulder-length wavy blonde hair with streaks of lavender throughout and the prettiest bright-blue eyes that pop against the dark winged liner along her top lash line and white eyeliner on the water line, giving that doe-eye look.

"Hi. Welcome to Beyond Broken Colors. Are you here for the four o'clock session?" Sometimes, the more anxious clients come in early to avoid the awkwardness of showing up when others are already here.

"Uh, no. I'm actually here to look into maybe signing up? My grams thought I should look into art therapy to try to help me work through my shit," she says. She looks around the studio, avoiding eye contact with me. It makes me wonder if she is nervous.

I try getting a read on her to help her feel more welcome and give her a sense she is safe here. She looks close in age to me, but I'm not sure I have seen her around Bellwood High before.

My phone vibrates again, but I ignore it. If it's Felix, I can message him later when I have a free moment. Right now, my focus is a potential client for Helena who may need a class to work through her trauma.

"How old are you?" I ask, causing the girl to finally look at me.

"Seventeen. Why?" she says, putting her hands on her hips.

"Your age will help me know which class to place you in. Helena likes to keep the ages close together since it makes it easier for her to determine the level and style of work you will be doing."

"So you're not the owner?" blondie asks.

"No, I'm her assistant. I help her where she needs me. Helena actually had a family emergency, so I'll be taking over and running the studio this evening. I'm Jenna, by the way," I say, reaching out to shake her hand.

"Hollis," the girl says, extending her hand.

"That's a pretty name. Do you go to Bellwood High?"

"Um, no." She shakes her head. "I went to Greystone Academy, but it wasn't working out there, so I've been doing a virtual homeschool thing. It's not working for me. It's driving me batshit crazy, and I'm trying to convince Grams to let me go to a public school. I need to be around actual teachers who can teach me this crap in person. She made an agreement with me that if I seek some sort of help she will consider registering me to go to a public school."

"In that case, I can give you a brochure and form to look over. You can share it with your grams, and if it feels like this is something that can work for you, we would love to have you." I grab the information from the front desk and give it to her. "And if you want my own thoughts, Bellwood is a pretty nice school. A little more class than Wimbleton High, as far as the public schools in this area. Just my personal opinion." I give her a sly smile and wink.

"I'll keep that in mind." Hollis smirks. "Thanks again, Jenna."

"No problem."

At that moment, the first few clients arrive, and Hollis makes her exit. I'm not sure what her story is, but I hope whatever demons she has, she finds her weapon to slay them away. Maybe art therapy can do that for her.

I make my way through each session this evening with no issues. Thankfully, it was a mild evening for my first time closing. The weekends tend to be more chaotic, as so many people need the weekend time slots to fit their busy schedules.

Once the last client leaves, I flip the sign to closed, lock the door, and make my way around the studio. After I gather all the paint trays and brushes, I take them to the washing station at the back of the room. I clean every brush thoroughly, hanging them in the brush rack to dry while I collect the table easels to place back in their proper cabinet. Going around the room, I gather the mason jars our clients use to clean their brushes and place them in the dishwasher Helena had installed in the back. Not going to lie, this was the best idea Helena came up with. Saves us from having to hand wash each one ourselves. After starting the wash cycle, I head out to the studio area to finish cleaning everything up. This part of the day is so time-consuming and why Helena needed the help. Doing it on your own takes almost two hours.

I double-check the front door is securely locked, then head to Helena's office in the back to make sure the money is in the safe. After grabbing my cell phone and backpack, I set the alarm and dash out the back door before locking it. The studio sits on Main Street, a mile long stretch of road in the center of Bellwood, so there is limited parking out front. Behind the stretch of small business buildings that line Main Street is extra parking. Normally, I park back here with Helena, but I was rushing to get here, so I parked out front of Beyond Broken Colors.

Walking along the small alley that runs beside the studio, making my way toward my car parked in front of the building, I pause. The hairs on the back of my neck rise, my pulse thumping loudly in my eardrums. I could have sworn I heard something behind me. Footsteps maybe? I quicken my pace, digging through my backpack for my car keys as I hurry toward the main road. My heart starts racing in my chest as I wrestle with trying to get my car keys out of my backpack.

The moment my fingers grasp the metal ring attached to my key fob, a strong hand grips my arm, and I swing my backpack around, attempting to smack my potential attacker.

"Hands off, fucker!" I shout in case there is someone walking along Main Street who may come to my aid.

"What the hell, Spitfire?" a voice I recognize shouts back.

"Nathan?" I cannot believe this. "What the fuck are you doing sneaking up on me?"

"I wasn't trying to sneak up on you. I was just following you—"

"Oh, so not sneaking. Just playing a stalker. Sorry I got it all wrong. Why are you stalking me, Nathan?" I sneer.

"It's not like that, Jenna."

"Oh, by all means. Please! Tell me what it's like, then."

"I was driving home and happened to see your car parked on the street, so I drove around back and parked when I saw you leaving that building." He points to the studio behind him. "I didn't like the idea of you walking in a dark alley at night by yourself, so I followed behind you to make sure you made it to your car safely."

"How thoughtful of you," I say, rolling my eyes. "Doesn't explain why you grabbed me."

"You looked like you got spooked or something, so I wanted to make sure you were okay. I tried calling your name, but it seemed like you didn't hear me. You almost walked out into the road without looking," he growled.

Why is he being so growly?

I glance behind me and realize how close to the road I had actually gotten. Nathan saved me from potentially getting struck by a car that I would have not seen or heard coming.

"Thank you. Although you don't deserve it," I say.

"And why is that?" he retorts.

"Had you not been *stalking* me, I wouldn't have panicked and nearly gotten myself turned into roadkill."

"Like I said, I just wanted to make sure you got to your car safely."

"Why?"

"Why what?" he asks.

"Why do you care so much? Why do you have this need to be concerned with me?"

Nathan stands there staring at me but says nothing for a few moments. "You know my dad's the chief of police."

I nod because it's true. Police Chief Gregory Ward and his kid moved here the summer before sophomore year so Nathan's dad could fulfill the job that was left empty after our former one retired.

"So you should also know that beautiful women are likely to be attacked in dark places, such as alleyways and street corners. Do you know how many times my father has arrested those types of vermin? I hear the stories. I know the statistics. Any creep could have seen you all by yourself and taken advantage of that," he states. "I couldn't allow you to be another one of those statistics, another victim."

The way he says it with clenched teeth does something to me. A small piece of me is slightly turned on at the hint of primal protectiveness, but I quickly brush it off. There can be no such feelings for this man. I mean, look at who he surrounds himself with.

"Thank you for your duty, *Officer Ward*. As you can see, I'm completely safe now. So why don't you mosey your cute butt all the way back to your car and go home!"

He scowls at me calling him Officer Ward, and I find it interesting. Why does the idea of being a cop seem to repulse him? Normally, the first son follows in their father's footsteps to be the next chief of police. At least, that is how it's been done in this town for as far back as I know. Only our former police chief, Garrett, had no sons to fill his spot.

He had two little girls, and his girls have kids who are just toddlers, nowhere near old enough to take his place.

"Did you say I have a cute butt?" He smirks.

*Shit. Did I?*

"No! No, I definitely didn't."

"Mmm … I'm pretty certain you did."

"I did not!" I firmly state. "You need to leave, as do I. It's late and we both have school in the morning."

"I will leave after I help you pick your stuff up," he says as he points to the ground. Some of my school items are sprawled across the sidewalk. They must've flown out when I swung my bag around.

I drop down onto my knees the same time Nathan crouches, and we gather my school supplies. Being this close to him, he smells manly, amber and mahogany with notes of vanilla, and is that … gasoline? I'm a bit distracted by his scent when he hands me my things before swiping my cell phone off the ground next to me.

"Hey! What are you doing?" I glare up at him as he pushes some buttons on my phone. After I shove everything in my backpack, ensuring my keys are in my hand, I stand in front of him with my other hand out. "Give me back my phone!"

"Calm down. I'm just adding my number to yours."

I lunge at him, trying to take it back, but the fucker just raises it out of my reach as he types whatever into my phone. A moment later, his phone chimes with an alert the same time my cell phone does. Whatever message came through wipes the smug smile off his face.

"Don't you know that's an invasion of privacy? You can't just steal people's phones and read their private conversations!" I shout.

"You really need to find a better boyfriend," Nathan snarls before thrusting my cell phone back into my hands. "The one you got is a piece of shit."

"You would know all about being a piece of shit, wouldn't you?" I spit back.

"You know ..." Nathan starts to say before shaking his head. "Nah. It doesn't matter."

"Know what?" I ask. He stands there glowering at me before giving me his back and heading toward the alley. "You got something to say to me, Ward, say it to my face like a man!"

"Go home, Spitfire!" he shouts before disappearing into the dark. After a quick glimpse to make sure there are no creeps around, I jump into my car and drive home, exhausted from this evening.

I pull into my driveway, parking behind Sadie's car, and stare out the windshield at my home. The white house looks dark, with only the front porch light on for me. Grabbing my things, I make my way up to the black door, letting myself into the house as quietly as I can. Ensuring the front door is locked, I creep through the entryway like a thief in the night in case everyone is asleep.

"Jenna? Is that you, babygirl?" my father's voice sounds from the room to my right. I hadn't noticed the soft light from his desk lamp was on.

"Yeah, Daddy, it's me," I say as I enter his office. He sits at his big walnut-colored desk, grading papers, I'm assuming. My father is a psychology professor at the community college.

"How was work?"

"It wasn't too bad. Didn't have any issues, but I didn't realize how tedious the cleanup process was for one person. I see why Helena needed an extra hand."

"I'm sure it was," he says. "I'm proud of you, kiddo. Choosing to help Helena out in her time of need was selfless of you. I know it was a lot for her to ask you to do this on your own, but she clearly trusts you enough to let you to take this task on by yourself. I had no doubt you could. But to go out of your way to ensure she gets to be with her mother, that proves to your mother and I that we are raising a wonderful young woman."

My heart melts at my father's praise. "Thank you, Daddy." I go around and give my father a tight hug and kiss his cheek. "I do my best to make you and mama proud."

"You have made it pretty easy for us, kiddo. You are truly our heavenly blessing."

My parents had a difficult time when they started trying for a family and struggled for years to conceive. They still are not sure why I stuck when my mom finally got pregnant, but they were over the moon with happiness that their dream was finally becoming a reality. I am their only child, their little miracle baby. Or as my parents like to say, their heavenly blessing. Hence why my middle name is Celeste.

"I'll let you be so you can finish. I'm going to shower and do some homework before calling it a night."

"Night, baby girl."

"Good night, Dad."

After heading upstairs, I walk pass Sadie's closed door. Her muffled voice comes through, and I am certain she's on the phone with Payson. I head to my bedroom, place my phone on the charger, then take a quick shower to cleanse away the sweat and exhaustion from work before throwing on my comfiest pj's.

Grabbing my backpack, I pull out my notes to start on my chemistry homework when my phone goes off. Deciding it was better to ignore whoever was calling me, I get to work, needing to get this done so I can get to bed at a reasonable hour.

I'm trying to make my way through my assignment when my phone keeps buzzing.

*What the hell?*

I finally cave and grab it, noting many missed calls and texts from Felix. My heart starts racing, my mind automatically assuming something is wrong, or worse, something bad happened. I call Felix back, and the phone rings twice before he answers it.

"Felix! Is everything al—"

"So she does know how a phone works," he snarls.

"Excuse me?"

"I have been texting and calling you all evening. Not a single reply back. What's worse is you saw my messages and couldn't bother to answer me back."

"I'm sorry, Felix. I had to cover for Helena tonight, so I had to work a longer shift—"

"Excuses! Just fucking excuses. If you really cared about me, Jenna, you would have taken the time to answer, or better yet, tell me you were busy instead of ignoring me."

"Felix, I didn't have a chance to—"

*Click.*

*Did he just hang up on me?*

I call back, but it rings a few times before going to his voicemail. After making a few more attempts to contact

Felix to try to talk to him, the calls stop ringing and instead go right to his voice message, as if he shut his phone off.

Seriously, what the fuck just happened?

I go to my text messages to figure out why he is acting out. It shouldn't have been a big deal. I mean, yeah, I could have sent a text telling him, but I didn't get a free moment tonight.

UNKNOWN

Save my number, in case you ever need me, Spitfire.

I roll my eyes at the text from Nathan. What is his deal? What is with the nickname? Spitfire? Really? The audacity of that man. To snatch my phone to get my number and have it in his head to think I could ever need him. I don't. I have a man for that. Technically two if you count my father, because my father would do anything for me. No one messes with his baby girl.

Felix is a strong man and comes off as someone who would protect the ones he cares about. I believe he would come to my aid if I needed him. Well ... maybe, if I still have him. I'm not so sure what is going on with him, and I hope I can rectify this situation.

I scroll through my text messages with Felix and note the first three messages I saw before I got distracted with work. Then I see them. Message after message of Felix trying to conversate with me to only go unanswered before he seemingly loses his mind.

FELIX

Hey beautiful.

I miss you.

How was school?

…

Hello? Jenna?

What are you doing??

Seriously, you can't answer a simple text?

It doesn't take a rocket scientist to reply back.

ANSWER YOUR DAMN PHONE!

Starting to think you're just playing with me and my feelings. Here I am, crazy about you and you're ghosting me? Real mature.

If you want to play games, I can play them too.

Fuck, Jenna. You're driving me insane. Plz talk to me!

Wow, you can read the texts but you can't respond. You do know I can see that you read these, right?

Ya know what? Fuck you. Fuck this.

My mind is frazzled. I read through the texts and then reread them, trying to make sense of it all between the messages and our brief conversation on the phone. He's upset and angry with me, even though tonight was out of my control. That part of reading the texts technically wasn't my fault because Nathan was reading them.

Felix, who is royally upset with me for ignoring him, which, again, wasn't my fault. Did he have any reason to insult me like he did, though? No! And what the hell did he mean if I want to play games, he can play them too? I don't play games. I'm too mature for that nonsense. Is he considering cheating on me? Because Jenna doesn't get cheated on. It's why I've always avoided serious relationships, especially after the shit show my bestie went through.



Since you clearly don't want to speak to me ...

I'm sorry I upset you, even though things were completely out of my control. My boss had a family emergency and asked if I would cover for her. I went directly to my job after school. I was going to text you back, but I literally got caught up in work and closed on my own for the first time. Which is a whole process for one person btw. By the time I was done, it was late. I got home, showered, and was working on my homework when your incessant calling disrupted me.

Here I was worried something bad happened to you when I saw all of your missed calls and texts only for you to be a dick? I read your messages, and quite frankly, I don't need the bullshit, Felix. If you want to be upset because I couldn't answer you for one evening, then clearly this isn't going to work, and we should call it quits now.

I hit send and let out a frustrated sigh, then plop back onto my pillows and stare at my ceiling for a moment before my phone chimes with incoming texts.



Baby, I'm sorry!

Please don't end us!

I was just upset at the idea of something happening to you or maybe you're just off with another guy and using me like my exes did.

I have trust issues, okay? It makes me upset, and I hate not being with you all the time. I just miss you :(

I don't know how to respond to that. A part of me wants to tell him off, to tell him I'm not one of his exes and it's no excuse for how he can just talk to me like that. If we can't have trust, then what's the point of us being together? I'm exhausted from work, and the whiplash he's giving me isn't helping. Maybe I should call it a night and save it to deal with in the morning. Ignoring him is what led to this outburst, why not just ignore him a little longer. What's the worst that could happen?

# Chapter 7

## Nathan



The smile on my face and the smugness I feel in my chest as I read that text should alarm me, but it doesn't. It came from Jenna late last night as I was getting ready for bed. I'm not sure what I supposedly did to cause such a status change in their relationship, but I can't say I'm mad about it.

I saw those texts he sent her. The anger and the gaslighting? Huge red flags. This guy is a problem, and I don't like the uneasy feeling I get over Jenna being with him. Cassidy hasn't sent me any updates with information on the guy, but to be fair, I didn't supply her with much of anything myself. I know nothing about him other than what he looks like and his first name.

"What's got you smiling like that?" Dom asks. I shove my phone into my jeans before grabbing my backpack from the passenger seat and locking up my car.

"Nothing," I say to my best friend.

"Pretty boy got a new toy?" Anthony asks, coming to stand next to Dom. Anthony is a junior and Dom's immature younger brother. He also plays on the football team with us. Another linebacker, who is set to take over his brother's spot next season.

"For God's sake, Anthony. When are you going to grow the hell up and stop objectifying women as only being something to get your dick wet. We are human beings!" Alora snarls before smacking her twin upside his head.

"Can you two not already?" Dom grits out. "Must you always get on each other's nerves. And mine? Why can't the two of you just get along for five minutes?"

Anthony and Alora look at each other with disgust before Alora rolls her eyes. "I'm not the problem. He is," she states, pointing at Anthony before walking off.

"Whatever!" Anthony shouts at her retreating form. "What the fuck!? Oh, hell no! Nuh-uh. Not on my watch!"

Baffled by the quick change in his demeanor, my brows raise as Anthony runs toward his sister after some guy hugs her.

"Fucking hell," Dom mutters.

"What's the matter? Don't like your little sister getting hugs from guys?" I taunt.

"Of course not. You know how it is. How our teenage hormones are all about one thing with girls, many girls.

But it's not just about that, especially with Anthony and *that* guy. There's beef between those two." He nods toward them as Anthony pulls her away from the guy and drags her through the school doors.

"Care to elaboarte?"

"Nah. Nothing to worry your pretty head about. Besides, you still haven't answered my question."

"Just got an interesting text, that's all."

"Mm-hm. Any chance from the pretty girl you've been eye-fucking the hell out of since the Halloween party?"

Damn this fucker. He pays too close attention to things around him. Great for on the field but can be annoying off it.

"First off, I don't eye-fuck her."

"Riiight. Right, right. Just like I'm still a virgin."

"Whatever man." I chuckle. "Nah. Seriously though, it's just her saying something about how I somehow ruined her relationship."

"Ah, now I see. You're smiling because now you can shoot your shot with her, right?"

"Nah, it's not like that, man. For starters, she clearly hates my guts, and I don't know why."

"Have you ever asked her?"

"Yeah, exactly how am I supposed to do that when the moment I'm within breathing distance of her, she has her claws out, keeping me at arm's length?" I'm not sure what I did to be on her shit list.

"Well, you have her number now. Not sure how you managed to swing that, but if talking in person doesn't work, you could, I don't know, just text her and ask." He shrugs.

"Who is to say she hasn't blocked me?" I mean, the best way to find out would be to ask her.

"Uh, maybe you might want to hold off on the whole shooting your shot thing," Dom says. He pats my chest and points toward Jenna's white Volkswagen Beetle. There's a big ass blue truck parked in front of it, blocking her in.

"What the fu—" A big ass dude hops out of the truck with a bouquet of flowers in his hands.

He goes over to the driver's side door and taps the glass in an attempt to get her attention. My eyes focus in on Jenna's face. If I spot an ounce of a flinch, I'm going over there and dealing with the fucker myself.

To my utter shock, she beams her big beautiful smile up at him. Did she not read those messages, not see the danger within those texts?

Anger simmers under my skin as she gets out of her car and wraps her arms around the ogre before he leans down to kiss her plump lips.

"Whoa, bro. You need to calm down," Dom says, breaking my focus. "Your jealousy is starting to show."

"I'm not fucking jealous." I seethe.

"Okay. You're breathing heavily, nostrils flaring, and your fists look two seconds away from wanting to punch something." He chuckles, shaking his head before walking off toward school. "That's jealousy, my guy!"

Dom is my best friend and I love the dude like a brother, but he has no idea what he is talking about. I'm not jealous. *I'm not.*

Jenna is blinded by the front this ogre is showing her. This isn't who he is. This is a facade, an act. The real him, the monster underneath, is biding its time. She needs to see that before it gets to be too late. Before something seriously bad happens to her. If what happened at Chad's party was a sliver of the rage her *boyfriend* has and what he let slip, what will he do if no one is around?

No! I won't let that shit happen to her. I need information on him, ammo to convince her she needs to be away from this fucker for her safety.

Before thinking better of it, I'm moving in their direction, staying clear of catching either of their attention. I pull out my cell phone and when I'm within camera distance, I snap a photo before sending it to Cass.



After I send the text, I look up in time to see the fucking ogre making his way in my direction. Jenna's eyes widen when she sees Felix coming for me.

"Felix! What are you doing?" she yells.

"I've got a few bones to pick with you," he snarls, ignoring his girlfriend.

"Oh yeah. Is that so?" I retort.

"Yeah. You got some kind of crush on my girl? You seem to be around an awful lot."

"Feeling a little insecure, are we?" Do I have some crush on Jenna? Yeah. Since the day I laid eyes on her in the hall on my first day of sophomore year. Am I going to tell this fucker? Hell no.

"I'm just going to make something very clear. She's *my* girlfriend. If I find out you're bothering her, I will see to it myself you are dealt with. Do I make myself clear?"

Standing toe to toe with him, I find it funny how he seems to think I'm the threat when in reality it is him who should be dealt with. Anger thrums through me, so I raise my voice, wanting everyone to hear my next words.

"Are you really threatened by me being close to her, or are you more afraid because I caught your ass laying hands on her? What kind of low life does that, huh? Lays a hand on a woman, leaving marks?"

Felix clenches his jaw and a vein in his forehead throbs. He's pissed because I'm exposing him to anyone within earshot. *Good.*

"Yeah. I saw the bruises you left on her, you piece of fucking shit!"

Some students gasp while others whisper among themselves.

"What do you have to say for yourself, *woman beater*?"

It happens so quickly, I wasn't prepared. He punches me in my face, knocking me back. Some people say "Oooh," and the sounds of heels clicking across pavement can be heard in the distance.

I take a moment to steady myself. My cheek split, a metallic taste fills my mouth, then I spit the blood onto the pavement.

"Felix! What the hell?" Jenna exclaims as she looks around. "You need to go. Now!"

I'm ready to retaliate, but I spot Ms. Everhart approaching us. Felix sees her too, then gives Jenna a kiss, deepening it and keeping his eyes on me as he does.

*Dick.*

He releases her before hopping in his truck and burning his tires as he flies out of the parking lot before Ms. Everhart can get to him.

My eyes move from the disappearing truck to Jenna walking toward me with the bouquet of red roses in her hand. She stops before me, a smirk displayed upon her beautiful face.

"Guess I was wrong. You didn't ruin shit for me, after all," she says before smelling the roses, a wide smile blooming across her face as she passes me on her way to the front doors.

I'm not sure how I'm the one to blame. I didn't even reply to that douchebag's texts for her. Even though I thought about it. How tempting it was, but I didn't need Jenna to hate me even more than she already does.

"Mr. Ward, may I see you in my office please?" Ms. Everhart says as she passes me to head into the school.

"Yes, ma'am," I say as I follow behind her. My phone alerts me to a new text, so I pull my phone out of my jeans pocket to check it.

CASSIDY

I'll look into it. Still no word to daddio?

I hope having that bastard's tag can pull up information for Cassidy. I need anything and everything on the fucker to help me protect Jenna from him. No matter how she feels about me, I know my gut is sending me warning bells for a reason. Even if we could never be, if she could never be mine, some part of me cares for her deeply. Cares enough to want to ensure her fire is kept safe and protected from anything wanting to diminish it.

"Please have a seat," Ms. Everhart says as she closes her office door behind her. She's a middle-aged woman with caramel-brown hair that hangs in long loose waves. Big black librarian-style glasses sit upon her face, and her brown eyes bore into me as she sits behind her desk.

"Mr. Ward, you have been an exemplary student since you have been at this school. No reports of bad behavior from your coach or teachers. You are excelling in your studies and, excuse my language, one hell of an athlete. So it's safe to say that I'm truly surprised and slightly appalled by what I came across as I was making my way in. Do you care to explain to me what transpired outside a few moments ago?"

I look away from her piercing gaze, unsure what I want to say. "Truthfully, Ms. Everhart, it's not my place to say."

"You seemed to have plenty to say to that gentleman outside."

I scoff at her calling Felix that because the guy is nowhere close to the definition of being a gentleman.

"Those things you were saying … is there something about that person that makes you think you can just slander him in front of your peers in the parking lot?"

"It's not slander because it's the fucking truth!" I shout, my heart racing. I don't know if it's the adrenaline still coursing through my body, but I'm crossing a line raising my voice and cursing at an administrator. "I'm sorry—"

Ms. Everhart raises her hands slightly. "There is no need to raise your voice. I'm not your enemy here. All I'm trying to do is understand what is going on. I overheard some of the things you were yelling back there, and those are some big accusations to be throwing around."

I refuse to say anything, not wanting to have to tell her how I know they aren't accusations. They're facts but stating that would only lead to her bringing Jenna in and questioning her. How much would she despise me if I allowed that to happen?

She studies me for a moment. "Are you usually this temperamental?"

"No, ma'am. I'm usually good at being level headed. It's why I'm a great defensive player, why I work hard at … school." I almost let it slip about the garage. I don't need word getting back to my father that I'm still working there, helping out my uncle. "At least not since before my sophomore year."

"Did something terrible happen before sophomore year, if you don't mind me asking?"

I take a deep breath, calming my racing heart before I speak. "I lost someone. Someone who was really close and important to me. Ryan was my older brother. We got into an argument one night over something so stupid and then ..." I swipe my arm across my eyes to wipe away the tears forming in them. "Then he was gone. Car accident took his life."

"I am so sorry to hear that, Nathan," she says, giving me that all too familiar sympathetic look. The very reason I never share with anyone about my brother. Everyone except Dom. "That must have been really hard on you."

I nod, refusing to look at her.

"It sounds to me like you're blaming yourself for the accident. Am I somewhere close to that hard truth?"

I refuse to say it out loud, admitting how I often blamed myself, still blame myself, for Ryan losing his life. It's why I am the way I am today. It's why I remain stoic. Why I refuse to speak the truth or say what's on my mind.

"Have you received therapy since losing your brother?"

"No."

"I see ..." Ms. Everhart takes a moment before she opens a drawer in her desk and pulls out a few pamphlets. "It's apparent that you have some unresolved trauma associated with the loss of your brother. I'm glad you have football as an outlet, but sometimes it helps to have a professional to guide you through the waves of grief. These"—she points to the booklets on her desk—"are just some of the local therapists in town who may be able to help you. I want you to take these with you, and in your down time, browse through them. Compare them. See what would fit you best, and then I want you to make an appointment. Can you do that for me?"

Ms. Everhart smiles as she pushes the pamphlets toward me.

"Sure."

"I'm holding you to it." She points a finger at me. "I'll be checking on you to see if you have either right before or after Thanksgiving break. That should be plenty of time for you to make your decision and at least get an appointment booked."

I grab the handful of papers, nodding at her before making my escape. Stopping by my locker, I shove the pamphlets inside before grabbing what I need for my next class. Maybe I will consider what the guidance counselor says, or I won't. How am I expected to find the time between everything else I have going on in my life?

# Chapter 8

## Nathan

"I'm a free man tonight! Whoop whoop! So what's the plan for the evening, fellas?" Brady says as he enters the weight room. It's the final period for the day and a free period for most of us seniors on the football team. So we work out to keep our bodies in shape since our season isn't quite over yet. We have the big championship game in two weeks, so we don't want to slack off. Can't afford injuries or risk any chance of us losing this game. We are hungry, starving to claim the trophy and the title of being South Carolina's football champs of the year.

I push the barbell, finishing out the last rep of my bench press before Dom helps me secure it in place so I can sit up.

"Got to work with my uncle tonight," I say.

"Yeah, I got some calculus homework I need to do," Dom replies.

"Same, bro," DeAndre says from the chest press machine.

"Yeah, I got to meet with Dylan after school to work on that stupid novel assignment Ms. Steinhall gave us," Chad says. "I need the grade to keep that hot piece of ass of a teacher from going to my parents."

"You guys! Do the homework later. You have all weekend to work on that shit," Brady says.

"Actually, man ..." Dom says, rubbing the back of his neck. "You might but we don't."

"What the hell do you mean?" Brady asks.

"Yeah, we have practice this weekend, dude," DeAndre states.

"No, we don't. Coach said practice starts back up again on Monday." Brady cannot participate since he's out for the rest of the season with an arm injury, but he helps the coaches with plays and formations so he can still be a part of the team. It was at the request of his father, Russell Thomas.

The guys and I look at each other, trying to decide who will break the news to him. Or if we should even say anything. He's been chill about talks of the game, but if anyone brings up Payson, he tends to lose his shit.

"Well, dude ... you see ..." DeAndre says but stops. He doesn't want to deal with the tantrum Brady will throw anymore than the rest of us do.

"Jesus. Clearly since no one is going to man up and say it, I will. We don't have time to do anything because Payson is pulling an extra weekend of practice before we start on Monday," Dom states. "Everyone agreed to it."

We all look at Brady, watching the emotions play out on his face. Surprised, hurt, then anger or annoyance.

"Clearly I was not included nor agreed to such a thing," he grits out.

"Yeah, well, we didn't think you needed to know." DeAndre shrugs before going back to his workout when Brady shoots daggers at him.

Chad walks toward Brady and places a hand on his shoulder. "Look, man. We didn't say anything because we all know how you feel about Payson since she took your spot and stole your girl."

"Payson didn't steal my girl. We have been over this! I fucking used Sadie and her father's status to appease my father." He seethes.

"Tomato, To-mah-to. Point being, we know you don't like Payson, and if you knew we were getting together with her, you would flip the fuck out." We all nod with Chad because he isn't wrong.

"Payson wants us to make sure we are still vibing like we have been. She wants us to win, and we agreed. Coach is aware of this because she went to him first and made sure he approved."

"I can't believe you guys," Brady says. "I thought we were bros."

"Why are you being so emotional about this, man?" Chad asks.

"Yeah, are Lydia's pregnancy hormones rubbing off on you? What's it called when the girl is pregnant and the father gets, like, the symptoms?" DeAndre asks.

"Sympathy pains," Dom responds.

"I don't have fucking sympathy pains!" he shouts. "I'm just pissed that for once I don't have to deal with Lydia clinging to me since her parents are taking her out of town for the evening and I want to be with my friends. I want to get fucking drunk and maybe find a willing chick to fuck."

The room goes quiet for a moment as we gawk at Brady.

"What?" Brady sneers.

"Dude, your girl is pregnant with *your* baby. And you want to disrespect both Lydia and your child by fucking some random chick while they are away?" Dom asks, shaking his head. Even if Brady doesn't have feelings for Lydia, it seems wrong to want to mess with anyone else. Especially since he has *two* babies on the way.

"You guys act like she's my fucking wife. She's just a clingy bitch, claiming her kid is mine, and wants me solely for the Thomas name."

"If you can't see that girl has been infatuated and obsessed with you since you allowed her near your dick, then you're fucking blind," Dom says. "That kid is yours. We all know it. She hasn't come near any of the footballers since you finally looked her way. Ask the guys. They will tell you."

"Do you think you should be getting laid? I mean, your track record of knocking up the ladies is—"

"Shut the fuck up, Chad!" Brady growls out. "You know what? You guys can go do your own shit, and I'll find something to do. Better yet, *someone* to do." Brady storms out of the weight room, leaving us all to our thoughts.

"That guy has some serious mommy issues," DeAndre says before making his way over to the treadmill.

Maybe there is some truth to that. No one knows anything about Brady's mom. We know his dad was a pro baller who got hurt and had to retire before he wanted. He became a successful businessman and has raised Brady on his own. Or with the help of a few nannies. Regardless, his lack of respect for women and their feelings may be rooted in the fact that his mom hasn't been in his life and his dad doesn't do steady relationships.

"Hey, kiddo. What troubles you?" my uncle asks. "Your old man isn't giving you a hard time now, is he?"

I'm sitting at the front desk of my uncle's garage, where I must have zoned out. My uncle is finishing with the last car for the evening before we close up shop. "Nah. Just thinking about stuff."

"What kind of stuff?"

I think about what I want to say and how much I'm willing to tell him. If I say the wrong thing, he may go to my dad, and that is the last thing I want or need him to do.

"Have you ever gotten a bad feeling about a situation or even a person?" I feel like this is a vague yet basic question. Doesn't give anything concerning away.

"Mmm ... not that I can recall," he answers. "Though, I think I recall a few times Sarah did."

I perk up at the mention of my mother's name. "Really?"

"Yeah. She called it her intuition. She said whenever she felt like something was off, it tended to be true most of the time. Same with people. I think it saved a friend's life once back in high school. Her friend was talking to this guy, and when your mother met him, she said she didn't like the vibe he was giving off. She felt like there was something bad about him. Told her friend too."

"Did the friend listen?" I had to ask, needing to know.

"She did, and I bet she's counting her stars everyday that she listened to your mother. The guy your mother had a bad feeling about? He ended up raping and killing the girl he dated after Sarah's friend. Now he's serving a life sentence for it."

*Jesus.*

"One of the infamous things I will remember about Sarah is her saying to always follow your gut when it's trying to tell you something. I don't know if it's a female thing or what, but clearly there was truth in it for her." He looks at me. "You got a bad feeling about something?"

I stare into his green eyes, the same green eyes I inherited from my mother, and nod.

"I have to ask, and I need you to be completely honest with me. Are you in any trouble, kid?" he asks.

"Nah. Not about me. Just something has me worried and I can't seem to shake it."

"If your mother was here, she would tell you to take her advice. Whatever is troubling your mind, don't ignore it."

"Thanks, Uncle." Just as he walks back to finish working on the current car, my phone vibrates with an incoming message from Dom.

DOM

Anthony just got home. He said him and some of the junior guys were at a party with Brady in the next county over. Said a lot of Greystone guys were there. One of them believes they saw Felix lay some girl out.

NATHAN

Like full out punch a girl?

DOM

From the sounds of it. Said she didn't get up and chaos ensued. Everyone was scattering when someone said they were calling an ambulance.

*What the fuck?*

NATHAN

Did he say if the police were called? Bc that's assault dude.

DOM

He doesn't know. They all bounced except for Brady. Said they didn't know where he went after they spotted him talking to some girl. But if it was Felix, man, you better warn your girl.

Fucking hell. I need someone to confirm if it was him. Better yet, I hope the police were called and there's a report. I could message Cass and find out if she heard anything at the station. If it was Felix, and he knocked some girl out at a party in front of others, what else is this monster capable of? That thought alone doesn't sit well with me, especially when I think about the fact he is still with Jenna.

*My Jenna.*

# Chapter 9

## Jenna

It's Friday night and the outlet mall is crazy busy. I'm not surprised. I mean, what else is there really to do on a Friday evening in a small town?

Usually, I work with Helena to help her prepare for the weekend appointments, but she gave me the night off as a thank you for closing for her last night. Her mom is thankfully okay and went home early this morning. Helena said since the sessions were small today, she could handle closing the studio on her own.

Since Sadie doesn't have cheer practice to command and her girlfriend is occupied with family, she agreed to have a girls night out. Manis and pedis, shopping, dinner from the food court, and then going back to the house to watch chick flicks with my bestie is exactly what we both need.

"How are things with your family?" I ask Sadie since I haven't had a chance to check in on her situation. To be fair, we haven't had a lot of one-on-one time lately with how busy our schedules are.

Sadie came out at homecoming, and word spread around town so fast it got back to her mom during Sunday church services. Her mom is homophobic, something that runs in her side of the family. After she kicked Sadie out, she banned her from having any contact with her two younger siblings, fearing her gayness would corrupt the other two. Mayor Adams, Sadie's father, came by after he found out what happened. Sadie confessed she kept her sexual identity a secret from them because of the homophobia and not wanting to embarrass her father's career. He reassured her she hasn't embarrassed him, and he is so proud of her for finally accepting herself for who she is. He ensured Sadie he will try to work on getting her mother to see reason as they seek marriage counseling to help them through some marital problems they've been having.

I'm just grateful my parents love Sadie like a bonus daughter, and since I'm their only kid, we had the space to give her a home to finish out her senior year.

"They're okay." She shrugs. "Mom is still not seeing eye to eye with Dad, especially with letting me see Hannah and Isaiah. I think it's causing more problems in their marriage," she says, her voice low, staring at the ground. Sadie spends time with her dad when her mother attends church services on Sundays. She's been doing better, but I know there are moments when she misses her family, especially her little brother and sister. She's worried for them and hopes their mom isn't poisoning their minds to turn them against her.

"Their troubles are not your fault, Sadie. This whole situation is not yours to blame. You know that, right?" If I know my best friend, I have no doubt she is blaming herself for the problems her parents are dealing with.

"Yeah … I'm trying to remind myself of that. I just feel guilty sometimes. You know? That my happiness to be with a woman I love is also destroying the happiness of another couple. It feels wrong sometimes."

"Your parents have been hiding their marital problems from you and your siblings long before you came out, so don't you dare think your lesbianism is ruining your parents' marriage."

Sadie gives me a soft smile. "Is lesbianism even a word?"

"I don't know, but it felt like the right word to say." I laugh. "Look, you get to be who you have longed to be. You are free to be you, and life is worth living so much more being happy than hiding from the world, afraid of what others think about you. I mean, look at how much happier you have been since Payson stole your heart? You practically glow! Hell, even your confidence has grown since you told the whole school you loved her. The difference I have seen in you from when you were with that jackass to now, it's incredible. This is who you are supposed to be, Sadie, and I'll knock a bitch who dares to say otherwise!"

"This is why you're my best friend," she says, squeezing me into a side hug as we walk toward the food court. We grab a pizza and drinks and make our way to one of the tables in the middle of the food court.

"Enough about me. Let's talk about you. I saw the roses Felix gave you this morning. That was so sweet! Are things going well for you guys?"

Sadie grabs napkins to dab up the grease off her pepperoni pizza. The girl has done it as long as I've known her.

"They're good," I say, shrugging.

"Are you guys having problems?"

"No, nothing like that. It's just that … I guess I'm conflicted. He got really upset with me last night because I didn't reply to his texts. Which I couldn't because I got caught up with work, then Nathan was being a pain in my ass, and by the time I got home, it was late. I had chemistry homework to do. Felix called—"

"Wait! Sorry for interrupting, but did you say something about Nathan? What did Nathan do?"

"Yeah. He fucking *stalked* me after work! Like dude, what the fuck is your problem?"

"Explain to me how he *stalked* you?" Sadie asks, eyes narrowed.

"I went out the back door of the studio after locking it up and took that alleyway that runs along the studio because I parked on Main Street. I had a creepy feeling like someone was following me which scared the shit out of me, so I moved faster. I was digging for my keys in my backpack and then someone grabbed my arm and I swung, trying to hit them with my bag. That's when I saw it was Nathan. Said he wanted to make sure I got to my car safely." I roll my eyes, remembering how it all went down.

"That's … actually kind of sweet."

"Come again?"

"I mean, you definitely should be aware of your surroundings at night and especially in darkened allies. The fact he was just making sure no harm came your way ... that is incredibly thoughtful."

"You cannot seriously be standing by him?"

"Why not? He was just making sure you were okay, that my best friend made it home safely to her family. I mean, he would know about that sort of thing. His dad is the chief of police. I can't imagine the stories he must hear, the cases his dad deals with."

"Yeah ... but ... Sadie. He's Brady's best friend."

"And?"

What the hell does she mean *and*?

"He's ... Brady's ... best ... friend."

How else can I spell that out for her?

"I'm still not following you, Jenna."

"Nathan cannot be sweet. We cannot admire him doing things that are clearly annoying."

"They are only annoying because it's happening to you." Sadie leans back in her chair and narrows her eyes at me, like she's trying to see something within me. "Awe! I get it now."

"Get what?"

"You're looping Nathan in the same category as Brady and Chad. You're still pissed at what Brady did to me, and you dislike him by association."

"Okay, and like that's a bad thing?"

"Yeah, it kind of is, Jenna. You cannot assume someone is like the people they hang out with. Nathan is his own person. He makes his own decisions, and honestly, out of the three, Nathan is far from being anything like the other two. If you stopped being catty with him long enough, you may even notice that."

Is she for real right now?

"Well, your *thoughtful* Nathan read my texts from Felix last night and it put a damper on my relationship."

Sadie takes a pull from her soda before speaking. "He read your texts?"

"Yeah. Nathan was helping me pick up my stuff before he snatched my phone to send me a text with his number. That was right before the nosy prick took it upon himself to read Felix's texts." Sadie looks confused, so I explain it to her. "Felix saw that the texts were read and because I didn't respond, he flipped out on me. I told him if he got this upset over me being busy, then we should call it quits. He tried apologizing, but I went to sleep. Figured I would deal with him when I was mentally capable. It's why he showed up at school with the roses this morning. He wanted to show me he was really sorry, no matter if it made him late for school."

Sadie ponders over everything. I'm not sure what is going through her mind, and I don't get to ask her because someone appears next to our table.

"Well, if it isn't little miss trouble."

"Holy shit! Deon?" I squeal, jumping out of my chair into my cousin's arms. I haven't seen him in so long. Deon is my Aunt Naomi's son and the oldest of three boys. He's attending Benedict College, majoring in computer science.

I pull away, taking in how much he has grown since we last saw each other. He's so tall, probably like six foot two and has a whole mustache and goatee now. He got that good hair going for him. Black curly hair on top and faded up the sides. He looks so much more like a man now, reminding me of a young Shemar Moore.

"You remember my bestie, Sadie?" I point to my gorgeous friend who stands and gives him a hug.

"Of course. How could I forget the beautiful Miss Sadie Adams?" Deon smirks.

"Watch it. She's got a girlfriend who could kick your ass." I tease.

"No shit! Sadie finally came out of the closet?"

"Wait. You knew?" Sadie asks, eyes wide.

"I didn't know … per se. Jenna might have let it slip a time or two," he says as he sits beside me at our table.

"Jenna, how dare you? You swore you wouldn't tell a soul!"

"To be fair, he lives in Georgia, a whole hour and a half away from here. Word wasn't going to get back to your parents. Plus, Deon is the older brother I never got to have. I can tell him anything and trust him to keep a secret."

"Fair enough," Sadie replies, going back to eating her slice of pizza.

"So, what brings you to my neck of the woods, cuz?"

"Shopping, obviously. Trying to find a gift for my girlfriend."

"Awe!" Sadie and I say in unison.

"You two can stop that!" he says as he points a finger at both of us. "Her birthday is next week, and I want it to be nice. Thought I'd check out here. Glad I did since I bumped into you ladies."

"Is it serious?" I ask. "Does auntie know about this girl?"

"Nothing serious. Well, not yet at least. I don't know … it feels different with this girl. She feels … special. And no, you cannot tell my mother!" He gives me a stern, *you better keep your pie hole shut* look. "Especially since we are coming to your house for Thanksgiving this year. I mean it too, Jen. Not. A. Word!"

"Okay, okay. Message received. Sheesh!" In all honesty, it's adorable to see my cousin sweating to find the perfect gift for a girl who's somehow stolen a piece of his heart.

"Will we get to meet her?" I ask.

"If things continue going well, yeah. I think so," he replies. "So, what are you two ladies up to?"

"Having a girls night," Sadie says. "Much-needed, long-overdue girls night."

"Yeah, and since you're of the male species, you should probably kick rocks. Otherwise, we may find a cute little dress for you, and we are not talking about one for your girlfriend either."

The way Deon's eyes bug out has Sadie and I bursting into a fit of giggles.

"You know, I saw a really gorgeous purple dress that would look impeccable on you." Sadie taunts.

"You know, I really do need to get back to what I came here to do," Deon says as he stands from the table. "Sadie, it was a pleasure. Jenna, see you at Thanksgiving."

I give him another big hug before he walks away. I hope he finds what he is looking for. Whoever the girl is, she is lucky to be loved by Deon because he loves so deeply when he cares about you.

"Well, I am stuffed. What do you say we blow this popsicle stand and head home, put on our pj's and watch some movies?" Sadie says.

"You've read my mind, girl." We gather our bags and throw our trash away as we make our way to the parking lot.

Sadie and I just finished watching *Purple Hearts* when her phone starts ringing.

"It's Payson. Do you mind? I want to see how things went with Judson."

"Go ahead. I'll make us some more popcorn before we watch the next movie."

Sadie whispers "Thank you" before answering her phone and heading to her bedroom.

"Hey, QB. How did it go?" she says before she disappears up the steps to her bedroom.

I make my way into the kitchen, grabbing drinks and placing a new bag of popcorn in the microwave when there is a pounding on the front door.

My parents went out with colleagues tonight and won't be back till later this evening. Plus they have their house keys on them, so who the hell would be at my door at almost ten thirty?

Unless ... Nope! No.

*Do not even think such a thing, Jenna.*

I push that dark thought out of my mind while racing to the front door, secretly praying I don't find a pair of officers on the other side of it giving me the worst news a young person could ever hear.

Pulling the door open, I'm surprised to find Felix pacing back and forth on my front stoop, then let out a breath of relief.

"Felix? What are you doing here? I thought you were hanging with your boys?"

"Who is he?" Felix growls out.

"I'm sorry. I'm not following. Who is who?"

"Don't play dumb games with me, Jenna. The guy ..." Felix grits out, teeth clenched.

I cross my arms over my chest.

"I'm not playing games with you, Felix. I seriously have no fucking clue who are you talking about? You're going to have to be a little more specific." What the hell is his deal? What is he even going on about?

"The one I saw you hug at the mall tonight," he says, standing at his full height. His muscular arms crossing over his chest as he looks down on me.

"You were at the mall?" I don't recall seeing him when Sadie and I were shopping.

"Don't change the subject. Who was he? Is he why you avoided answering me last night? Is that who you were with, claiming you were busy?"

"No, Felix. I really was busy with work last night. I worked 'til close, then Nathan was being Nathan—"

"Who the fuck is Nathan?" he snarls. "Is that the fucker you were hugging?"

"First off, do not cut me off," I say, jabbing my index finger into his muscled chest. "Nathan is a nobody from school and someone you don't have to worry about. Trust me, I can deal with him. And for your information, the only guy I hugged tonight was Deon, my *cousin*. I haven't seen him since summer break, and we were catching up before he left."

"Jesus, Jenna. Do you see how crazy you make me?" Felix says, back to pacing before he stops and grabs my face between his big meaty hands. "You swear to God that's all he is to you? Your cousin?"

Grabbing his hands, I gently remove them from my face. I know how strong his grip can be, and I don't want to chance him leaving any bruises on my face, giving Nathan more reason to annoy me. "I swear to you. Deon is my cousin, but he's more like a big brother to me. He was out shopping, saw Sadie and I eating, and we were just catching up before he had to go." I look into his eyes, but one thought keeps nagging me. "Why were you at the mall tonight and how come you didn't come say hi?"

"It was a quick trip. One of the guys had to grab something before we headed out." He quickly averts his gaze to the road before returning to me. "Look, I acted out. Let me make it up to you, beautiful. Come over to my house tomorrow evening. I can order us takeout, get whatever you want. My parents won't be home, and we can do whatever you want."

I think it over for a few seconds. We haven't really had any alone time, just the two of us. Between his football practices and my work schedule, we have both been fairly busy. Maybe that is what we need to help fix whatever these issues are plaguing Felix.

"I can have anything I want?" I ask slyly.

"Anything you want, gorgeous."

"Well ... I could go for some sushi ..."

"Say less," he says, and leans down to give me a kiss. He is gentle with me, taking his time tasting me. His tongue flicks with mine before he nips my bottom lip and pulls away.

"I gotta get going. I'll call you later," he says as he makes his way to his truck.

I wave him off, taking a deep breath before returning into the house. I'm not sure what his past relationship experiences were like, but his lack of trust is alarming. He should trust me better, trust I'm nothing like the girls before me. He just needs to see that. A thought crosses my mind as I grab the drinks and popcorn. If Felix needs to be persuaded, I know just the thing to convince him I'm not like the rest.

# Chapter 10

## Nathan

I'm making myself a protein shake when my father steps into the kitchen, his uniform crisp and clean, ready for another day of duty.

"Working again, Dad?" I ask, even though it's obviously clear. The man has worked every day this week, and I wonder if he will ever take a day or, hell, a weekend off.

"Yeah. Got some cases to work through. Crime never sleeps, you know?" he says as he pours coffee into his thermos. He glances up at me, taking in how I'm dressed. I'm wearing dark-gray athletic shorts with white compression pants underneath and a white thermal undershirt. "Where are you headed off to?"

"To the park. Most of the team is getting together for some extra practice time." The local park has a wide, open field that allows plenty of space for us to move around and run plays.

Dad nods, acknowledging me. "And after?"

I shrug. "Don't know yet. I'm not even sure how long Payson wants to run these practices, but I might go hang out with some friends afterward. Is that okay with you?"

"It's fine. Just shoot me a text letting me know what you are doing," he says. I grab my shake along with my football bag when Dad says, "Oh, and Nathan?"

"Yeah, Dad?"

"Be careful."

"Always, Dad."

"Another thing, before you go. I'll see if I can grab a practice test today for you and drop it in your room."

"Dad, I've already taken like … five of them. I'm pretty sure I've had plenty of practice."

"Listen, son. The more you practice, the better chances you have of passing and getting into the academy after graduation. The sooner, the better."

I stare at my father, wanting to tell him how I've actually not been studying the handbook. How I attempted the first practice test he gave me, but my heart wasn't in it. The others ended up being shoved in a drawer somewhere in my room, forgotten and untouched. I just don't have it in me to tell him to stop forcing this on me. He didn't do this shit with Ryan …

I swallow the lump in my throat and blink back the tears threatening to make their appearance.

"Just put it on my desk," I say, then make a dash through the living room and out the front door to my car to drive my ass to the park. I have never been more grateful for Payson deciding to put this extra practice together. Football distracts me and gives me a way to release these feelings I harbor inside, and today feels like a good day for some football.

I make it to the field just as Colton and some guys finish spray painting the grass to look like an actual field. Orange cones sit on both ends, marking where the goal line will be while we practice. I don't think I've seen anyone take football as seriously as Payson Moore. Not even Brady was this committed.

I stand next to my quarterback, watching our teammates paint solid white lines in the green grass. "How did you manage to get all of this?"

"I have my ways." Payson smirks.

"You really don't play around, do you?"

"Nope," she says, emphasizing the p. "Especially when it comes to a championship. We have worked hard all season, given certain situations. Everyone on this team has earned their ticket into one of the biggest games they will play. And everyone deserves to show what they are made of when they enter that stadium. I want this but not as much as I want it for them. This may be the only chance some of these guys get seen to earn scholarships or full rides, so it's imperative we be ready, as one working unit."

I can't help but feel inspired. Payson has always had heart. You can see it in how she plays and commands the offense, but this chick has fire and leadership too. Something Brady didn't quite grasp as a quarterback, and even though he is my friend, this team has done better since she came along.

"Can I talk to you about something?" Payson asks.

"Yeah, what's up?"

"Sadie seems to have some concerns about Jenna. More specifically, that guy Jenna is seeing," she says. This grabs my attention. "She was on the phone with me last night and paused our conversation when she heard shouting coming from the front of the house. Took her a few moments to realize Felix showed up and was going off on Jenna."

"What was he saying?"

"She couldn't really make out what was said, but it was more how he was saying it. Sadie said he was aggressive, that it made *her* nervous and she was inside the house on a whole other floor. No lie, I don't like anyone making my woman feel unsafe. I was tempted to go over there, but Sadie said not to since he wasn't there long. But she did say hearing him like that, it's giving her a bad feeling and she doesn't know how to approach Jenna about it."

Sadie has a bad feeling about Felix too?

I look to the sky, as if I could ask my mother if this is her way of telling me to keep following my own intuition.

"So ... why are you talking to me about this?"

"Sadie may have mentioned you showing up the other night after Jenna got off work, wanting to make sure she got home safe. You have also been a little extra observant of my girlfriend's best friend as of late." Payson smirks at me. "Something tells me there's a reason for it, but I'm not trying to snoop. I just need to know if Sadie has anything to worry about."

Damn. I was not expecting this, but what do I tell her when I don't know for sure myself?

"Look. I won't lie and say I don't have concerns regarding that ogre. Something isn't settling with me when it comes to him." I glance around, ensuring no one is near us before looking back at Payson. "I may have someone on my dad's payroll already looking into him. I don't have much and she hasn't given me any updates, but I'm trying to do what I can. I need proof, evidence that fucker is dangerous so I don't look like an idiot if I'm wrong about him."

Payson nods. "If I find or hear anything about him, I'll pass it along."

"Thank you," I say. "And what about Sadie?"

"I'll do what I can to reassure her, to not press Jenna about him. Especially since it seems Jenna is very much into this guy."

Hearing that causes a weird ache in my chest, but I try not to let the hurt show on my face. Last thing I need is Payson knowing that part of my behavior with Jenna is because of feelings I harbor for her.

"Now, with that out of the way. I need you to run defense today. Are you cool with that?" Payson asks.

"You know I am." We bump fists before grabbing our helmets and making our way to the field when the rest of the team arrives. It's definitely a great day to play some football.

It's almost 6:30 p.m. and the sun is setting for the day. Payson called it quits about a half hour ago so we could clean up the field and head home for dinner with our families. Well, the majority of us who have family dinners.

"Hey, some of us are meeting at Munson's Diner for food, then going to Chad's to hang out afterward. Want to join?" Dom asks as we get to our vehicles.

"Sure. Not like I have anything better to do since Dad's working." It beats having to go home to an empty, quiet house.

Thirty minutes later, I'm freshly showered and ready to stuff my face with the best burgers in Bellwood. Munson's Diner is your classic old-school diner, with its checkered flooring and neon lights. Red and white booths line the windows. They even have what looks like a bartop with round stools lining it in the center, something pulled from the 1950s, and there is a jukebox in the far-right corner.

A cute girl with blonde wavy hair and lavender streaks approaches me when I enter.

"Welcome to Munson's Diner. How can I help you?" she says, face flat and hand on her hip.

"I'm looking for a group of guys. Football players who are probably loud and obnoxious?"

The girl points behind her. "Last booth in the corner," she says before walking off to clear an empty booth.

"Pretty boy is finally here!" Anthony shouts once he's spotted me. "Now we can eat!"

"You guys haven't ordered yet?" I ask as I take a seat next to Dom.

"Ignore my brother. He's just messing with you. We ordered a shit ton of burgers and a couple baskets of fries for all of us to split," Dom says.

"Well, I hope you ordered plenty because my ass is starving!" I say.

"Yeah, I'm famished!" Chad says. "That practice totally kicked my ass."

"No kidding. My calves are on fire. And we are supposed to do another practice tomorrow?" DeAndre says.

"Payson just wants to go over formations and stuff. No actual running or hitting," I say. "Not to mention, it won't be as long as it was today. She has big family dinners on Sundays, so she has to make it home for that."

"You know this ... how?" Chad asks.

"Payson and I discussed it this evening," I state, looking at my fellow teammates. Chad stares at me as if I have an extra head. "What?"

"How come she's discussing this shit with you?" Chad asks with a scoff. "You know, considering she's the enemy and all that."

"You only look at her as the enemy because of being friends with Brady, but I view her as a teammate. A leader. She is only looking out for the best interest of the entire team, including you and everyone who was against her playing with us when she first got here. Yes, Brady was a pretty good quarterback, but he got hurt and Payson stepped up, even after all the shit she had to deal with. If it wasn't for her, our season would be over right now. You do realize that, right?"

"He makes a valid point," Dom says. "I mean, you are the one who is hyped up for this game the most. Hell, you even threw that party to rub it in the faces of our rivals."

"Yeah ... but ..." Chad stammers. He hates when he gets called out on his shit. "Whatever, dudes. Where is this chick at with our food?" He leans out of the booth, looking around for the waitress before he waves her over.

The blonde girl with the lavender streaks from earlier appears at our booth.

"Can I help you?"

"Yeah, beautiful. You look like you've been on your feet all evening. Why don't you take a seat"—he leans back and pats his lap—"right here. I bet your feet are killing you." He gives her what he likes to call his *charming* smile.

"Mmm ..." She tilts her head. "You know? My feet are a little tired ... but I'd rather my feet fall off before I sit on the lap of little boys who wet themselves."

Chad quickly glances to his lap before smiling up at the girl. "Sweetheart, as you can see. My lap is completely dry, and I'm not so little—"

She grabs Chad's cup of water and pours it all over his lap. "I don't know. Looks pretty wet to me," she says as she slams the cup on the table and looks at the rest of us. "I will be back with your order."

DeAndre, Dom, and I burst out laughing as the waitress storms her way to the kitchen.

"Fucking bitch," Chad says as he takes napkins from the dispenser to try to dab up his pants but fails.

"To be honest, Turner, you had it coming," Dom says, only agitating him more.

"I'll be back!" Chad grits out. He stands and leaves the booth, headed toward the mens room.

Shortly after, our waitress returns with three trays loaded with our food. She has a tray in each hand, but I'm more impressed how well she balances the one sitting on top of her head. She places the trays with the baskets of fries down onto the table first before reaching for the one on top of her head. As she is pulling the tray off her head, another waitress stumbles into her, causing the tray with our burgers to go flying.

As if she was a female version of the Flash, she snatches one arm out to grab the tray, managing to collect almost all the burgers except one. With her free hand, she grabs the burger that was within inches of colliding with DeAndre's face. He grabs her wrist of the hand holding the burger she caught, and while staring into her blue eyes, he takes a bite.

"Mmm." DeAndre smacks his lips. "Delicious."

"What are you doing?" the waitress asks, staring at him in disbelief.

"I'm enjoying this burger that you so graciously saved from ruining my face," he says.

"You still want this after I've touched it with my bare hand? That's against the health code here."

"I won't tell if you don't." DeAndre winks.

She shakes her head and mumbles "Whatever" before releasing the burger to DeAndre.

"What's your name?" Dom asks.

"Hollis," she replies.

"Hollis, have you ever played football?" Anthony asks her.

"No ... why?" she asks.

"The way you just snatched that burger, you got impeccable hand-eye coordination," I say. "You'd be one hell of a wide receiver." The guys all nod in agreement.

"Psh. Please. As if girls could ever play that sport." Hollis crosses her arms and looks at the floor. She sounds like she has thought about it. Was she never given an opportunity? Then again, how many girls have ever gone out for football? I didn't know of any until Payson came to Bellwood.

"Why not?" I ask. "Our quarterback, Payson Moore, is a girl." This catches her attention.

"Wait. You have a girl who plays on your team?"

"Sure do, and she's a badass on the field. She's the one taking Bellwood High to the state championship game," DeAndre says before stuffing his mouth with fries.

"You're joking?"

"Have you been living under a rock?" Anthony asks around a mouthful of burger.

"Jesus, dude. Chew and swallow before talking! Mama raised us better than that!" Dom says before turning to Hollis. "Excuse my little brother. We are still training him on how to be a civilized citizen."

Hollis lets out huff. "Sorry, I don't have social media. And I don't go to public school. I'm homeschooled—"

"If you think you're getting a decent tip after that shit you pulled, you're sadly mistaken," Chad says, returning from the restroom. "Unless ... you care to meet me in the bathroom to make it up to me." He stands next to our waitress, staring down at her with a cocky smirk, but the girl has courage. She stands toe to toe with him, her chest against his, not backing down.

"So I can, what? Fake choking on your centimeter peter to give you an ego boost and catch an STD? No thanks."

"Hollis!" someone shouts from the kitchen. "You're needed!"

"Coming!" she yells back before facing Chad again. "Just an FYI ... I don't need nor *want* your tip money. So you can go to hell!" Then she walks away, leaving the rest of us to laugh and not choke to death while we eat our food.

"Can you believe that bitch?" Chad says, taking his seat next to Anthony and DeAndre. "She definitely isn't getting my money."

"To be fair, she said she didn't want it. Just be grateful you were in the bathroom and not out here. She would have embarrassed you more than she already has," Anthony says.

"What the fuck do you mean by that?" Chad asks.

"Let me think. How can I put this delicately ..." Dom says, tapping his fingers together.

"She would make a way better wide receiver than you," DeAndre states after swallowing his bite. Chad leans back in the booth, crossing his arms and frowns. "You weren't out here to see it. The way *that* girl caught a burger before it smacked into my face? Shew. I think I saw my life flash before my eyes! I also may have been turned on by her reflexes."

"Dude!"

"TMI!?

"What? I mean, apart from that prickly persona, she is quite the looker. Am I wrong? Besides, I'm pretty sure we had a moment when we were looking into each other's eyes. I think I'm going to leave her my digits when we leave."

I shake my head and continue stuffing my face. I'm glad I came out tonight with them. It feels good to be with my friends and laugh, even when some of them can be dickheads.

The guys and I finished everything, no burger or fry left in sight. Then we all paid for our share of the food before heading out, but I stayed behind to wait for Hollis to return.

"Did I forget something?" she asks as she approaches the booth to clean it off for the next customer.

"Oh, no. I just wanted to make sure you received your tip," I say as I hand her the wad of cash.

She stares for a moment before she reluctantly takes the cash from my hand and pockets it into her apron. "What about the blond-haired dickhead? Did he leave a tip?"

I rub the back of my neck. "Uh … no. He didn't. That's why the rest of us wanted to make sure you got paid what you deserve."

"You guys didn't have to do that."

"Well, we did. Sort of an apology for our friend. He reverts to being an asshole when he's embarrassed or doesn't get what he wants."

"So, what I'm hearing is I embarrassed him, huh?" A villianish smile slowly crosses her face.

"Yeah, you did. I think he would have been far worse had he been out here when you caught those burgers. He's one of our wide receivers, and his hand-eye coordination is nowhere near your skill level."

She shrugs as if the comment meant nothing, but I caught the slight smile before she forced it back.

"Anyway ... you impressed us, so we wanted to make sure you got your tip. You should definitely consider going out for football if you ever get the chance."

"I'd have to go to public school for an opportunity to play. Trying to convince my grams to let me, but I have to prove to her I can handle it. I'll do anything if it means I don't have to do another virtual class again."

"Can I see your phone?" I ask her.

"Why? Is this your way of giving me your number? You're cute and all, but I'm not interested—"

I put my hands up, halting her. "No, no. Nothing like that. And I say this as respectfully as possible, I'm not interested either ..." I make sure she isn't offended, and when it seems like she's okay, I move forward. "My one friend might be, though. The one whose face almost got attacked by the burger? Just a heads-up, his number might be tucked in along with his tip. Do with it what you will, but I thought I would give you Payson's number. She's the quarterback for our high school's football team and has played football for years. I think she would be very helpful if you ever consider it."

She thinks over what I said, then grabs her cell from her back pocket and hands it to me, so I put in Payson's number and give it back to her.

"Thanks. I appreciate it," she says.

"You're welcome. I'll be sure to let her know you may be in contact," I say before I walk away and head out the door.

Hollis clearly has an interest in football, and with that hand-eye coordination, she would be a phenomenal wide receiver. She just needs someone to encourage her, and no one is better suited than Payson Moore.

My pocket vibrates, so I retrieve my phone and see a text from my uncle.

UNCLE DEAN

Hey, kiddo. Any chance you can run by the shop and make sure the alarm is set? I had to leave a little early to go check on Mom.

NATHAN

Yeah. No prob. I'm leaving the diner now and can swing by to check before I head to my friend's house. Is grandma okay?

UNCLE DEAN

Yeah, she's fine. Nothing for you to worry about. & Thanks kid! Appreciate it!

I walk into the cool evening air and spot the guys waiting by their cars in the parking lot.

"Hey, I got to run by the garage real quick and check on something for my uncle. I'll meet you all at Chad's," I say as I approach them.

"Yeah, man. Just let us know when you head that way," Dom says as we slap hands and pull each other into a hug.

After my friends leave, I get in my car and head in the direction of the garage. I try not to think about my grandmother and why Dean would have had to leave the shop to go tend to her. If he had to close shop earlier than usual and couldn't recall setting the alarm, then it must have been something serious. I hope he's right, that everything is okay. It's been a fairly good day, and the last thing I want is something terrible happening to someone I care about.

# Chapter 11

## Jenna

It's been a little chaotic for a Saturday morning, but that usually goes in hand with the younger group of clients. It also hurts my heart knowing these children have endured some trauma in their life for their parents to sign them up for these sessions to provide them with a way to heal.

Helena and I are cleaning up after the latest group when I ponder over what I'm about to ask her.

"Hey, Helena. Can I ask you something?"

"Sure thing."

"There's an art competition for high school students to enter for a chance to win some scholarship money."

"That sounds like fun. How much is the scholarship?" she asks.

"Fifty grand."

She lets out one of those long whistles. "That's quite the scholarship money."

"It is. It's why I've entered. If I can win that money, I can pay for college myself and take that burden away from my parents."

"That's pretty admirable of you." She pulls her long wavy auburn hair up into a messy bun. "I've also met your parents, and something tells me they probably have some sort of college fund set aside for you already."

"They do, but I rather them use that money for themselves. They should be off traveling the world and paying off their debts so they can enjoy retirement when the time comes."

"Can you be my daughter?" she asks, and we laugh as we wipe down the tables.

"Anyway, what I wanted to ask is if it would be okay if I work on my piece here? I would bring my own materials, of course. Just figured it would be easier if I can work on it here when I have some free time."

"I don't see the harm in that. You can even use the spare room if you want."

It would be the perfect spot to paint. There's a room across from Helena's office that sits fairly empty, apart from a few tall easels she uses for sessions. I could set up everything in there, and it would be out of the way. Not to mention, it's quieter and I can focus on my craft.

"Thank you! I appreciate it."

"You're welcome," she says with a warm smile. Her hazel eyes glance down at her watch. "If you want, you can go ahead and clock out. I have a private session coming in fifteen minutes and nothing after, so I'll be closing early tonight."

"Are you sure?"

"Absolutely! I can take care of everything. You just go on and do … whatever it is your generation does for fun. I'm sure you have plans, right?"

"Helena, you're only thirty-two," I quip.

"That's old. When you hit thirty, you'll know what I'm talking about," she says, pointing a finger at me. I just shake my head at her. The woman looks young, like someone who just graduated from high school.

"You sure you're not lying about your age? I mean, you really could pass for someone in their late teens," I say.

"Okay, for that, I'm giving you a raise."

"Really?" I mean, I wouldn't object to a pay raise.

"Go home, Jenna. I'll see you Monday evening."

I go to the front desk to grab my stuff and head out to my car. Before I drive home, I send Felix a text to make sure we are going through with our plans for the evening.

As I head home, I'm thinking about what I will wear when I remember the sexy little dress I picked up while shopping with Sadie. The moment I saw the dress, I knew I needed to have it. The dress would make any grown ass man drop to his knees, and I want it to make Felix *beg* to touch me, to worship me. I want him to dream of all the ways he could take me and then act them out. Hopefully, he won't have to question our relationship anymore after tonight.

I pull the front of my black peacoat closed as I make my way to Felix's front door. It's early November and the nights are getting cooler, and tonight, it's extra breezy. With this dress, I need the extra layer of warmth, not to mention, it gave me the ability to get out of the house without my parents noticing. Their eyes would have bulged out of their sockets if they saw this dress. No way was I going to let them see me in it and formulate whatever ideas of their "innocent" daughter not being so innocent.

I knock on the door and wait for my handsome boyfriend to answer. Anticipation of seeing his reaction when I get to remove this coat thrums through me. A few moments pass and I'm greeted by my own personal Herculean god. His dirty-blond hair is neatly styled to the right with some gel, and he smells of wood and spice. His light-denim jeans hug his massive thighs while the white tee pulls tight across his muscled chest. He has a black, long-sleeve button-up over top of the white tee. It's hanging open with the sleeves rolled to the elbows, showcasing forearms of corded muscle along with his tribal wolf tattoo.

I bite on my painted red lip, admiring how delicious he looks standing in his doorway barefoot and dressed like this.

*Mmm. Maybe we should skip dinner and go straight to the bedroom.*

"See something you like?" he asks while his hazel-blue eyes take me in.

"Maybe," I reply with a smile. More like I want to devour him right here and now.

"Come on in." He gestures for me to enter, and I walk into the warm house, spotting pictures upon pictures hanging on the walls in the front entryway.

"Are these your brothers?" I ask, noting the family portraits of Felix with two other guys who look so similar to him.

"Yeah. That's Hendrix and Knox. Hendrix is the taller one. He's a junior in college, and the one just a little shorter than us is Knox. He's a sophomore at Greystone."

"Are you close to them?" I don't have any siblings myself but was always curious to know how the relationships were between those who did.

"Kind of." He shrugs. "There's a bit of an age gap with Hendrix, and Knox tends to prefer his buddies, as do I. But are we really going to stand here and talk about these two? Because I much rather enjoy tonight with you."

I smile, feeling the heat rush to my cheeks.

*Don't be nervous. You have nothing to be nervous about. Just take off the coat and let the night go where it goes.*

I lock my chocolate-brown eyes on Felix's hazel-blue ones as I untie and slowly unbutton my peacoat. Reaching up, I grab the opening of my coat at my shoulders and slowly remove it as I watch the expressions play out on Felix's face to seeing me in the dress.

The dress is black and lacy, mostly see-through, showcasing my light-brown skin. It has thin spaghetti straps, and the v-shaped neckline gives my B cups a bustier appeal. The lace over the bust is sheer except for a solid-black section covering my nipples. The lace continues from the midsection to my midthigh, with a mini split over my left thigh. The solid black, high-waisted hipster undergarment ensures my lady bits are covered while making my ass look extra plump in the backside. I paired the dress with some strappy black heels, giving my legs that long, lean appeal.

"What do you think?" I ask. He just stands there, soaking every inch of me in.

"Turn around," he demands, his voice low and husky.

I do as he says, taking my time so he sees every inch of me. As I'm about to face him again, he rushes me and shoves me against the wall.

"What the hell are you wearing?" he grits out. He seems upset, and I'm confused by his reaction.

"It's a dress. What's it look like I'm wearing?"

"It looks more like lingerie!" he yells in my face. "Who the hell has seen you like this? Huh?"

"N-n-no-no one. I went home from work, changed, and came right here. It's brand new. I just bought the dress last night."

"Did you try it on at the mall? Did anyone see you in it?"

"No! I took it home and tried it on to see how it looked. No one has seen me in it. You're the first and only one!" I yell back.

He snatches me by my ponytail and pulls so my face is tilted toward the ceiling.

"You better not be lying to me or so help you ..."

"I'm not." I swallow deeply. "I saw the dress and thought how sexy I would look wearing it just for you. Only you, Felix." It's the truth, even if it comes out more like a plea.

He leans down, taking my mouth into his and kisses me roughly. I kiss him back, trying to match his energy, but he pulls away. "Let's go eat. I'm starving, and I spent a good bit on the sushi you wanted. I don't want to waste it."

Guilt consumes me as he backs away and walks off to what I'm assuming is his kitchen or dining room. He told me he would get me whatever I wanted, but I hadn't considered the price of sushi. I mean, he attends Greystone Academy, and the tuition for that private school is insane. Plus, he lives in a gated community.

None of that factors into why I'm with him or what I feel for him. I'm not some gold digging, materialistic girl. I believe in hard work and earning a dollar, just like my parents. They worked several jobs paying their way through college to earn their degrees. My father is a psychology professor, and my mother earned her doctorate as an obstetrician-gynecologist. Hell, they are probably still trying to pay off those student loans to this day. It's why I have a job, and why it means so much to me to win the art competition.

I follow Felix into what looks like the dining room. A few white candles are lit surrounding a vase of red roses in the center of the table. As I approach, I see he grabbed his parents' good china. These plates are so antique and beautifully decorated, no way should we be using them. They belong on a display in a beautiful cabinet, untouched to be passed down to the next generation.

"Felix, I'm perfectly okay if we use paper plates. You didn't have to do all of this." I point to the place setting on the opposite end of where Felix takes a seat.

"Are you seriously suggesting I use cheap, disposable plates for our dinner?"

"I feel wrong using these—"

He slams his fist on top of the oak table, making me jump. "I practically begged my parents to allow me to use these for us this evening, Jenna! I even offered to clean the whole damn house for them to let me use them."

"I never asked you to make it some extravagant dinner."

"If that were the case, then why the hell did you show up dressed like that?" He shoves a hand in my direction.

"I wanted to dress up *for you*! I bought this dress last night while shopping with Sadie because I liked it. Figured I would save it for a special occasion with my man. When you wanted to do this dinner after you accused me of cheating on you, I knew this was the dress I wanted to wear, to show you how much I only have eyes for you. Not because I was expecting sushi on fine china!" I cannot believe this is how he is acting. What the hell is even happening right now?

A sting of tears swells in my eyes, but I blink them back, preventing them from falling. I take a deep breath, swallowing the golf-ball sized lump in my throat.

"I don't even know what I'm doing here if this is how the night is going to be." I turn on my high heels and walk back toward the front door to grab my peacoat.

"Where the hell do you think you are going?" He storms after me and snatches my coat out of my hands before blocking the front door, preventing me from leaving.

I fold my arms in front of me, staring at the man I was pretty certain I was going to confess I was starting to fall in love with.

"I'm going home, Felix. This was not how I foresaw the night going. I thought I was coming to eat sushi and enjoy the evening with you. All I wanted was to spend some time with you, to connect with you so you could overcome these trust issues you have, but clearly, this isn't working."

Felix swallows deeply. "What's not working?"

"Us, Felix! You and me. You don't trust me. You are basically insinuating I'm some materialistic girl when I'm far from it. If sushi was too expensive, then here ..." I reach forward, putting a hand into the pocket of my coat Felix is still holding and pull out my wallet, yanking cash out and shoving it into Felix's chest. "That should cover my half of dinner, because if you even knew me, you'd know I am very capable of paying for myself. Enjoy the dinner all alone because I'm no longer hungry."

I make a grab for my coat, but Felix drops it when he falls to his knees and wraps his muscular arms around my bare legs.

"Baby! Please don't leave! Don't walk out that door, don't end us. I'm sorry. Okay? I'm so, so sorry. Baby! Please stay! Let me make the night better. I'll make it up to you, I promise. Just ... please ... stay." I stare into his eyes glistening with wetness.

*Is he going to cry? Oh, God, please don't cry.*

I look up, forcing back the tears that want to fall down my face. I hate when people cry, especially men. It's a weakness for me. Men are taught to not show emotions because it doesn't make them masculine, when it's quite the opposite, at least in my opinion. Once I've composed myself, I look down at Felix.

"Felix ..." I whisper, unsure of what to say, of what to do.

"You walk out that door, Jenna, not only are you breaking us, you will break my heart. How am I supposed to deal with that, huh?"

"I don't know, Felix. The same way I'll deal with mine," I say, shrugging before reaching down and picking up my coat.

"You know how I'll deal?" He quickly stands and towers over me. "I can go to a party. I'm sure some of my buddies know where there is one right now. I can go and just drink myself until I pass out. Or better yet drive completely drunk out of my mind! I can break into my dad's office. He has plenty of liquor—"

"Felix, stop!" I yell, horrified that he would even consider that option. Is he seriously considering drinking himself to death or worse, driving under the influence?

"You know my dad owns a gun, right? I know where he keeps it. I could just blow my brains out, because the mere thought of losing you would drive me to do it!"

Before I think about it, my heart racing in fear he may go through with something as insane as shooting himself, I reach up and grab his face with both of my hands. "Stop it! I'll stay, okay? You hear me? I'll stay."

His hands cover mine, and he stares into me, taking a deep breath before speaking. "You'll stay?"

"Yes," I whisper, "I won't leave. I'll stay right here. I'm just going to put my coat back up on the coat rack and then we can go eat."

A smile slowly moves across Felix's face before he leans down, pressing a soft kiss to my lips. "You have no idea how much that means to me. How much *you* mean to me."

I don't know what to say, my mind is still spinning, so I just give him a soft smile back, hoping it reassures him I'm not leaving. At least, not yet. I will allow him to show me he can turn this whole evening around. He seems so adamant about it, why not give him the chance? I mean, what's the worst that could happen?

# Chapter 12

## Jenna

Felix and I make our way back to the dining table to eat dinner, only this time Felix moves to sit beside me. For a few moments, neither of us say anything until he fills the silence with talk of football, classes he hates, and a teacher he doesn't like. I'm too in my head to be paying attention, thinking about what we went through, when Felix rubs my leg.

"What's on your mind, babe?"

"Hmm … Oh … um … just this art competition I enrolled in. I'm trying to figure out what I'm going to paint now that Helena has given me permission to work on it at the studio."

"You do art?"

"Yeah …" Didn't I tell him all this when we were getting to know each other? Or did he forget? "Art is my passion. It's why I work with Helena at the art therapy studio. I've also applied to a few different art schools, but I'm really hoping to land my dream school out in California. I want to major—"

"Wait ... did you say California? Babe, that's so far away."

"Far away?" I ask, unsure what he means.

"Yeah ... from me."

"I'm not following, Felix ..."

"I'm applying to Ole Miss, and I want you to apply there too. I want you with me when we go off to college. I'm sure they have a degree to be an art teacher or whatever you want, and this way, we can be together." He smiles at me, like this is the best thing for us, and I wonder how long he has been thinking about this.

"You see us being together after high school? Like, in college too?" I'm taken back. I figured he would want to break up after graduation so he could be single and do as he pleased in college, not be tied down to one girl.

"Of course I do. You and me? We are endgame, baby," he says as he leans in to kiss me. The kiss is gentle and sweet, then he grasps my neck and tugs me closer to him.

His tongue caresses my lips before pressing for entry into my mouth, and I let him. Our tongues twist and tangle in a slow dance before he pulls away.

"Why don't we go watch that movie?" he says as he grabs our plates and takes them to the kitchen. He returns and leads me to the massive family room.

The walls are light gray with more family portraits neatly adorned on them in distressed white wooden frames. There's a large white sectional couch, big enough to seat what looks like fifteen people, placed in front of a fireplace.

A big flat screen TV hangs above it with a movie ready to be played on the screen.

"We're watching *The Blind Side*?" I ask, spotting the familiar movie on the screen.

"Yeah. I thought it would be perfect for us to watch while we cuddle," he says, pulling me toward the couch. "It's got football and that sappy shit you women like."

Sappy shit women like? The hell is that supposed to mean? I would have enjoyed a good action or thriller movie. In fact, I know I told him *Halloween* is one of my favorite scary movies.

"We don't have to watch this," I say before recalling the fiasco with the paper plates, then quickly change my tone. "Uh ... it's actually quite perfect."

I give him a warm smile as we sit, and Felix drapes a muscled arm around my shoulders as I snuggle into his side, finding comfort in the warmth of his body.

We are halfway through the movie, and I may actually lose my mind. Or nod off. In all honesty, it's a terrific movie, but I have seen it one too many times before. I don't know if Felix has, but he seems to be into it, and I don't want to ruin this evening.

Then again, I haven't had sex in a while and will honestly go a little crazy if I don't get to ride his dick soon.

*Oh, what the hell ...*

Grabbing Felix's chiseled jaw, I turn his face toward me. Leaning into him, I bring his lips to mine, giving him a heated kiss in hopes it conveys how needy I'm feeling.

Felix pulls back, resting his forehead to mine. "Jenna ..." His warm breath caresses my face. "What are you doing?"

I look into his eyes. "I don't want to watch the movie, Felix," I say as I straddle his lap. The lace on my dress rides up, with my thighs resting on each side of his muscular ones. "I want to kiss you and feel you inside of me. You can't tell me you actually want to watch a movie, do you?"

He stares at me, just for a moment, before his lips latch onto mine and he devours my mouth. His big hands reach around and grab my ass, pulling me closer. As his dick hardens underneath the denim, I grind down on it, the friction eliciting a soft moan from me.

"Oh, god ..." It has been too long. I want this, no, I *need* this.

"Damn, Jenna. I want to fuck you so bad right now. Do you have any idea how long I've wanted you."

"Why make me wait?" I whisper before kissing him again.

"You seemed to want to take things slow, and when I fell in love with you, I knew I wanted to wait it out a little longer," he states.

I pull back and look at him. "Did you just say you fell in love with me?"

He smiles. "I mean, it's not that hard, Jenna. I love you. Do you understand why you make me so crazy? Why I say insane things and do stupid shit? I'm in love with you."

He grabs my face, pulling me into him, and kisses me with hunger. His hands skim my arms until they reach the black straps of my dress, pulling them down and exposing my darkened areolas. His lips move away from mine to kiss along my jawline, down my neck, and toward my breasts, where he pulls a nipple into his mouth and sucks on it with the right amount of pressure.

I let out another moan as he switches between my breasts, ensuring each gets the same amount of attention from his mouth.

Grinding harder and moving faster on his hardened cock, my panties get wetter, and I worry I may leave a spot on the front of his jeans.

Felix grabs hold of my hips and flips us to where his body is above me. He quickly removes his shirts, and I take in the muscles displayed upon his body. It's like this man was chiseled from stone in the Greek era. A well-defined six-pack and those v lines direct my eyes to the very appendage my body aches for. Felix makes quick work of unfastening his jeans and pulling them off. His erection stands at full attention, tenting the front of his black boxer briefs.

He climbs over me and tugs my dress off, leaving me bare before him, as his gaze roams me from head to toe.

"Damn, Jenna. You are so fucking sexy," he rasps before pressing against me and taking my mouth with his.

My fingers roam over his abs, feeling the hard ridges and creases before I move toward his back and pull him closer. I wrap my legs around his waist, seeking that friction I so desperately need.

I rake my nails down along Felix's back toward his underwear and am about to pull them down to release his dick when I feel a dip in the couch near my head.

*Did someone sit down? Oh, my God, are his parents back!?*

I quickly release Felix and push on his chest to get him to stop kissing me.

"What the hell?" Felix says before a chuckle sounds next to us.

"Well, don't stop on my account," the deep voice says. "I'm just enjoying the show."

Felix's head snaps up, and I'm frozen in place. Someone is definitely in this room!

"You fucker! You should have called," Felix tells the person who sat on the couch. He reaches over my head and does one of those hand clap things guys do with their friends.

"I did, but you didn't answer. I was concerned and came over, but clearly you were a little ... occupied." I can hear the smirk in the guy's tone.

I move to sit up so I can pull my dress back on, but Felix shoves me back down.

"What are you doing?" Felix glares down at me.

"I'm getting my dress back on ..."

"We're not finished."

Is he for real right now? There is another person right here in this very room. Why would he want to go through with sex? I'm not into that sort of thing.

"Felix, I'm not having sex with you when there is someone else here." As I grab for my dress again, Felix snatches it away. I cross my arms over my breasts, trying to keep as much of me obscured from other eyes.

"It's just my buddy Drake."

"Okay ... and? I'm not about to let someone I don't know see me naked. Or having sex with my boyfriend."

"Why not? It's not like we haven't done this before."

"We haven't, Felix, because this is our first time together."

"Not what I meant," he says.

Puzzled by what he means, *Drake* takes the moment to clarify.

"What he means, sweet cheeks, is that this isn't our first rodeo. Felix and I have had many occasions where one of us has been in the same room while the other has sex."

"What the hell?" I spring up, keeping my breasts covered with my tawny brown arms. "You have had sex with other girls in front of each other?" I'm honestly horrified by this tidbit of information.

Felix leans back on his knees and shrugs. Shrugs! As if this is nothing new. "Yeah. It's not a big deal to us."

"Well, then, here's some news for you, Felix. It's a big deal to *me*! I'm not that kind of girl, and I will not be doing this. I'm not going to be just like every girl you had before me."

I go to stand up, reaching for my dress, and Felix grabs my wrist. "I said, we are not finished here," he growls out.

I tilt my head at him, thinking he's lost his mind. "What part of I'm not doing this do you not understand? Give me my dress, Felix, so I can go home." The whole situation is making me uncomfortable. I feel vulnerable. Exposed.

"The fuck you are," Felix snarls, gripping my wrist tighter. "You wanted to have sex with me, remember? You came onto me, Jenna, so now we are going to finish what *you* started."

"Yeah, well, I've changed my mind. I'm not having sex with you. Now let go of me so I can leave!" I'm trying to pull my wrist free, but aftr a few tugs, there is no point. His firm grip holds me in place. "Felix, you're hurting my arm!"

"Awe, c'mon, sweet cheeks. Don't be like that." Drake taunts. I turn my head, eyes glaring as I finally get a good look at the uninvited guest.

His brown hair is parted to the side. Stubble aligns his chiseled jawline, and bright-blue eyes pop under thick dark lashes. His blue eyes rake over me, moving down, and I realize I'm no longer covering my breasts. I make an attempt to cover them up the best I can with my free arm while Felix still has a hold of my wrist.

"Aren't you a pretty thing?" Drake says. My stomach rolls with disgust, feeling like some sort of object or caged animal on display.

"Don't fucking look at me, you pervert!" I snarl.

"Ooo ... she's a feisty one you got there, Felix."

"She definitely has a mouth on her. I can't wait to shove my cock in it and teach her some lessons on how to be respectful toward my friends," Felix says. I turn my focus back on him.

"Put that thing anywhere near my mouth and I'll bite the fucking thing off!" I sneer.

*Smack!*

My head snaps to the side from the force of Felix slapping me across my face. The sting of his hit causes my eyes to water, and I'm left speechless, unable to move or react.

Felix shoves me back down onto the couch, raising my arms above my head and pinning me under his massive body.

"Felix, get off of me!" I attempt to use my body weight to push him off, but it's useless. Of course, it's not going to work. The guy has more muscle to weigh me down than I have to fight back.

"Felix ... please ... Felix, if you love me like you said, you will listen to me and let me go."

A few tears escape and glide down my cheeks.

"Aren't they pretty when they cry?" Drake says.

Felix looks at his friend with a sly smile on his face. "You're the one who enjoys making them cry."

"Mmm ... you're not wrong there. There's just something about it that gets me so hard, though ..." The sound of a zipper being undone fills me with panic. I kick and wiggle in hopes to free myself from this nightmare.

*Is he going to do something to me too?*

"Felix, listen to me, please. I ... I-I-I don't want to do this anymore. I just want to go home!"

"Shhh, calm down, babe. You're sooo ... tense. Let me help you to relax," Felix says as he places wet kisses on my neck. He's trying to be seductive, but all I can think in my head is how gross it feels, the moistness of his saliva as it coats my skin combined with the heat of his breath. He releases one of his hands from my wrists and glides it down my body, then shoves two of his thick fingers inside of me. I jerk at the intrusion, as the wetness that was there dried up the moment I realized we weren't alone.

A moan comes from the other side of my head, and more panic fills me.

"Felix, stop! I said no!" I say, but he acts like he doesn't hear me. "This doesn't feel good!"

He pauses his movements, his hazel-blue eyes looking like storm clouds as they glare down at me. "You owe me this, Jenna."

In a moment of anger, or maybe stupidity, I spit directly in Felix's face. Clearly pissing him off, Felix's hand leaves my body, then latches around my neck and squeezes with enough pressure to make me regret what I just did.

"You're going to pay for that," he snarls. With his hand still on my throat, Felix picks me up off the couch and throws me to the floor. A screech escapes me as my body collides with the hardwood floor.

Ignoring the pain, I try to push myself up, figuring out how I can escape. I can grab my coat and just leave. Maybe Sadie can meet me somewhere with clothes.

*Then you would have to tell her what happened …*

Fuck. I can't do that. She has enough on her plate with her own family problems. Why add mine to it?

Before I'm even halfway up, Felix slams his massive body on top of me, shoving my head to the side. His friend still sits on the couch, masturbating as if he is getting off on this shit.

"Your ass looks so good in this position. I think I may just take you like this," Felix says into my ear while rubbing his erection into my back side.

I swallow back the bile rising and make another attempt to reason with him. "Felix, please stop. I don't want to do this. I'm not into being shared. There is no way in hell I will have sex with you or your friend!"

The deep rumble of his laughter fills the room. "You think I'm going to share you with Drake?"

"Y-y-yes …"

"Oh, baby. I don't share my girls with him. Drake just gets off watching other people have sex. Our little foreplay is just turning him on, and he is just chasing after his release."

For a moment, I breathe a sigh of relief, but then Felix thrusts his erection into my pussy, and I scream out.

I'm driving along some backroad in a mindless fog, unsure of how I walked out of that house or got into my car. I'm not even sure where I'm driving. I am just completely ... numb. So numb thinking back on this night that I miss the turn in the road and my car collides head-on with a fence.

# Chapter 13

## Nathan

I send a text to my uncle, informing him the shop is locked and the alarm is set before I get in my car to head toward Chad's house. Since he lives on the outskirts of Bellwood, I decided I would take the backroads to save some time.

As I make my way along Pine Hill Road, I notice something large off to the right side. When I get closer, I realize it's a white Volkswagen Beetle with a convertible top. There's only one person I know who drives that car in Bellwood.

*Oh my God, Jenna!*

With my heart pounding against my ribcage and my pulse quickening, I pull my car behind Jenna's wrecked vehicle and jump out. I walk around the car, noting all the damage and scanning for any signs of potential gas or oil leaking.

The last thing we need is something to make the vehicle explode.

I'm about to go check on Jenna when the driver's side door opens and she steps out of her car. She stumbles a little, so I rush to her, checking her from head to toe for any serious injuries.

"Jenna, are you okay?" I reach for her hand, wanting to steady her. "Are you hurt anywhere?"

Jenna squints as she takes my hand. "Nathan?"

"Yeah. It's me. Are you bleeding anywhere? Does anything feel like it may be broken? Do you need me to call you an ambulance? Do you need to go to the hospital? Because I can take you—"

"No!" She shouts, pulling away from me to lean against her car. "I mean … no. No hospital. I'm fine."

Warning bells go off in my head at how quickly she dismisses a trip to the hospital, but I brush it aside. My sole focus is making sure she isn't seriously injured.

"Are you sure?"

"Yes, Nathan, I'm sure. It's just a few scratches and bruises," she says as she looks over her arms.

"I should still take you to get looked at. To make sure you don't have a concussion."

"Nathan, I said no! God, what the hell is wrong with guys who don't understand—you know what? Nevermind."

"Don't understand what?"

She doesn't answer and instead walks around me to the front of her car. "Oh, God. This is so bad! How the hell am I going to explain this to my parents? This is the last thing they need to be worried about!" She places her hands on top of her beautiful raven-black hair, pacing back and forth.

"It's not too bad." I shrug.

"Not too bad? Are you blind, Nathan!? Look at my car!" She lets out a frustrated sigh before lowering her voice. "You don't get it."

"Then explain it to me."

Jenna releases another sigh. "Look, my parents have busted their asses to be where they are today. To fix this"—she waves her hand toward the car—"is going to cost them money, and they shouldn't have to pay for this. Especially since it's my fault."

She looks down at the ground, shame clear as day on her face. I'm not sure how the accident happened, but the fact she doesn't want her parents to pay to fix her car, fix her mistake, shows how mature and responsible she is.

"If you take it to the dealership where you got it, then, yeah, it's going to cost you a pretty penny to have them fix it up. Not sure what you make with your job, but you could bargain out a payment plan with the dealership."

"This car was a gift for my eighteenth birthday from my Aunt Naomi," she says before dragging her delicate brown fingers down her face. "Ugh ... what the hell am I going to do?"

"You probably won't like this but ... I may be able to fix it for you."

Jenna tilts her head at me. "You? Fix my car?"

I shrug. "Yeah. Why? Does that surprise you?"

"A little ..."

"Look, I know my way around cars since I work with my uncle at his garage. I'm sure you know of the place. Wesley's Auto Repair and Detailing?"

"Yeah, I drive by it on my way to work," she says. "Hold up! Your uncle is Wesley?"

"Wesley is actually a family name on my maternal side. Dean Wesley, my uncle, took it over when my grandfather passed."

"Oh ..." Jenna mutters.

"Anyway, I know a thing or two on how to fix up cars. If I can get your Beetle to the shop, I can get a better look at the damage and see if I can fix it for you. No charge."

Jenna's head shoots up, her chocolate-brown eyes wide as she stares at me. "No charge? Seriously?"

I simply shrug. "I mean, well ... yeah."

"So, let me get this straight. You expect me to not pay you, *at all*, for you to work on my car?"

I nod in response to her question.

"Nah ... it can't be that simple." She mockingly laughs. "What is it that you want?"

"Pardon?" I ask her.

"C'mon Nathan. Guys don't do favors for girls without wanting something in exchange. So ... what is it that you want?"

"Nothing." I shake my head, but she still doesn't believe me. "I'm being serious. I don't want anything from you, Spitfire."

*Lies! You want her.*

"You're lying!" she states. Am I being too obvious with my own thoughts?

"Jenna, only little boys want favors. I'm simply just trying to help you out. You don't want your parents to pay to fix your car, so why can't I do the same for you?" It's honestly the truth, with maybe a little motivation to get her to talk to me so she can get to know me better.

"For real?" Jenna asks, as if this is some kind of abnormality. Is she finally getting it through her pretty head I just want to help?

"Like I said, I just need to get your car to the shop." I look over her car once more before I pull my cell phone out and text my uncle, asking if I can use the tow truck. It may be a family business, but I rather ask instead of just taking it. Don't need my uncle to freak out, thinking someone is stealing his only tow truck, then my dad showing up. When my uncle replies giving me the okay, I look up at Jenna. She's zoned out, staring off into the darkness of the backroad.

I pause for a moment, now that I know she's okay, to take her in. I note the lacy black dress and heels and how stunning she looks in the glow of the moonlight. The moment a breeze blows through, breaking her from her daydream and sending a shiver down her spine, she turns to open her car door. Only then do I see the globes of her ass peeking out the backside of what looks like a thong. Blood instantly rushes to my dick, and I groan inwardly. What is she doing wearing something like that in early November? It's too chilly out for a dress like that.

*Do not get hard. Think of something that isn't Jenna in her dress. Like kittens or puppies.*

My brain reminds me of the ogre she's seeing and in an instant, I'm annoyed. Angry. *Jealous.*

Fuck. Okay, it's definitely jealousy, but anyone would be if the girl who's always in your head makes you want to drop at her feet to kiss the ground she walks on is with someone who isn't you.

Jenna pulls out a long black coat and covers herself. As she goes to pull it in to keep out the breeze, a look of horror crosses her face before she removes it and throws it onto the hood of her car.

"Something wrong with your coat?" I ask, curious as to why she wouldn't wear it to stay warm.

"It just smells ... awful," she says with her lip curled. She wraps her arms around herself, her hands rubbing up and down her bare arms.

"Here," I say, removing my Carolina-blue letterman jacket and holding it open for her to place her arms through the sleeves. "Put this on so you stay warm."

She hesitates for a moment before sliding her arms into the jacket sleeves. "Thank you," she mutters.

"My uncle just gave me the okay to use the tow truck, so I can move your car to the shop. But in order to do that, you're going to have to ride with me to the garage. Are you okay with that?"

She nods and walks toward my car. Meeting her at the passenger door, I open it so she can climb in, and ensure her seatbelt is on before closing it. I jog around to the driver side, getting in to start the car and turn the heat up so she isn't freezing.

I check the roadway before making a U-turn and head toward my uncle's garage. It's about a ten-minute drive before I pull into the lot and park around back.

As I help Jenna out of my car, my jacket covering almost all of the dress she is wearing, I keep my eyes focused on her face, refusing to let them roam anywhere else. The last thing I need is a boner when I'm trying to help her after an accident. She has never been a fan of me, for reasons I'm unsure of, and I don't want to make the situation awkward for us. Plus, she has a boyfriend.

I walk toward the back door of the building with Jenna close behind me. Looking around, a force of habit to make sure no one is watching, I reach for the cinder block where my uncle hides the spare key. Quickly, I unlock the door, then place the spare key back in its original hiding spot before making my way inside. After punching the code on the alarm to ensure it doesn't go off and alert the police of a break-in, I lead her into my uncle's office.

"You can sit in here while I grab the tow truck. I shouldn't be longer than twenty-five, thirty minutes tops. Unless you want to call your parents to come pick you up?" I'd mention Sadie, but last time I did that, she nearly snapped my head off my shoulders.

"I don't mind waiting here until you get back," Jenna replies from the chair behind my uncle's desk. "I can just play a game on my phone to pass the time." She gives me a soft smile, probably the first one she's ever given me.

If she only knew how much that smile affected me, warming the cold heart that beats inside.

I reach across my uncle's desk to get the tow truck key, and Jenna flinches, causing me to pause.

"I just need the tow truck key out of the drawer," I say calmly so she knows I'm not trying to do anything. She nods before pushing the chair back, allowing me access to the drawer. Once I grab the key, I back away slowly to not spook her. "You're safe in here."

"What?"

"I just wanted you to know, you're safe here." With that, I make my way out of the office and outside to where the tow truck is parked. I don't look back, forcing my feet to keep moving forward. The fury within me wants to ask questions, but the anger I feel would be no help. It could frighten her, causing her to freak out and run off. I can't let that happen. Instead, I take the spare key with me and lock the door, ensuring she is safe inside.

NATHAN

I locked the door and have the spare key with me. It's late and I don't expect anyone will come by but on the off chance someone does, DO NOT open any doors for anyone while I'm gone. Don't turn on any lights. I won't be long.

I climb into the truck, allowing it to warm up for a few minutes when Jenna's text comes through.

SPITFIRE

You got it, shop boy.

I smirk at her attempt to mock me and head off to go get her car. My mind replays the way she flinched, and I grip the steering wheel harder, my knuckles turning white as the anger boils my blood. In my father's line of duty, I've come to learn that a person only flinches like that when they've been hit. Domestic violence and violence against children are the calls my dad hates the most. I don't blame him. What kind of monster thinks it's okay to lay a finger on anyone, especially a woman or child?

I send up a prayer, praying to God I don't find out someone has laid a finger on my spitfire, or there will be hell to pay.

# Chapter 14

## Jenna

I glance around the office space after Nathan leaves, impressed with how tidy and organized everything is with a man running a mechanic shop. Not saying men can't be tidy, but to run a whole car shop in a small town, he must be busy. When does he find the time?

Swiveling in the chair slowly, I notice pictures on the wall behind me. I know little about Nathan Ward, but since his family runs this place, the pictures might tell me something about him.

*Or you could just try being nice and talk to him like a normal person.*

I laugh at my inner thoughts. As if!

*He did come to your rescue. Is he really such an awful guy?*

I shake my head to silence my thoughts, then refocus on the photos and take in every face on display. My eyes are instantly drawn to a grainy photo that must have been taken in the '70s. The adorable couple is hugging while standing outside the front of the shop with huge smiles upon their faces. I can only assume these are Nathan's grandparents from when they opened their doors for business in Bellwood.

Another picture shows a couple at the beach with two little boys. I recognize the gentleman as our much-younger police chief. Though, I have to admit, the guy ages nicely. Next to him is a beautiful brunette woman with the perfect sun-kissed tan and green eyes. I have no doubt in my mind it's Nathan's mother. They share the same gorgeous olive-green eyes that stand out against their bronze skin tone. The picture next to that one shows a slightly younger Nathan with another young man looking up from under the hood of a car and smiling for the camera. He looks similar to Nathan, but I don't recall Officer Ward having two children. Maybe it's the uncle? A cousin? Or maybe he has an older brother who's off at college, like Felix's bro—*Nope!*

I close my eyes, forcing back the tears that want to fall from my ducts at the mere thought of him and what happened earlier and trying to not let my memories take me back to when I knew the only way out was to give in. I recall little after that. It was as if I crawled into the recesses of my mind to escape reality.

Fear trickles into my mind, thinking about Felix possibly coming after me for leaving or worse, for another round. The thought sends a shiver through my body. I pull the jacket tighter, forcing the chill to leave, then I smell a scent

I've only ever smelled once before. Only this time, there's a lack of gasoline and oil mixed with it.

Inhaling a little deeper, I absorb the aromas of Nathan's cologne, and a sense of calm and peace wash over me, pushing the fear aside. I think of Nathan and how he literally came to my aid tonight. How crazy it is that he happened to be on the same road and came across my path. How he ensured I was okay above everything else. Not once did he comment about how I was inappropriately dressed for the chilly weather or say something perverse in reference to how I looked. Maybe there is some truth to what Sadie said about Nathan not being anything like Brady and Chad. Those two are complete womanizing pigs. Brady kept his affairs quiet until he got busted, but my oh my, did karma bite him hard twice! As for Chad, he boasts his conquests like he's going for a Guinness world record of how many females he can sleep with.

*Barf!*

As I look over all these photos, I try to piece together the story behind the Wesley family name and find something that could just give me a little insight into the mysterious six-foot-three linebacker.

My phone vibrates on the desk, and when I glance to see who the incoming call is from, I freeze. My heart beats quicker and nausea swirls in my stomach. I think I may throw up.

Oh, God ...

I let the phone ring through until it goes to voicemail. Then there's a momentary pause before it goes off again. The same name appears on the lock screen.

*Felix Martin.*

I let it ring through and go to voicemail a second time, hoping he gives up on calling me. Is he calling to apologize? There are no words to excuse his behavior and what he did. Yet, once again, my phone vibrates on the desk. What would I even say? I refuse to hit the ignore option because then he would know. He would know I'm purposely avoiding his calls, and that could set him off, which would be bad. His anger ... his temper? There is no telling what he could do. Especially since he hinted to a gun being in his house.

*Just turn off the phone.*

No, I can't do that. That would really set him off, especially since he's already called three ... make that four times now. He would know I'm avoiding him, then he would go crazy. He could show up at my house again, angry and ready to yell in my face like he did last night. I'm not sure if my parents are home or if they went out. They haven't met Felix because, thankfully, I haven't introduced them to him. I was waiting to see if we were going to be serious first, but now I know there is no future with him. If he is really heated, he could show up to my house and possibly hurt them. Or Sadie.

I shudder at the thought. Like hell I would let that happen to the people I love. He may have hurt me, but I'll be damned if he touches anyone else.

*Don't go home.*

*He won't show up if he doesn't see your car.*

*But what if he is waiting and someone else takes me home ... that could be bad!*

I pace back and forth, my heels clicking against the linoleum flooring the only sound I can hear. Where would

I go? Sadie lives with my family now. Who could I possibly stay with? Especially since I am without a car. Shit! How am I going to explain this to my parents?

"You going to get that?" a deep voice says, breaking me from the whirlwind of questions running through my head.

"Jesus Christ, Nathan, you scared the shit out of me!" I halt in my pace, my heart hammering against my rib cage.

"Sorry … I didn't mean to," he states. "Are you sure you're okay?"

"Yes, I'm fine. Could you stop asking me that?" I snap at him.

*Breathe, Jenna. It's just Nathan and he's concerned.*

I let out a deep breath before facing Nathan. "I'm sorry. I'm just … It's been a long night, and I'm going through some stuff."

He leans against the doorframe, arms crossed as he stares at me. His narrowed eyes make me nervous, as if he can see through me. The last thing I need for him to do is find out what happened tonight and go on a man hunt. I don't need him involved in my problems.

"You really should answer that. It could be your par—" He moves from the door to the desk and reaches for my phone.

"No! Don't answer that!" I yell as I reach for my cell phone, but Nathan grabs it before I can. Damn him and his football reflexes.

He glares at the screen. "So, you are not going to answer your boyfriend?" he asks through clenched teeth.

I snatch my phone out of his hands and place it back on the desk. "It's none of your business! But you should know … he's not my boyfriend. Not anymore," I mutter, turning around to face the wall of photos to wipe the tear that escaped so Nathan doesn't see.

"Come again?"

"He's not my boyfriend anymore. I mean, technically, he still is, but I'm breaking up with him. I just need a day to pull myself together and wait for him to calm down."

"Wait for him to calm down ..." There's a silent pause, and he swallows before he speaks again, this time with concern. "Did he hit you, Jenna?"

I shake my head, refusing to turn around and face him. I'm afraid he will see the tears and the lies upon my face. I just can't bring myself to tell him what Felix did because I let it happen.

*No one will believe you are a victim.*

"You're lying. I saw you flinch, Jenna, and the only reason you would flinch like that is if someone laid a finger on you. I may not have grown up in Bellwood all my life, but for the past three years that I have lived here, I have never heard a horrible thing said about your parents. Everyone has nothing but good praises about the Altwoods in this community. Even more so since they took in the mayor's daughter after she came out at homecoming and Mrs. Adams kicked her out. That to me says they are good people. There is no one else that you have been around that I know would hurt you except for one person that came into your life recently. I saw the bruises after the party. If he was capable of doing that, what else is he capable of? So, tell me the truth, Spitfire. Did. Felix. Hit you?"

I can hear his heavy breathing and the tension of him holding back from losing his shit. But why?

"N-n-no, he didn't hit me," I say, but I know it's not convincing enough.

"Wow. You are really going to stand there and lie to me? To what? To protect that fuckface? I don't understand, Jenna. If he did something to you, you need to tell someone. Tell me, for Christ's sake! I don't get why you can't just be up-front with me and tell me the truth. What have I ever done to you to make you hate me so much? Huh?" His voice rises with each statement.

I spin to confront him, anger rising in me. "I'm not fucking protecting him! If anything, I'm protecting you and everyone I care about from him! Don't you get it, Nathan? I'm afraid of him! I'm afraid he will hurt the people I care about and nothing can be done about it, because his anger consumes him. He flies off the handle, and God only knows the dangers if I put everyone I care about in his crosshairs. You don't know what he's capable of ... what ..." My anger dissipates, and I swallow the lump that forms in my throat and blink away the tears welling in my eyes. "You don't know what he's already done," I whisper as I look away from him.

Nathan steps in close. His hands slowly reach toward my face, as if he is being careful not to spook me. With the pad of his thumbs, he brushes away the tears on my face before taking a hand and lifting my chin so I'm looking directly into his olive-green eyes.

"I find it ... interesting ... that you want to protect me when you seem to despise me," he says. "But you don't need to protect me from him, Spitfire. I can take care of myself."

"I don't despise you—" He pushes a single finger against my lips, promptly silencing me.

"We will come back to that. The only thing I want to hear right now is what did he do to you?"

I shake my head, pleading with my eyes for him to understand. I can't tell him. His father is the police chief, and he could say something to him. What if they arrest Felix and then nothing comes of it? It would place a target on my back because Felix will despise me for wrecking his life.

"Jenna, *please* ..."

"Were you able to get my car?" I ask, trying to change the direction of this conversation. Nathan holds my face in his hands, but I refuse to look him in his eyes. When I say nothing else, he releases me.

"Yeah, I did. I need to pull it into the garage so I can put it on the lift to get a good look at it. I just came in here to check on you to make sure you were okay before I head into the bay area to open the door."

"Can I go see it? I would like to see how badly I fucked up," I say. Nathan simply nods and signals for me to follow him.

We walk out of the office and across the hall to a door that leads into a nice-size garage area that looks like it fits four to five cars in it. Nathan flips a switch, causing the long white overhead lights to buzz to life. He moves around to what looks like a desk to press a button, and one of the big garage doors slowly opens.

My damaged Beetle is hooked up to the navy-blue tow truck waiting outside. He goes to the truck and backs in, placing my car on top of the lift before he hops out and unhooks it.

I'm not sure how I missed the gray muscle tank he is wearing, but watching his biceps flex as he works to get my car detached? *Jesus.* Talk about arm porn.

*When did he remove his hoodie? Isn't he cold? He has to be cold.*

Before I know it, Nathan pulls the truck forward so it's no longer in the bay, then shuts the engine off and locks it before coming back into the garage—a man on a mission. Then he closes the garage, shutting us in from the outside world.

"Just a warning, the lift gets to be kind of loud, especially with nothing else in here, so it's going to echo. You may want to cover your ears."

I clamp my hands over my ears as the lift starts, the noise ricocheting around us. My Beetle rises in the air, my eyes following Nathan as he scans the underside of my vehicle.

"Well, I've got good news and bad news. Which do you want to hear first?" he asks once he finishes looking around.

"Obviously, the good news."

"There doesn't appear to be any damage to the underside of your car. It looks like the front end took the brunt of the damage."

"And the bad news?"

"Your headlights are busted, so I'll have to order new ones to fix them. Pretty easy fix. Your bumper is cracked and busted pretty badly. I'm going to have to rip this entire piece off and replace it. Then obviously find the right shade of paint to match your Beetle and paint it to make it all look seamless again, but it should look good as new when I'm finished."

"How long do you think it will take to fix it?"

"One to two weeks. Two tops."

"That sounds like a lot of work."

Nathan shrugs. "It is, but I can do it all. It may take me about a week or two, but I can definitely get it done."

"When would you find the time? Don't you have football practices coming up? Which means you will have practice after school before the sun goes down. Not to mention, I'm sure you have other customers to tend to on your shifts."

"Nothing to worry your pretty little head about. I'll get it done. Even if I have to put in extra hours on the weekend."

I sigh, feeling overwhelmed for him. This is too much work for one person to do. Unless he asks his uncle to help him, but I can't see his uncle wanting to take on extra work. Then again, I don't know much about what their relationship is like.

"So, you're going to fix all of that, by yourself, and not charge me anything?"

"Precisely," he says, giving me a toothy smile. "If you were to go to an actual dealership or any other repair shop, you're looking at thousands of dollars to get your car fixed. I can do all this myself, right here where I have all the tools I need, and anything I have to order, I can. If it helps you feel any better, you'd actually be doing me a favor."

"And how is that?"

"It gives me the practice I'll need to do this for a living. I want to take on the family business, possibly expand it. Here, we make sure people are able to have a place where they can count on the work to be done correctly and affordably. Times are tough for a lot of people, and most garages charge out the ass just to do basic maintenance. It doesn't seem fair for families to have to choose between paying their bills or putting food on the table for something their car needs done. They shouldn't have to jeopardize their safety by simply choosing to live in this economy."

Wow. How sweet and admirable of him to think of his customers that way.

"Wait. So you're not planning to follow in your father's footsteps?" I figured the police force was where he would go, so hearing him talk about taking over his family's garage surprises me.

"It's what my father expects, as I'm sure most people in Bellwood. It's what I let him believe."

"And your uncle?"

"Believes he's preparing me for this line of work."

"That sounds exhausting." I stand there fully taking him in before asking him the one question I don't think anyone has ever asked him. "What do *you* want to do?"

"I thought it was obvious," he says, and a sly grin stretches across his face as he gestures around the garage.

"Does your father know you work here with your uncle?"

"He does. Or he did. He suggested I quit to focus on studying the handbook to prepare for the academy. I let him think I quit, working here under the guise of football practice or studying after school."

"Nathan, have you ever sat down with your father to discuss with him what it is you want to do with your life?"

His smile quickly disappears, and he moves his eyes downward, shoving his hands into the pockets of his jeans.

"It's something I can't really discuss with him."

"You can't? Or you won't?"

"Does it matter," he responds with sadness.

"It does when it concerns what will make you happy in life," I say.

"Yeah, well, if you knew anything about my life, you would know life hasn't exactly been too kind to me," he grits out before storming off and disappearing behind a door on the other side of the garage.

I stand grounded in my spot for a moment, not understanding what just happened. Pulling out my phone, I open the Uber app to order a ride, but the next car won't be available for another thirty minutes. I have a lot to figure out, like transportation for the next few weeks, but at least for tonight I will have a ride home. With the Uber taken care of, I follow after Nathan, hoping I can rectify whatever I did to upset him.

# Chapter 15

## Nathan

Staring at the baby-blue Chevelle, lost in my thoughts, I hear the door shut behind me and the clicking of Jenna's heels crossing the concrete flooring.

"She's beautiful," Jenna states as she comes to stand beside me, looking at the car I have worked tirelessly on for the past few months.

"Yeah, she is. I put a lot of work into getting her fixed up so I can drive her someday. Hopefully soon."

"You fixed this car all on your own?" she asks, with surprise in her voice.

"I told you, Spitfire. I know my way around cars. This one"—I pat the black rooftop of the Chevelle—"is all mine when I'm done with her. A gift from my uncle."

"Color me impressed, Shop Boy." She teases. "It's a really beautiful color. Did you paint it yourself?"

"I did. I still have the hood piece to paint." I point to where I have the hood sitting along a wall against a thick sheet of drop cloth. "I've been back and forth on what I should do with it, though. If I want to do solid black to match the roof of the car or if I want to paint it the same blue and just add some white racing stripes. I think that's what Ryan would have chosen, especially since this was his favorite color."

"Ryan? Who's Ryan?"

I clear my throat, trying to push away the emotion that consumes me anytime I think or talk about my older brother.

"Ryan—" I clear my throat once more. "Ryan was my older brother, about two years older than me. He was kind of like my best friend until he got his driver's license, then he was barely home. I felt betrayed … hurt. Like he was leaving me. Dad was picking up more shifts with work, so I was constantly home alone and hated it. So one day he decided to take me with him, and I finally got to see where he was going. Even though it's a forty-five-minute drive from Dartmouth, where we lived, he had taken on working part-time to help here at the garage. He enjoyed being around all the cars and helping our grandfather and Uncle Dean. It was his happy place and one he was planning on taking up after he completed all the necessary schooling."

"You said *was* your brother … what happened?" Jenna looks at me with a softness I haven't seen from her before.

"He died in a car accident the summer before my sophomore year. He was just eighteen years old." I use my arm to swipe away the tears that threaten to spill. "Him and

I were really close, but we became closer when it came to cars. It's how we bonded. Most siblings don't get along, you know, but us? Nah. We loved each other. Sure, we had our fair share of arguments …" I pause, giving myself a moment to breathe through the memory. "But at the end of the day, we loved each other."

"I"m so sorry, Nathan. It doesn't feel like enough, but I'm so sorry for the loss of your mom and brother. I can't imagine that losing those two has been easy for you." She extends her arm and gently squeezes mine, igniting a sensation when her fingertips touch my bare skin.

"After we lost Ryan, Dad took the position at the police department here in Bellwood and we moved here that summer. He said he felt like we both deserved a change. Not be stuck in a house where we lost not just one but two people who meant everything to us. I think in some way he felt I should be closer to the remaining family members I still have. People who can look after me while he grieves by throwing himself into his work."

Jenna wraps her arms around my waist, giving me a slight squeeze, and just holds me. I hesitate for a moment before wrapping my arms around her.

"Is this okay?" I ask, wanting to make sure she understands if I'm making her uncomfortable, she can tell me.

Jenna looks up at me, a slight wetness to her brown eyes, and smiles. "Just hug me, Shop Boy. You look like you could use a hug as much as I do, especially after tonight."

I give her a gentle squeeze, enjoying the warmth of her body next to mine. My cold heart warms as I breathe in her sugary, warm vanilla scent with notes of jasmine mixed with my cologne. Our scents mingling draws out the primal beast within, wanting my scent always to be mixed with hers on me ... on her.

"I was thinking ..." Jenna says, bringing me back from the space I zoned off to. She pulls away from me, my body instantly missing the warmth of hers. She walks over to the Chevelle's hood and tilts her pretty head side to side as if she is sizing the sheet of metal. "What if there was a painted mural on the hood? Like a portrait of your brother? Or something in regard to your family?"

"That isn't a bad idea, but how do I go about doing that? I'm not an artist. Painting one solid color or doing lines? Easy. Painting a full out image that includes actual people and not stick figures? I'm not Picasso." I softly chuckle.

"I could do it for you," Jenna states. "Think of it as a trade off. You want to fix my car for free? Let me paint the mural on the hood of your car, then we can call it even. What do you say?" She holds out her dainty hand, waiting for me to shake it.

"On one condition," I say, holding my hand close but not yet ready to shake hers. "You stop being catty with me and try being nicer when we are in public."

Jenna scoffs, but I give her a pointed look.

"Fine. But just so you know, I'm only *catty* with you, as you so put it, because you need to find better friends."

"Care to elaborate as to why?"

"They're players. The biggest manwhores in the school who think they're God's gift to the ladies, and I ... might have ... loopedyouinwiththem." She mumbles the last part of her statement.

"I'm sorry, what was that last part?" I ask, wanting to hear why she treats me the way she does.

She releases a heavy sigh. "I might have misjudged you and assumed you were just like them. I mean, you hang out with them, and I've never seen you with the same girl. Plus, you never spoke up about Brady sneaking around with Lydia. I mean, clearly you had your boy's back instead of telling Sadie he was stringing her along with that skank or telling your boy how wrong he was."

"Ah," I say, pulling my bottom lip into my mouth and biting before releasing it. I grin at the realization. "Now it makes sense. I kept questioning what I could have possibly done to be on your bad side. Now I get it," I state. "May I clear a few things up for you?"

Jenna crosses her arms. "I guess if we are exchanging services, I could hear you out."

"Thank you," I say. "First, you are correct to misjudge me, but I am nothing like those two, and if you ever paid closer attention, I'm not nearly as close to Brady and Chad as everyone thinks I am. I tolerate them because we play football together. If I'm being honest, I hang with them when Dom isn't able to. He's my best friend, the one I prefer to hang with. We used to go to school in Dartmouth together, but his family moved here when we were in fourth grade. Brady and Chad just always found a way to hang out, and when your dad picks up shifts because he can't stand being home with his only living kid ... well ... would you stay home or go hang around people to keep the darkness away?"

Jenna fiddles with her fingers, her eyes focused on me as I explain. "As for the girls, there hasn't been anyone, apart from one girl, who intrigues me enough to bother with. I had a friends-with-benefits arrangement in tenth grade with a senior, but I was also in a really dark place. I had just lost my brother and then moved to a new town, a new school. I was dealing with some shit and went about it the wrong way. We ended things when she graduated, and I've just never had the interest to be with anyone. Yes, I talk to girls who approach me, but I do it out of politeness because that's how my mother raised me to be. I don't particularly like being a dickhead like Chad, or flirtatious to get pussy from a girl the way Brady does. It's not me, it's not who I am."

"So, who's the one girl?" Jenna asks, and I furrow my brows. "You said there hasn't been any girls apart from one who intrigues you enough for you to bother with."

Shit. I hadn't realized I let that slip. Do I tell her it's her? *She has a boyfriend, remember?*

I clear my throat. "It … it doesn't matter. She doesn't really seem to know I exist."

"Did you ever think, oh, I don't know, maybe telling this girl how you feel? I mean, she could possibly feel the same way you do."

"It's not that simple," I mumble, but she still heard me.

"Afraid of rejection there, Shop Boy?" Jenna says as a taunt, and I begin to lose my resolve.

"I'm not afraid of being rejected. It's because she has a fucking boyfriend!" I raise my voice with each word, causing her to flinch.

Fuck! I didn't mean to do that.

I take a deep breath before speaking in a softer tone. "I'm sorry. I shouldn't have raised my voice at you. You didn't deserve that. It's … just … the girl has a boyfriend, someone who doesn't deserve her, but I have to accept it and move forward."

"Nathan—"

"As for Sadie and Brady, I had no idea he even messed with Lydia in that way. I warned him several times to watch out for her. As did Dom and some of the other guys on the team. We all warned him about Lydia's obsession with him, but I swear to you on Ryan's grave, I didn't know that was going on. I've got my own problems to deal with, and with the clock ticking on the graduation countdown, I have been too consumed with my personal shit to worry about other people's drama."

Jenna nods and extends her hand once again. "Look, I'm not great with apologies, but I do apologize for misjudging you. I promise you I will do my best to show you more kindness. Deal?"

She gives me an assuring smile, so I shake her hand.

"Deal." I release her hand and go over to the work bench along the wall where I keep the tools and materials I need to work on the Chevelle.

"I've already sanded down the hood and applied the basecoat, so all that is left is to paint the design." I grab the airbrush tool I use for the finer line work. "Have you ever used one of these before?"

"No, but I've always wanted to try it out. Is it hard?"

"Not really. It's fairly easy once you know how it functions. Come here, and I can show you how to operate it." I gesture for her to come to me so I can demonstrate how the equipment works. "First, make sure the gun is connected to the hose and compressor. Very important that they are completely connected."

I pull Jenna in front of me, her back pressed to my front, and hold back the groan I want to release at her body against mine.

*Control yourself. The last thing you want to do is ruin the agreement and make things uncomfortable!*

I place her hands on the airbrush gun, her left hand on the hose and her right hand on the top while putting her finger onto the trigger, before taking a step back.

"This is where you will pour the paint into." I point to the paint cup that sits on top of the airbrush gun. "It's not very big, so be cautious not to overfill it. The little joystick-looking button your finger is on is called the trigger." I place my hand over Jenna's to guide her finger and direct her on how to work the tool. "What you want to do is press down so you start the air, then pull the trigger back to start the paint flow." She follows my guidance. "That was nicely done. Now, to stop the paint flow, you will want to push forward, then release the trigger." I move her finger forward, then release her finger as she releases the trigger.

"That's it?" Jenna asks.

"That's all there is to it, Spitfire," I whisper.

She turns to face me, her eyes bouncing between mine before darting to my lips.

"Do you know how incredibly beautiful you are?" I whisper as I lose myself in her eyes. The air in the room seems to warm, and my heart thunders against my ribcage as Jenna and I stare into each other. I wish I could read her thoughts, be in her head, to know what she is thinking at this very moment.

She leans in toward me, pressing her soft lips with mine. I return the kiss, a kiss I've only ever dreamed about since I first laid eyes on this beautiful woman. Her tongue probes my lips, wanting entry, so I open for her, tasting her, my tongue caressing hers.

She presses her luscious body into mine, pulling me closer with her free hand. I graze my hand along her curves 'til I reach her face and deepen our kiss.

A moan escapes her lips, and my dick twitches, getting hard. I back off before I'm full out tenting the front of my pants.

"Jenna ... Jenna, wait," I say as it takes everything in me to break one of the best kisses in my life. "We can't be doing this. We shouldn't be doing this."

"Doing what?"

"Whatever you are doing."

"It's called kissing, Nathan."

"I know ..."

"So, what is it, then?" she asks. There's anger in her voice. "Is it me?"

"No, Jenna. Of course it's not you. The kiss was incredible. Really. It's ... you have been through a lot tonight—"

"Yeah, Nathan. I have. I have been through hell tonight, more than what you know." Tears start streaming down her face, and my heart aches wondering what could have been worse than the accident.

"Tell me what happened, then. Talk to me, Spitfire," I plead. "I opened up to you about Ryan. I have never been able to talk about him with anyone except for Dom, and that's only because Dom knew I had a brother. So, now it's your turn to share."

She shakes her head, wrapping her arms around her tightly. "I can't ... it's embarrassing. And if I tell you, you'll just run to your dad and just make everything worse!"

"My father throws himself into work and is rarely home. We don't speak much except when he is trying to shove practice tests down my throat and pushing me toward being a cop. His way of trying to control my life so I don't end up like my dead brother. So believe me when I say this, whatever you tell me will stay between us. I give you my word!"

"You give me your word, huh?"

I nod, telling her she has my promise.

"So you won't go running to our beloved police chief when I tell you I initiated sex with Felix tonight? You won't go tell your father that in the process of this, one of Felix's friends showed up and plopped himself right on the couch, unbothered that we were practically naked, and Felix wanted to keep going. And when I told him I didn't want to, he kept pushing for it, saying that him and his friend have done this sort of thing before ... I begged and pleaded for him to stop, but he didn't listen to me ..."

Pure anger rolls through me. "Are you telling me you were raped?" I grit out, forcing the rage that wants to go full Hulk mode and smash shit.

"How can it be rape when I wanted to in the first place?" she says solemnly, unable to look at me.

"Doesn't matter. If you wanted to at first but changed your mind and he didn't listen, that is rape! No is a full sentence. It means no, Jenna. If he kept going ..." I clench and unclench my fists. "Jenna, you have to report this.

Tonight! I can take you to the hospital and request a rape kit—"

"No!" Jenna shouts back.

"Jenna, we have to press charges!"

"We don't have shit to do because it doesn't affect you, Nathan. It only affects me, and I'm not reporting this."

"Why not? You want him to get away with this? How many other girls has he raped before? How many more girls will be a victim if we don't put a stop—"

"Who's going to believe me? Huh?" she yells. "Who is going to believe the brown girl dressed like this?" She opens my letterman jacket, showcasing the dress she wore tonight. "I go to a hospital and tell them I need a rape test done, they are going to take pictures. The moment those people see pictures of me in this dress, telling them I initiated sex first, that I ... gave up ..."

I remain quiet as the strong, fiery woman I've known her to always be breaks down, and it rips me to pieces.

"I gave in, Nathan. I dissociated and have no recollection of what happened or for how long it went on. I don't know how I was able to dress myself or drive. It's why the accident was my fault ... I got lost in thought, missed the curve, and wrecked."

"Regardless of if you mentally were there or not, you said no and he kept going. That. Is. Rape!"

"You don't know the kind of monster he is. If he gets arrested and we go to trial, they will spin it to make it look like I'm the girl who cried rape, and he'll walk freely. That only puts a target on my back, and I'll be damned if I become his sitting prey!"

"Jenna, we will figure out a way to make sure he's locked up and you're safe."

"How, Nathan? How?"

I don't answer her because truthfully, I am not sure how. All I know is I would do any and everything in my power to ensure she feels safe, safe from anyone who dares to harm her. Felix included. That piece of shit will get his, I swear on my own life, I will see to it.

"See? You don't know how," she says when I don't respond. "By the way, I kissed you because I wanted to. I kissed you because you have done nothing but respect me, ensure I was safe, and look after me all evening, and I was certain that we were having a moment. I guess I was wrong. Way to make a girl feel rejected, Ward!" she grits out as she checks her phone. "Look at that. My Uber is here. Talk about perfect timing."

She storms through the door, but I follow after her.

"Jenna, wait. Can we please talk about this?"

She ignores me as she unlocks the front door and heads toward her ride waiting in the parking lot. I don't miss how her head is on a swivel searching the parking lot before she climbs into the car, driving off into the night.

"Fuck!" I yell as I kick the ground. Just then, my phone rings with a call from my best friend, but I decline it. I can't talk to him right now. Not while I'm like this.

My phone alerts me to a new text.

I go back inside the shop, locking the front door, and head straight for Jenna's vehicle to start working on it. I'm still furious over finding out what she endured tonight, and sleep won't come easily for me. Not that it has since the night Ryan died. So I do what I do best, throw myself into work to quiet my mind and busy my hands that want nothing more than to seek out that piece of shit and beat him within an inch of his life. The last thing my father needs is his own kid being arrested and charged with assault while he believes I'm on the path to becoming an officer of the law.

# Chapter 16

## Jenna

I'm woken up by the sounds of someone knocking on a door nearby.

"Jenna?" *Knock. Knock.* "Jenna, you awake?"

Sadie? What the ...?

I lift my head off the pillowy bedding beneath me and look around. With groggy eyes, I recognize the pastel-yellow walls of my bedroom. My gaze falls to my body, still wearing the same dress and heels I wore last night, along with Nathan's letterman jacket.

*So it wasn't a dream?*

She knocks on my door again, my head throbbing with each hit.

"Yeah, Sadie. I'm up!" I shout as I remove the jacket and stuff it under my pillows. After tossing my heels into my mini walk-in closet, I grab my big fluffy bathrobe and wrap it around me, ensuring it covers up the dress.

My bedroom door creaks open, and Sadie walks in dressed in her fuzzy cherry pajamas. Her blonde hair is thrown up into a messy bun on top of her head, no makeup in sight.

"Looks like someone had a good night." She smirks as she enters my room and plops down on my bed. "I didn't see your car in the driveway, so I'm assuming Felix gave you a ride home since it was so late. Did you two finally take that trip to pound town?" She wiggles her eyebrows at the mention of pound town. If only things had gone as I had wanted them to.

I fight back the grimace as I look at my best friend, unsure of what to say.

"Actually ..." I take a moment, thinking of what to tell her. Like I told Nathan, I can't go to the police about what happened. No one will believe I was raped, especially if I don't believe it myself, and he will more than likely get off with nothing more than a slap on the wrist. "The date didn't go so well. I realized he will never fully trust me because of his past relationships, and I can't be with somebody like that."

"Oh ..." Her smile drops. "I'm so sorry, Jen. I know you really liked the guy."

"Yeah, well ... it's senior year. I got plenty of time to worry about men later. I just need to keep myself focused on school."

*Yeah, let's lie to our best friend.*

If lying protects her from Felix's wrath, then it's worth the little white lie.

"So where's your car?"

"At Wesley's … I kind of, sort of … wrecked it last night."

Sadie jumps up. "What!? Oh my God, Jen! What happened? How come you didn't call me? I would have come to you!"

I hold my hand up, silencing her rambling. "Sadie, I'm fine. I'm just a little sore, but I'm okay, and it wasn't anything major. I just missed a turn on my way home and wrecked into a fence. Had Nathan not been driving along, I don't know what I would have done."

She tilts her head. "Wait. Did you say Nathan? As in Nathan Ward stopped to help you?"

"Yeah … why do you sound so surprised?"

"Uh, because whenever he comes around, you're defensive and abrasive with him."

I roll my eyes. Yeah, I know I was always harsh toward Nathan, but that was before last night. After getting to know him a little bit, I realized how wrong I was to judge him. Sadie doesn't need to know that bit though. "As shocked as we both are, I'm just grateful he stopped and helped, considering I wrecked on Pine Hill Road. You know how there's hardly any cars that travel through there, especially at night. Nathan made sure I was okay before he took me to the garage and went back to tow my car. Did you know he works at Wesley's?"

She shakes her head. "I knew he had a job but didn't know exactly where or what it was he did."

"Apparently, Wesley's is a family-owned business on Nathan's maternal side."

"Oh … I had no idea."

Everyone in town knew our police chief was a widow, but I wonder how many know he also lost a son. I want to ask Sadie if she knew or heard about it when she was dating Brady, but I feel like that would just violate Nathan's trust in some way. He willingly opened up to me last night, and it seems like something that isn't easy for him to do with just anyone. Which makes me question ... why me?

There's a soft knock on my door before my mother's beautiful face appears. "I thought I heard your beautiful voices in here. Jenna, sweetie, I didn't hear you come in last night. Where is your car?"

Crap. I am not awake enough to do this right now.

"Um ... that's a good question," I answer with a soft chuckle. "There is something I need to talk to you and Dad about, if he's home."

"Your father is in his office. Why don't the two of you get dressed and come downstairs? I will make us all some lunch and you can talk to us while we eat."

I nod. "Sounds good, Mom."

She flashes us her beautiful smile again before leaving us alone in my room. At that moment, my phone starts to go off somewhere in the room. Sadie and I both search for it before she finds it under my pillow in the pocket of Nathan's letterman jacket. Her eyebrows furrow, and she tosses me my phone. One look at the caller ID and my spine goes ramrod straight. Again, I am not awake enough to deal with this. I take a deep breath, ignoring Felix's call as I walk to my bedside table where I put my phone on silent and place it on the charger.

"Do I want to ask how or why you have Nathan's jacket stuffed under your pillow?" she asks, amusement in her voice.

"I got cold, so Nathan let me borrow it." Sadie gives me a pointed look. "I forgot I still had it on, okay? Don't worry. I'm going to give it back to him tomorrow at school."

"What about Felix?"

"I'm going to deal with him later. Right now, I want a hot shower and to take some ibuprofen for this headache I have."

Sadie gives me a soft smile as she leaves, and I take the opportunity to get a hot, steamy shower. The kind that leaves your skin all red. As I lather the body wash into my loofah, I spot the bruises along my wrists and forearms. I look at them closely, noting how I can almost see the fingerprints when a flashback of last night runs through my mind. Blinking away the memory, I shake my head and take a few deep breaths to calm my racing heart.

*You can get through this. You will get through this!*

After scrubbing my entire body trying to erase every touch Felix placed, I make my way into my closet to grab clothes. I throw on some black leggings and my favorite Aaliyah T-shirt, dressing strictly for comfort today. It's Sunday, after all.

I stand in front of my full-length mirror and gasp when my eyes land on my neck. More finger-shaped bruising marks my slender neck, and panic rises in me. Mom and Sadie didn't say a word, so they must not have seen it because of my bathrobe, but I can't just walk around wearing a robe everywhere until the bruises disappear. That would be weird. I will have to find a way to cover this up, keep this from my parents and Sadie. Plus, everyone else at school. If anyone sees these marks, they will know something serious happened. There's no mistaking what they are.

I grab my gray Bellwood High hoodie from my closet and make sure the bruising is hidden. Thank goodness we are entering fall, and I can get away with wearing a hoodie. Once I've ensured there are no other marks visible to the naked eye, I head downstairs to the kitchen.

Mom and Dad are setting plates with sandwiches and chips down at the table while Sadie grabs the pitcher of sweet tea to fill up our glasses. I grab the big bowl of mixed fruit from the kitchen island and take it to our dining table where we all take our places.

"Jenna, your mother says that you need to talk to us about your car," my father says. I chew and swallow before I answer him.

"Yeah, about my car—" I take a deep breath. "So, I was coming home from Felix's house and took the backroads. I wasn't paying attention and missed the turn in the road and collided with the fence."

"Jenna!" My mother gasps, dropping her sandwich onto her plate.

"Are you okay, sweetheart?" my father asks as he gets up from his chair to come over to look me over.

"I'm fine! I'm fine. It wasn't anything too bad. I swear!" I say, assuring them I'm okay. "I just have a slight headache and I'm a little sore, but I took some ibuprofen before I came downstairs."

"You said you weren't paying attention," my mother says. "Please tell me you weren't on your phone, Jenna Celeste.

You know when your auntie gifted you the car, that was a strict rule we made."

"I wasn't. Felix and I"—*careful how you word this so you don't alarm anyone*—"things didn't exactly go well, and we broke up. I was just in my head about the fact and allowed it to distract me. For that, I'm sorry."

My mother and father momentarily glance at each other, reaching for the other's hand while Sadie remains quiet as she chews her lunch.

"We are so sorry to hear that, honey," my mother says. "We are, however, thankful you're okay, but you should have called us."

"Where is your car now? I should probably call to get it towed—" my father says, but I raise a hand, shaking it back and forth.

"No need for that, Dad. Nathan helped me out."

"Nathan? Who is Nathan?" my mother asks.

"Police Chief Ward's son," Sadie answers for me.

"Yeah, he was driving along shortly after the accident happened and came to my aid. He actually works at Wesley's with his uncle and was kind enough to give me a ride to the shop before he towed my car there."

"Oh ... well ... how thoughtful of him," my mother says. "Why don't we head there after lunch and see what we can do about the cost of repairs."

"No need to!" I blurt out. "Uh ... Nathan and I came up with that last night. Payment will all be taken care of by me since I was not in the right state of mind. I will be paying for the damages myself so you guys don't have to."

My parents look at me with lifted brows. I'm not sure if it's shock or if they are impressed. "Well, honey, I have to admit that it is very responsible and grown up of you to decide."

Their praise for my actions warms me. "You guys have done so much for me, not to mention taking in Sadie. It's the least I can do since I am the one who wrecked the car. My car, my accident, my responsibility. And don't you two think about trying to sneak in there to make any payments either! I will have Nathan tell me if you do."

Sadie coughs, and I glance at my best friend as she guzzles her glass of sweet tea. "Sorry! Wrong pipe," she says after finishing her tea.

The doorbell rings through the house, and I inwardly begin to panic.

"Who could that be?" my mother asks.

"I'll go get it," my father says as he gets up to go toward the front door.

*Please, oh please, don't let it be Felix!*

I sit and listen carefully, my heart racing as I wait for the aggressive yelling that is sure to come from the monster I'm avoiding.

"Jenna," my father says my name loudly. "There's a gentleman at the door for you."

*Fuck.*

I feel a squeeze on my hand under the table and glance over to look at Sadie. She gives my hand another gentle squeeze, letting me know she's here for me and has my back. I give her a soft smile before I make my way to the front porch. When I open the door, I'm met with two olive-green eyes, a warm smile, and two dimpled cheeks.

"Nathan? Hey, hi." I'm surprised to see him while, at the same time, relieved it isn't who I thought it was.

Nathan's eyes roam over me, and the inside of my body warms as he takes me in. I'm not sure if he is checking me out or looking me over after what I admitted to him last night.

"Hey. I just wanted to come by and check on you before I head to practice. How are you feeling?"

"I'm okay. Just a little headache, but I took some medicine for it. Just waiting for it to kick in."

"Is that all?" he asks as he tilts his head, and it doesn't take a rocket scientist to know what he's asking.

"I swear to you on my own life, I'm okay." I give him my best fake smile, hoping he buys it. Nathan smirks, shaking his head.

"I don't believe you, Spitfire, but I'll let it go. For now," he says as he glances around as if looking for anyone who could possibly show up. I'm guessing he is waiting for Felix to show his face, but I pray to God he doesn't. "That's not the only reason I came by."

Green eyes meet my brown ones, and there's a seriousness to his tone. "Oh … um, you mean your jacket? Yeah, I'm so sorry. I forgot I had it on. Give me a second and I'll go grab it—"

"Not the jacket." Nathan flashes me his most handsome smile that makes me feel some type of way. "I wanted to come by to tell you that I started on your car last night and already ordered the parts to fix it. I should have it done before I leave for the championship game."

Refocusing my mind from the way his smile lights me up to what he said, I realize what he is saying. "Wait, the championship game is in thirteen days."

"Yes, but I will do my best to get it done before we leave that Friday, so hopefully, it will be more like within eleven days."

"Is that doable?" I ask.

With a grin that reminds me of the Cheshire cat, Nathan replies, "It's very doable."

I roll my eyes.

"Get your head out of the gutter, Shop Boy." I pause for a moment, realizing that for almost two weeks I will be without transportation, and groan. "Fuck! How the hell am I supposed to get to and from school or work?"

"Me."

My eyes shoot to Nathan's face. "You?"

"Yeah, me. Who else?"

"Uh, there's Sadie."

"Does she even drive her own car?" Nathan asks.

Crap. No. Ever since her and Payson began dating, Payson picks her up, wanting to spend every second with her she can get.

"Well, no. She rides with Payson, but I can just ask Payson to give me a ride too."

"You could, but where would you sit?"

"In the back?" I mean, where else would I sit?

"You could, but that would be quite a tight fit, considering she also gives Colton and his sister a ride too. Jeeps are not very spacious vehicles."

"Then I'll take the bus."

Nathan crosses his arms and leans against the pillar that holds the porch up. "Are you really going to ride the bus with all the noisy, immature teenagers who have yet to get their licenses?" He gives me a knowing smirk, as if he knows how much I despise the loud noise.

God, no. I don't want to ride the bus. Besides the noise, it puts a crunch on making it to my first class on time, and I don't like being late for art.

"Is there a reason you are refusing to ride with me to school, Spitfire?" he asks with an amused expression on his face. "Correct me if I'm wrong, but didn't we make a deal last night about you being nicer to me."

This man is infuriating, but I can't say that to his face because of our *deal*. I did promise him I would be nicer.

"I don't want to burden you," I state. "You have football practices after school in preparation for the championship game. I know how Payson is. She takes this shit seriously. Not to mention, my house is not quite on the way to school, which means you would have to get up earlier if you were to pick me up and get us both to school on time."

"You let me deal with football practice and Payson. I'm sure they will be more than understanding. And I have no qualms about getting up a little earlier to pick you up for school, Jen. I wouldn't be telling you this if I hadn't already thought it through."

I stare in awe at him willing to go to such lengths to help me.

"Why?" I ask.

"Why what?"

"Why are you doing all of this? The car? The repairs? Offering me rides? Why are you so willing to help me? You clearly rejected me last night—"

"I didn't reject you," Nathan says, and moves to stand in front of me, forcing me to look up into his eyes.

"I kissed you and you shoved me away," I grit out, recalling the hurt I felt when he didn't want to kiss me although I was certain there was a moment where he wanted that kiss as much as I did.

"You went through something traumatic last night. Not only were you ra—" He pauses, clenching his jaw and taking a breath. "You also wrecked your car. I wasn't sure if the kiss was out of a response from being traumatized or if it was pity for all the shit I opened up to you about. No one knows all that personal shit about me except my family and Dom. It was never rejection, Spitfire. Trust me. If you knew how long I have wanted to …"

He closes his eyes, taking a moment to gather himself.

"How long have you wanted to … what?" I want to hear what he was going to say. Before he can answer, his phone rings and he pulls away from me.

"It's Dom. I've got to go pick him and his brother up and get to practice."

I nod, wrapping my arms around myself. "Thank you, by the way. For helping me last night and with my car. I should have said it last night, but I didn't, so I wanted you to know I appreciate it." I'm about to turn around to go inside when he grabs my waist and pulls me back into him. He gently clutches onto my chin, tilting my face to look up into his.

"I'll be here in the morning to pick you up. You better be ready if you don't want to be late to art class." Nathan leans in and presses a kiss to my forehead. "And just so there is no confusion …" He leans in again, only this time, his lips caress mine before he slowly pulls back. "See you in the morning, Spitfire."

He jogs off my porch to his car. As he opens his car door, he takes a moment to glance my way. With a wink, he climbs inside and drives away, and I watch until I no longer see the red of his taillights.

I press my fingers to my lips. *He* kissed *me*. It wasn't a passionate kiss, but it was a kiss that left me with those butterfly sensations in my stomach and a warmth in my chest. He said just so there wasn't any confusion. Did he mean he wasn't rejecting me? Does Nathan feel some type of way … for me?

# Chapter 17

## Nathan

I pull up in front of Jenna's house at exactly seven thirty, ensuring we have plenty of time to make it to school so she won't be late. I even calculated a few extra minutes in case she decides to argue with me about giving her a ride. If I know anything about my spitfire, she enjoys sparring with me like she did yesterday morning when I stopped by.

After knocking on the front door and waiting a few moments, the door opens to a woman who looks like an older version of Jenna.

"Can I help you?" she asks.

"Good morning, Mrs. Altwood. I'm here to give Jenna a ride to school. I'm Nathan Ward, Police Chief Ward's son," I say while reaching out to shake her hand. One thing my mother taught my brother and me was to always use our manners and show respect to anyone we meet. She shakes my hand in return and gives me a pleasant smile.

"So nice to meet you, Nathan. Please, come inside out of the cold."

"Thank you, ma'am," I say as I walk into the entryway.

"Oh, please, Mrs. Altwood or Veronica will be just fine. Ma'am just makes me feel extremely old." She laughs.

"With all due respect, you look like a woman in her late twenties, Veronica. Are you sure you're not Jenna's older sister?" I give her a smile, the one I know showcases my dimples. It's not a smile I show often, but this is Jenna's mother and I want to be in her good graces, especially if they got to know *him*.

"Oh, I like you," Veronica says with a grin. "Why don't you follow me into the kitchen. I was just making myself some coffee before I leave for work."

My heart fills at her praise, and I follow her into their kitchen that complements the outside of their home. Light-gray wood flooring complements the white cabinets and black kitchen appliances. A white island sits in the center, taking a seat at one of the black bar stools lining one side.

She gets to work making a pot of coffee. "Nathan, can I get you anything to eat?"

"No, thank you. I ate before I came here."

She leans against the cabinets and stares at me for a moment. "Nathan, I want to say thank you for what you did for my Jenna the other night. I'm so glad you came across her accident and helped her out."

"I am too."

"Jenna says it wasn't that bad, but I need to know, from someone that isn't her. I'm not saying my daughter would lie to us, but she also has this way of wanting to ease things for her father and myself. Was it ... was it worse than what she is saying?"

I see the worry there in her eyes, like any loving mother or parent would have for their child.

"I give you my word, Mrs. Altwood. The front of her car took a bit of damage, but it was nothing too serious. If she had been speeding, I can't say the same though. I did offer to take her to the hospital, but she refused me, claiming she was fine."

Relief washes over her face, as if she had been preparing for me to say it was worse. That Jenna lied to protect them from worrying about her. Did she bring up what she went through beforehand? I doubt it. I don't think I would be sitting here about to take her to school, and I'm certain my father would have mentioned it in passing if they'd reported it.

"Thank you. Seriously, thank you. I wanted to press her more. Hell, I was prepared to go to the garage to look at the car myself to see how badly it looked. I appreciate Jenna trying to shield us from this, wanting to own up to her mishaps. I just wish she would have called us when it happened." She leans across the island and squeezes my hand. "I'm so grateful you showed up and helped my girl when you did, though." She pats my hand before releasing me to go pour her coffee into a thermos.

At that moment, Sadie and Jenna enter the kitchen but stop when they see me sitting at the island. I keep my face schooled at the sight of Jenna wearing my jacket, not wanting her to see how feral it makes me to see her in something of *mine*.

"Nathan?" Jenna asks. "What are you doing here?" Her eyes bounce back and forth between her mother and me.

"I'm giving you a ride to school. Remember?" I give her a pointed look, daring her to argue with me in front of her mother.

"Y-y-yeah, but I just didn't expect you to actually show up in my house."

"He came to the door for you, and I invited him inside," her mom says as she takes a sip from her thermos. "If you will excuse me, I have to get to the office. Lots of expecting mamas are waiting for me." She says it so cheerfully, as if she looks forward to going to her job. Veronica heads to Sadie, kissing the top of her head. "Have a good day, girls."

She then walks to Jenna to kiss the top of her head. "The boy has manners and helped you with your car. The least you can do is take him up on his offer."

"Yes, mother," Jenna grumbles.

Her mom smirks at her and turns to give me a wink before she exits the kitchen to leave. "See you girls tonight. Love you!" she yells from the front of the house.

"Love you too!" Sadie and Jenna shout back before the door closes.

"Shall we?" I stand from the kitchen island and walk over to Jenna who is glaring daggers at me. "What?"

"You just had to be all charming and well-mannered. Thanks! Now my mother is smitten with you, and I'll never hear the end of it!" she says before she turns and storms out the front door.

"Is that a bad thing?" I yell after her, confused why she would be so infuriated.

Sadie steps beside me, smirking. "To Jenna, it is. Her parents have never met a single guy she has dated because she doesn't bring them around. She has this weird superstition that the guy who gets to meet her parents is the one she is meant to be with and well ... you're the first guy to meet the parents so ... congrats!"

"Really?" Something like pride fills me before it dawns on me what Sadie said. "We ... uh ... we aren't dating though. I'm just helping Jenna out."

"Give it time. I've seen the way you look at her. Reminds me of how I looked at Payson when I fought those feelings she stirred within me before I smartened up and claimed that woman."

"Jenna hates me."

"If there is one thing I have learned from reading romance, Nathan, it's that there's a thin line between love and hate. Sometimes, the hate is louder, especially when it's somebody one is unsure of. With just the right amount of patience, respect, and obviously communication, two people can change it into something beautiful. You just have to show her the real you."

"Are you two coming or what?" Jenna yells from the front door.

"One more thing," Sadie says, catching my attention, halting me in place. "The characters that seem to hate each other the most? Deep down, they secretly have feelings for the other."

With that, she leaves, and I let her words sink in. Is she trying to tell me that maybe Jenna has feelings for me?

The drive from Jenna's house to school was quiet, apart from the constant vibrating coming from her cell phone. After about the fourth one, she avoided looking at her phone, leaving it to sit on top of her backpack. She averts her eyes out the window, watching as the scenery passes us. I glance her way a few times, trying not to be obvious, before she catches me smirking.

"What?" Jenna asks.

"Uh, nothing. Just … you look good wearing my jacket."

She glances down. "Oh. Yeah, sorry about that. I put it on so I wouldn't forget to take it with me. When we get to school, you can have it back."

"What if I tell you no?"

"You don't want your jacket back?" Her eyebrow raises, questioning me.

"I mean, it is my jacket." I smile at her. "But honestly, I like it on you even more."

She doesn't say anything, but a tinge of pink flushes her cheeks. If I knew no better, I would think maybe there was some truth to what Sadie said back in the kitchen. Maybe Jenna has feelings toward me.

I pull into my parking space at the school, making it ten minutes before the late bell rings. I'm about to ask her how she is doing since the events of Saturday when she picks up her phone.

"Jesus Christ," she mutters as she ignores the phone call yet again. When the next alert flashes across her phone screen, her face pales.

"Is everything okay?"

"Uh ... yeah. It's nothing," she says as she turns her cell phone off and stuffs it in her backpack.

"Doesn't sound like nothing." I press her. "Is it ... *him*? Is he bothering you?"

She avoids looking at me, which is all the answer I need.

"It's not your problem to worry about, Nathan." Jenna opens the door and gets out of my car, shoving her backpack onto her shoulder. I grab my backpack from the back seat and follow suit, ensuring to lock my vehicle in the process. She speedwalks toward the school building, but thanks to my tall genes, I'm able to catch up to her.

"You see, that's where you're wrong, Spitfire. It is my problem, and it's been my problem since that night at the party when he put his hands on you." Remembering those marks he left on her skin makes my blood simmer.

Jenna stops abruptly and faces me. "I appreciate the concern, Nathan, but this is *my* problem to deal with, not yours. The less people involved, the better."

"What do you mean by that?" I ask as we cross the drop-off lane to the sidewalk leading to the front doors.

She lets out a frustrated sigh. "Just forget I said anything. Okay, Shop Boy?"

The sound of tires squealing catches our attention. We turn to see a blue truck coming directly toward us. Without hesitation, I shove Jenna out of the way, placing myself in the direct path of the vehicle. If it is going to hit anyone, it will be me.

The truck comes to an abrupt stop, mere inches from hitting me, as the driver partially parks on the sidewalk before getting out. The moment I see Felix, I see red. Hot rage consumes me, knowing what he has done to Jenna, and I storm toward him, ready to beat him into a pulp.

"Nathan, don't!" Jenna yells. She reaches for my arm, but I pull it away before she can grab it. This fucker has no reason to be here, and I'll be damned if he thinks he will get anywhere close to my girl.

"You have a lot of nerve showing your ugly face here," I snarl as I get right up in his face. "So why don't you take your sorry ass back to the privileged rich boy community you came from."

"Ugly? Really? That's the best you can come up with?" he retorts, looking me up and down. He laughs as he steps back, putting some space between us before his stare moves to Jenna. "Is this fuckface the reason you broke up with me? You told me he was nothing to you, but clearly, that's a lie. Is this why you won't answer my calls, you stuck up little bitch?"

"You don't get to talk to her like that!" I grit out. It's taking everything in me not to beat his fucking face in. I won't throw the first punch, but I will make sure I get in the last one if this turns physical.

"I have my reasons for breaking up with you, Felix. None of which include him. You need to just accept that our relationship ran its course. I'm sorry if that upsets you, but I just can't be your girlfriend anymore. You're free to go and date some other girl who will make you happy, because clearly, it isn't with me. We are over. Stop calling me. Stop texting me. Just leave me alone! *Please.* I have nothing else to say to you," she says as she comes to stand beside me. She's trying to put on a strong front, but I hear the slight tremor in her voice. Knowing she's afraid of him makes me want to protect her even more. I gently grab her arm, moving her to stand behind me as I do my best to keep her out of his sight. Every fiber of my being wants to hold her, to comfort her, and get her as far away from him as possible.

I place my hands behind my back and stand tall, showing that I'm not here for a fight, but I'm also not backing down. Showing Felix there is no way I will allow him access to her. Jenna's hand latches onto mine, squeezing it as if she is trying to take some of my strength for herself. I gently stroke my thumb over her smooth skin, soothing her and offering her the smallest ounce of comfort I can give her in this situation.

"Is that so?" Felix says, rubbing his grubby hand over his jaw. "Tell me, sweetheart. Did the relationship run its course after you got your expensive sushi dinner or before you wanted to ride my cock? Or was it just not good enough for your dirty cunt, so you had to break my heart and go run to the next willing dick who would fuck your skanky ass?"

I'm two seconds away from flying off the handle.

"Answer me, you fucking whore!" he yells.

Students everywhere stop and stare. Some pull their cell phones out, most likely recording the scene unfolding before them. I couldn't care less. It's just more evidence that will be out there showcasing what a violent jackass he is. I'm willing to bet I can find one of these guys to send me a video so I can forward it to Cassidy. Hopefully this will help build a case against him to at least get a restraining order to protect Jenna. Not that those are actually effective.

"Hey, whoa. Calm down man. There is no need for all the drama this early in the morning. My caffeine hasn't even kicked in yet." Dom appears out of nowhere, placing himself at my side. His younger brother, Anthony, is behind him, always ready to have his brother's back if shit goes down, and from the looks of it, mine as well. "Look. I get it. No one likes to be dumped, especially by a girl as hot as Jenna."

I let out a low growl, and my friend has the audacity to smirk.

Shit! I basically all but admitted to him I feel some way for the girl I'm trying to protect.

"You fucking her too?" Felix snarls.

"Me? Nah, man. Jenna is way too good for me. I'm man enough to admit that. But clearly, she's too good for you too, bro because, ya know, she dropped your ass."

People within listening distance laugh at what Dom says, infuriating Felix a little more.

The passenger door of the truck opens and another guy steps out. He walks over to stand next to Felix, radiating cocky little trust fund baby energy. He's shorter than Felix and dressed in the usual Greystone Academy uniform, looking like the poster boy for one of those fancy rich people's country clubs. A gasp comes from Jenna, and her hand begins to tremble.

She had mentioned Felix had a friend come over when they were being intimate which led to Felix raping her. Judging by her reaction, this must be him, and now I'm ready to tear the two of them from limb to limb.

"Dude, forget these middle-class degenerates." He pats Felix's chest. "We're going to be late, and I can't afford another tardy on my record. Forget the bitch and move on. There's plenty of pussy waiting for you back at school."

"Yeah, Shrek. You may want to listen and do as your donkey friend says," I say.

"What the fuck did you say?" The shortened friend comes at me, but Dom and Anthony block him.

"Nah. This one is mine to deal with Drake," Felix says. He comes to stand toe to toe with me. "If I were you, I would watch your back. You don't know the things I'm capable of and can get away with."

"Right." I lower my voice, ensuring only he hears me. "Like I don't know how much you like to manipulate girls before you rape them?"

Jenna moves around me, pushing me back. "Nathan, that's enough! Just forget about him!"

"Can you really rape the willing?" Felix tilts his head to look at Jenna.

I make a move to charge him, but Jenna shoves herself in front of me. "Nathan! Stop it! He's not worth it!" Worry shines bright in her eyes.

"What exactly are you going to do? Huh? C'mon, pretty boy. Hit me! I dare you." Felix taunts.

"Hey! Everyone to class!" a commanding female voice says, and some students start scrambling. Dom and Anthony refuse to budge, still blocking Drake from coming near me.

"What is going on here?" Principal King asks as she approaches us with Phil, the school officer, following close behind. "Is there a reason why two Greystone students are on Bellwood High property? Or are the two of you lost?"

Drake and Felix don't answer her, which only infuriates her more. "You two have thirty seconds to get your behinds off this property before I ask this officer to escort the two of you off in handcuffs. And rest assured, I will be in touch with your school's principal to inform him of this situation. The same with your parents! If I were you two, I would move those asses and get gone!"

Felix smirks before he takes a few steps off the sidewalk and onto the pavement of the parking lot. "I believe this is a public road. Therefore, I'm not on school property."

Principal King is fuming. If it were possible, there would be steam coming out of her ears. "Do not test me, young man!"

A few moments pass before Felix relents and heads to his truck with Drake following behind him. As Felix opens his door, he looks at Jenna and blows her a kiss. "Just so you know, sweet cheeks, this isn't over. You'll come crawling back to me. You know why? Because I was the best thing that could have happened to you. You'll see." He slams his door and speeds off, burning rubber on his way out of the parking lot.

Principal King looks around. "What are you all doing standing around? Get to class!" At that moment, the late bell rings and everyone rushes to head inside.

"You good, man?" Dom asks as he fist bumps me.

"Yeah. Just wish I could have pummeled his ass into the ground," I grind out.

"Mr. Ward, I'd like to have a word with you in my office," Principal King states. "Right now, please."

"Yes, ma'am." I nod.

Almost out of nowhere, Sadie scoops Jenna into a hug, and I can't tell if she is upset or worried by how she's looking at me before she's quickly guided into the school by Sadie. Payson gives me a quick nod, as if to say "nice job" before following behind the girls.

"Bro, I hope you're not in some deep shit," Anthony states. "We need you in that championship game."

"Same, man," I say before I follow after our principal. Not how I was expecting this Monday to go.

# Chapter 18

## Jenna

"Jenna, are you sure you're okay?" Sadie asks as she walks me to my art class, her arm linked with mine.

"I'm fine. I swear to you."

*Liar.*

"No lie, Jen. That whole spiel out there? I was so scared for you and Nathan. We were behind the truck when he pulled into the parking lot, and when we saw him speed up, I thought for sure he was trying to run you guys over."

"I think he was trying to scare them. That dude has some serious issues," Payson says. "Did Nathan really shove you out of the way?"

I nod. "Yeah. He basically put himself in danger, the fucking asshole." There's no heat or venom when I say it.

I was scared too, but the fact Nathan was going to sacrifice himself to save me? Why would he do that?

"I find it incredibly brave." Sadie swoons.

"Hey! I would take a car for you too, Cherry Pop," Payson says, as if she is offended.

"Calm down, QB. I'm not interested. I didn't sacrifice my family for you to go back to dick." Sadie grabs Payson's hand and kisses it before she turns to me. "Honestly, Jen, I think you should take it easier on Nathan. He practically saved your life today."

I don't tell her that my views of Nathan have changed since the weekend.

We make it to my classroom door, and I bid my friends goodbye as I enter my favorite class. I head to my seat along with several other classmates. Seems like the shit show outside has made many of us late.

"Take your seats so we can begin!" our art teacher calls out.

Rebecca greets me as I sit down. "Why is everyone so late?"

"Some craziness went down before school," I say as I take out my sketchbook and art supplies, ready to calm my nerves with my creative mind. Especially after the text message I received.

I dumped Felix in the worst way, by texting him last night. I couldn't bring myself to call him, and there was no way in hell I was going to break up with him face-to-face. As soon as I texted him we were over, he started excessively calling my phone, leaving numerous voicemails and text messages. I almost expected him to show up, but then I remembered my car was in the shop. If he drove all the way over to my house, he wouldn't have seen my car and would assume I wasn't home. The accident was a blessing in disguise. What I hadn't counted on was for him to show up to school this morning.

Felix

> If I find out there is someone else, I won't hesitate to hunt them down and rid this world of them. I have ways of making it happen.

> We belong together. You are perfect for me and I will stop at nothing until you are mine again.

I stare at those text messages on my screen while Mrs. Wailing goes over today's lesson. The first text I read before I got out of Nathan's car. The second one appeared shortly after I turned my phone on as I entered the classroom. After Felix nearly ran the two of us over, I'm starting to worry he will make good on his promise. Nathan can't be involved with me or this maniac. What would I do if Felix brings harm to Nathan? The pain he would inflict on Nathan's family? They have suffered so much loss, and I'll be damned if I allow any more pain to come to them. The only way to keep Nathan safe is for me to avoid being seen with him, which means no more car rides.

Fuck. How am I supposed to get around now?

I glance over at Rebecca. "Hey," I whisper to get her attention.

Rebecca looks in my direction. "Yeah?"

"Would you be able to give me a ride to work tonight? My car is getting fixed, and I have no transportation at the moment."

"What time do you have to be there?"

"You can drop me off at the studio right after school. I start a little later, but Helena's giving me space to work on my piece for the competition, and I want to get started on it before I clock in."

"Yeah, it shouldn't be a problem."

"Thank you!" I give her my biggest smile, relieved I can avoid Nathan for tonight. I just have to figure out how to get out of these car rides for the rest of the week. Anything to keep Nathan safe from Felix.

Somehow, I made it through the day avoiding Nathan. Lunch was easy since I went to the library instead of the cafeteria. Not hard to skip lunch when you have no appetite because your nerves are shot.

I stop by my locker to grab Nathan's jacket. I'm planning to give it to Payson so she can give it back to him before I meet Rebecca at her car.

I glance around the hall when I spot that Dom guy and some of the football players walking toward the door leading to the football field. It's not Payson, but Dom seems like he can be trusted to give the jacket back to Nathan.

"Hey!" I shout, gaining some of the guys' attention. When Dom sees me coming his way, he tells the guys to go ahead.

"You're Nathan's friend, correct?" I ask.

"His number one best friend. I don't care what anyone else has to say."

His comment is a breath of fresh air against the anxiety ridden roller coaster of emotions I've been riding today, so I giggle.

"Would you mind giving him his jacket for me?"

"Isn't he giving you a lift to work after practice? Coach done gave him permission to leave early so he could get you to work on time."

Damn that man for having a solution to everything.

"I actually have to go in earlier to help Helena, and Rebecca offered to drop me off. But I wanted to make sure he got his jacket back. Can you give it to him for me?"

Dom hesitates, so I attempt my best puppy-dog eyes and pouty lip to try to persuade him. "Pretty please?"

"With a face like that, how can I say no?"

"Thank you so much! You're the best!" I give him Nathan's jacket and a kiss on the cheek before making a dash to the student parking lot.

As I head across the parking lot, I can't help but to briefly look around in search of a blue truck, worried he will come for me. I breathe a little easier when I don't see him anywhere.

"Brady, you promised me you would come to this appointment," Lydia shrieks.

I roll my eyes as I walk by them and head toward Rebecca's silver Honda Accord.

"Hey! Sorry I'm a little behind. I had to take care of something."

Rebecca finishes her text message before unlocking her car, and we climb in. "No biggie! You caught me on a good day. My tae kwon do class starts a little later on Mondays, so I'll actually be on time for once."

"Aren't you always on time?"

"In my family, you're late if you arrive five minutes early and you're on time if you arrive ten to fifteen minutes early."

"Well, then I guess to your family I'm late."

Rebecca drops me off out front of the studio and drives off. With all this shit about Felix, I'm thinking maybe I should ask Rebecca about her classes or look into some self-defense ones.

The bell above the door chimes, making my presence known. Helena comes out of her office but stops when she sees me.

"Welcome to Beyond—Jenna! What are you doing here? You're not scheduled to come in until five o'clock."

"I know, but I'm kind of without a car at the moment, and a friend dropped me off on her way to a class. I was hoping it would be okay to come in early to start working on my art competition piece until I need to clock in?"

She doesn't need to know the shithow that has become my life since Saturday night.

"Of course! Please. By all means! Don't let me hold you up from creativity. If you need anything, you know where to find me." She gives me a hug before she's off to set up for her next session of clients.

Heading to the spare room, I grab an easel to place my blank canvas upon it. Once I set up all the supplies I will need, I begin prepping my canvas. I go over the entire canvas in white paint before letting it dry. Priming before painting helps the colors to appear brighter, and I want my colors to pop. As I wait for the paint to dry, I pull out my sketchbook and begin working on my design for the competition. I'm halfway through when the alarm on my phone alerts me it's almost time to clock in for my shift.

# Nathan

I'm in the locker room changing into my practice pads when Dom approaches.

"Hey, man. Jenna wanted me to give this to you," he says as he hands me my letterman jacket.

My lips press firmly together as I stare at the blue and white jacket with my name stitched on the front. I told her I wanted her to hold onto it this morning, and she seemed content with doing that. What could have possibly changed from then to now?

"Did she say why?"

"Nah, man. Just asked if I could give it to you before calling me her hero and giving me a kiss."

My eyes fly up to glower at my friend. "What do you mean she kissed you?"

There's a shit-eating grin on his face and a sparkle in his eye hinting at mischief. He likes to pull my strings because I'm the *serious* friend who needs to learn to let loose. "Calm down, calm down. It wasn't like that. She just gave me a peck on the cheek before she darted off to the parking lot."

"Wait a minute. She left?" My heart beats faster. This wasn't something I planned on. She was supposed to hang out here until Coach let me go a little early so I could give her a lift to work.

"Yeah. She mentioned she had to go in earlier and a friend was dropping her off."

"What friend?" I grit out. My hands start trembling, so I clench them into fists, opening and closing them to try to ease the anxiousness coursing through me. What if Felix shows up again? He nearly ran us over this morning. What would he do if no one was around?

"Uh, some girl named Rebecca?"

"Rebecca Chang?" I ask. They have art class together, and Rebecca tends to eat lunch with all the art students, but I know she's one of Jenna's friends. "Did you follow her to make sure she went with her friend?"

"Uh ... no. Should I have?" Dom asks, side-eying me.

"Yes!" I say a little too loudly, causing some of the guys to stop their conversations and stare at us.

"My bad, man. I was trying to get to practice on time."

"No. I'm sorry. It's nothing toward you. I'm worried. Okay? After what happened this morning, I'm worried he could show up and hurt her."

"I get it, man." Dom crosses his arms to think for a moment. "Aren't the cheerleaders holding practice tonight since they'll be cheering us on in the championship game?"

I get where he is going with this and flash him a smile, then toss my jacket into my gym locker. "Thanks, man."

"Anytime, bro."

I grab my helmet and quickly make my way to the track where the cheerleaders are running through a cheer. When they finish, I walk over to Sadie.

"Nathan. To what do I owe this meeting?"

"Hey. Any chance you can message Jenna for me and find out if she made it to work?" I'm trying to keep the worry out of my voice so I don't scare her. Jenna is like a sister to Sadie and the last thing I want to do is project my fear onto her about the girl we both care about.

She tilts her head. "I thought she was going to wait here and ride with you?" She turns to the stadium seats to glance around. Some of the girlfriends and boyfriends usually hang out in the stadium to watch us practice. When she doesn't see her friend, she darts to her cheer bag and pulls out her cell phone.

"She was, but then she told Dom that she had to go in early and Rebecca was giving her a lift. I just want to make sure she made it to work okay."

Sadie's fingers flick across the screen, and within a few minutes, it chimes with a message. She looks up at me with a smile and shows me her screen.

"And just so you're reassured ..." Sadie makes a few quick swipes before she pulls up a map with Jenna's beautiful face in a small circle, zooming in to show she's at Beyond Broken Colors. "Jenna and I always share our locations so if there is ever an emergency, we can find each other. She's at work, Nathan. You can breathe a little easier."

I exhale as relief washes over me. She's safe. "Thank you, Sadie."

"You're welcome."

I turn to head toward the field when Sadie calls out. "Nathan?"

"Yeah?"

She walks over to me and pulls me so we are a little farther away from the rest of the cheerleaders. "Listen, I'm worried about Jenna too. That night when I heard him go off on her outside? I was scared. I've heard anger before, but that was a whole different level of anger. Then what happened this morning? I'm ..." Her eyes start to glisten. "Thank you for shoving her out of the way. For protecting my best friend. It means the world to me how much you want to protect her. But don't you dare think about putting yourself in danger like that again!" She jabs a dainty, french manicure nail into my stomach.

I chuckle at how it feels. "Just so you know, Captain. I'll do whatever it takes to protect Jenna, *including* sacrificing my life for hers." I give her a slight shoulder shove, then jog off toward the field.

"That's an interesting way to say you love her!" Sadie yells. I don't give her a response or any reaction. I have never been in love before and I don't know what that feels like.

Am I falling in love with Jenna?

# Chapter 19

## Nathan

After football practice, I head home so I can take a shower and work on some class assignments since I will have time to kill before I get Jenna from work. The parts I need to work on her car won't be in until tomorrow, and Uncle Dean said he didn't need me tonight, as he had Jerry and Steve to help him get today's workload done. He also mentioned cutting my hours back some now that I have football practices again to prepare for the championship game.

He's so stoked for our team; he's even closing the garage the day of the game so he and my grandmother can be there to watch me play. He asked if my father was going, but I couldn't give him an answer. Dad hasn't brought it up, but I wouldn't put it past him to not go, no matter how much a small part of me wishes he would. To have my dad watch from the stands and see me play my final high school game like he used to do would be everything, but grief has stolen that father from me.

As I pull into the driveway, I park beside my father's patrol car. I'm surprised to see it sitting here when he's hardly home as it is. The man prioritizes his job over his kid. What can I say?

I head inside, making my way toward the stairs when my dad says my name. "Nathan?"

"Yeah, Dad?"

He enters the small living room from the kitchen. Our house isn't big, nothing like Jenna's or Chad's house. I mean, we don't really need much since there are only two of us living here.

"Hey. How was practice?"

"It was good. Coach was pretty happy with how things went."

"Good, good." There's a pause before he speaks. "Listen, I got your practice exam scheduled for after school on Wednesday down at the precinct."

I internally groan. How the fuck am I going to get out of this one? I've never taken the ones he would bring home. "Wait, this Wednesday?"

"Yeah. Is that going to be a problem?"

"Dad, I have football practice for the championship game. Remember?" I actually don't have football practice. Wednesday is a rest day for us, but my father doesn't need to know that tidbit of information. I'm planning on working at the garage so I can get more work done on Jenna's car with Dean's help.

"How is Coach Watson having you guys practice everyday? That's absurd! Didn't you practice this weekend?"

"The weekend was actually something Payson put together, and the team agreed to it. Coach is just pumped up as much as we are and wants us to be at our best. Plus, it's not everyday practice. He's giving us the weekends off."

My father just nods. "Well, the exam is at four, so I expect you to be there and ready to pass it. John's going to drop it off on my desk after he grades them. So, make sure you study up."

Without another word, my father leaves through the front door, and moments later, he pulls out of the driveway.

I sigh as I make my way to my bedroom, tossing my football bag and backpack onto my bed before crossing the hall to take a much-needed hot shower. After throwing on some gray sweatpants and one of Ryan's old favorite band tees, I sit down at my desk to work on my assignments.

My phone chimes with a text and my heart starts to quicken, hoping it's from Jenna. Instead, I see it's from Cassidy.

CASSIDY

I checked out the tags on that truck. It's registered to a Franklin Martin over in Fairhaven, which is close to Yacht Cove.

NATHAN

Must be Felix's dad.

CASSIDY

That's what I was thinking. The truck's been registered to Franklin for over a year now.

If Felix is under the age of 18, it makes sense for his father to be on the car's title. I did look into Franklin to see if I could find anything. Franklin Martin is an investment banker. Married with 3 boys - Hendrix, Felix, and Knox Martin. Hendrix is in college and Knox attends Greystone Academy with Felix.

The only thing I was able to find on this Felix guy was a doctor's referral for him to seek therapy pertaining to some anger issues. Not sure if he ever seeked out help. Does this guy seem to have anger problems?

I send Cass the video I got from one of the guys, and after a few minutes, she replies.

CASSIDY

Wow, someone is in need of anger management.

NATHAN

He also almost ran us over. That part wasn't filmed though. They caught all of this when he started yelling after that happened.

CASSIDY

Jesus, Nate! This guy seems pretty dangerous. Are you sure you don't want to take this to your dad?

NATHAN

I can't. I need some kind of evidence or proof, a justifiable cause for him to be locked up. He did something horrible to someone I know over the weekend, but she's too scared to come forward.

CASSIDY

I hate to be the one to say this but there are probably other girls who have been through similar situations. I haven't come across any police reports which means they either never came forward or daddy Martin paid hush money to make it go away.

The thought of other girls going through what Jenna experienced and Felix getting away with it makes me sick to my stomach.

CASSIDY

The only thing I can think of is to try to find other girls who have a past with this Felix person. I'm sure if you used that charm of yours, they would be willing to tell you.

;)

I don't respond. She makes a valid point about finding other girls who have been with Felix, others who have been through what Jenna has. But how do I go about that? I glance at the time on my phone, realizing it's almost eight thirty. Jenna will be getting off soon, and if I'm going to get there on time, I need to leave now. I grab my Bellwood High football hoodie, along with my jacket so I can give it back to her.

A short drive later, I park my car behind the studio. I wait patiently in my car for her and her boss to exit through the back door. A few moments pass before the door opens, only there is one person leaving instead of two, so I exit my vehicle and call to the red-haired woman.

"Excuse me, miss!"

She turns when she sees me. "Yes?"

"I'm Nathan. I go to school with Jenna. I was supposed to be giving her a ride home after work. I was positive she mentioned she was working until close."

"Oh. She didn't get in touch with you?"

"No ma'am, she didn't."

"Oh ... I let her go home a little early since my last session was smaller. Lots of people are already coming down with some sort of sickness. You know, cold and flu season is upon us."

"Did you happen to see who she left with?" I rub my palms against my sweatpants, wondering who came and got her.

"I think it was a girl from school. Blonde, curly hair, I believe? Really pretty."

I sigh in relief, pretty certain she is describing Sadie.

"Okay. Well ...Thank you!"

I watch her get in her vehicle, making sure she gets out of here safely, before going to my car to drive back home. You can never trust these parking lots at night. Never knowing who lurks in the shadows.

On the way home, my thoughts are everywhere trying to figure out why it feels like Jenna has been avoiding me today. First it was the jacket and lift to work? Now she's not contacting me about leaving early? Does she not trust me?

Sitting in my car after I make it home safe and sound, I send Jenna a text.

NATHAN

> I know we never got to talk about what happened this morning so idk where your head is at. But it feels like you're avoiding me. Did I do something wrong?

After I hit send, I make my way inside and up to my bedroom. Dad isn't home yet, and I'm grateful for the silence that welcomes me.

As I remove my hoodie, my keys fall out of my pocket onto the floor. I go to pick them up and spot some papers peeking out from under my bed. They must have fallen out of my bag when I grabbed my assignments.

I browse through the stack in case there are any important papers for my teachers until I come across the pamphlets Ms. Everhart gave me after that first altercation with Felix. I skim through them until I come across a dark blue pamphlet with paint splatters and one of those stands artists use to put their paintings on.

Beyond Broken Colors
Art Therapy that Soothes the Soul with Our Creative
Minds

I check the address, and sure enough, this is where Jenna works. An idea forms in my mind, and I make a note to call this Helena woman tomorrow morning to schedule my first session. Ms. Everhart said I should look into therapy, and art seems like a fun way to work through my demons.

I place the pamphlet on my nightstand and crawl into bed. As I lie there staring at the ceiling, I check my texts frequently to see if Jenna responded. Maybe she just needs space after the whole fiasco Felix caused this morning. I can understand that. Tomorrow, I'll show up at her house to take her to school and hopefully, things will get better.

Jenna never responded to my text. I stopped by her house to pick her up for school, only for her mom to tell me she got a ride with Sadie and Payson. I didn't see her in the halls between classes but made sure to get to the cafeteria a few minutes early, hoping to catch her walk in. Sitting at the table with Dom and some guys from the team, I watch the doors like a hawk in search of the raven-black-haired girl with beautiful brown skin. When I see Sadie and Payson walk in sans Jenna, I'm out of my seat and headed in their direction.

Sadie and Payson are talking but cut their conversation off when I approach.

"Sorry. I don't mean to interrupt, but do you know where Jenna is?"

Payson gives Sadie a quick kiss. "I'll save you a spot in line."

As soon as Payson walks off, I turn my attention to Sadie. "Is Jenna avoiding me on purpose?" I ask.

Sadie lets out a sigh. "I don't want to say because I honestly don't know what's going through her head. Also, kind of been sworn to keep her whereabouts on the downlow."

I drag my hands over my face. All I want to do is check in with her and make sure she is okay.

"When you need the answers to something you don't know, where do you go to look for them?"

I frown at Sadie. "What?"

"Figure the answer to the riddle and you'll find Jenna." That's all she says before she walks over to stand in line with her girlfriend.

*When you need the answers to something you don't know, where do you go to look for them?* It takes me a few seconds to realize where I need to go. I dart out of the cafeteria, almost colliding with Ms. Everhart.

"I'm so sorry!" I reach out to steady our school counselor, but she brushes me off.

"I'm fine! I'm fine! But I'm glad we ran into each other, Mr. Ward. I've been meaning to ask you. Did you ever get a chance to look at those pamphlets I gave you?"

Pamphlets? What—Oh ... the therapy pamphlets.

"Yes. After carefully looking them over, I finally was able to pick one. Called this morning to schedule my first session. Appointment is all set for tomorrow evening."

"Wonderful! I'll be checking in after Thanksgiving break to see how it's going. Try not to knock into anyone else." She smiles at me before walking off, and I continue on my way.

I walk around the library until I spot Jenna sitting at a table toward the back, headphones in her ear as she doodles. Taking the seat across from her, I tap her foot to get her attention. When she looks up at me, I smile and my heart beats slightly faster.

Damn, this girl is beautiful.

"What are you doing here?" she asks, removing the headphones from her ears. "Did Sadie tell you where I was? She pinky promised me!" She slams a fist onto the table.

"No, no. I figured it out all on my own. There's only so many places a student can go if they skip lunch."

Jenna leans back in her chair and crosses her arms, glaring at me.

"Aw, don't be like that with me, Spitfire. I thought we had a deal? I fix your car for free, and you treat me nicely, remember?"

She softens her features, glancing around the library. "Sorry. I'm not trying to be rude, Nathan. It's just that ..."

I wait with bated breath for her to continue, but she doesn't. When a few students walk into the library, she grabs my hand and pulls me to a secluded corner in the back of the library where no one else is around.

"You haven't done anything wrong, okay?"

"You read my text?"

"I saw it and read what I could when the notification came up on my phone. It never was about you doing anything wrong, Nathan. It's just that … I'm scared but not scared in the way that you think. I'm worried if Felix catches you with me, he could make good on his threats."

My nostrils flare at the mention of threats. "Is he threatening you?"

"Not really, no. It was more of him threatening you. It's basically what his text implied yesterday. I-I-I couldn't have it on my conscience if he made good on his word. How much hurt it would put your family through. Especially your dad. Your family has suffered so much already, and I don't want to be the reason there's more."

"You're trying to protect me?" I ask, in awe of this gorgeous woman standing before me.

Jenna licks her lip, then nods.

I smirk at her. "Can I get a verbal response, beautiful."

Her eyes stare into mine, a small gasp escaping through her parted lips as I brush a strand of loose hair behind her ear and drag my fingertips down her jawline before gently cupping her chin.

"Nathan, what—what are you doing?" Jenna whispers.

"Something I've been dying to do ever since we kissed for the first time." I lean in close to her, my lips hovering near hers. "But only if I have your permission first. You are in control here, Jenna. You are *always* in control. Of your mind. Of your body. Of your choices. I will never force you or manipulate you to do anything you are uncomfortable doing. You hold all the power with your words. So ... what's it going to be, Spitfire?"

Her eyes bounce between mine and my lips, as if she's having an internal battle.

"You can tell me no, and I will back off."

"Nathan?"

"Yes, Spitfire?"

"Shut the hell up and kiss me already."

"Yes ma'am." I smirk before I pull her body against me, taking her mouth with mine. I let out a low groan the moment her soft, plush lips make contact. Jenna's tongue pushes forward, prodding my lips to part for her, and I do so willingly. Our tongues cross, allowing us to taste each other as tiny nerve endings send tingles through my body toward my cock.

Her hands glide up my chest, over my shoulders, and around my neck as her nails dig into my skin, dragging me closer. I move my hand from her chin to the back of her head, tugging her gently, wanting to deepen our kiss even more.

The soft ding of a bell sounds in the distance, alerting the school that lunch is dismissed and it's time to get to our next class. I press my forehead to hers, breathing her in and feeling at peace.

"What now?" Jenna whispers, her eyes still closed.

"Like I said before. You're in control here. Everything is up to you."

"And if I want to see where this goes?"

I kiss her forehead and lean down so we are eye level with each other. "I want to be with you, Jenna. I want to be everything for you, including taking care of you and protecting you. I'm in this if you are."

Her smile widens, showing off her pearly white teeth. "That's a really good answer, Shop Boy."

"Just one more thing," I say.

"What's that?"

"I'll be giving you rides from here on out."

"What happened to my choice, my call?" She taunts.

"Can't a guy just want to make you his passenger princess and drive you around wherever you need to go while he admires your beauty?"

"Well, when you put it like that ... I guess I can give that to you."

"Thank you," I say as I lean in and give her a soft kiss.

Taking her hand in mine, we make our way back to the table to grab our things before leaving the library. I loosen my hold on her hand as we step into the hall in case she doesn't want us to be seen together. When she holds on firmly, my body warms on the inside, and I couldn't be happier than I am at this very moment.

# Chapter 20

## Jenna

It's been quiet on the Felix front. I don't know if I should be relieved or constantly looking over my shoulder. After he showed up to school on Monday, I blocked him on all socials as well as his number while I sat in the library during lunch. I didn't want him to have any way of contacting me.

My thoughts drift to yesterday when I pulled Nathan to the secluded little corner in the library, away from any prying eyes and ears. I had no intentions of things going the way they did, but I don't regret them. The way his lips melted with mine. That groan that made my pussy weep and dampen my panties. I was ready for him to push me against those bookshelves and take me right there.

I felt horrible when Helena messaged me after she got home Monday evening. She informed me that *a handsome gentleman had waited for me after work in hopes to take me home* and how he also *waited for her to get in her car to leave before he did.* I knew it was Nathan the moment she said he waited because what other guy would stand around in a dark parking lot with little lighting to make sure a woman was safe and secure in her car before he drove off?

The guilt that swarmed me over thinking he must have been disappointed or hurt I didn't contact him to let him know I had gotten a ride home gutted me. It wasn't fair to him. He did nothing wrong, and I mean every word of that.

The truth is, I feared someone would see us together and word would get back to Felix. Call me paranoid but some of my peers are friends with or have relationships with Greystone students. Greystone Academy is in Fairhaven, South Carolina which is only about a twenty-five-minute drive from Bellwood. Felix already assumes I dumped him for Nathan and being seen together would only make it seem like I lied to him.

Not that it would matter. Where Felix is aggressive and harmful, Nathan is compassionate and caring. How I could have been so blinded by the mask that covered the red flags of Felix makes me cringe. I was a complete fool.

I'm busying myself with my art piece for the competition when a chime comes from the front of the studio. I place my brush down and leave the room to go tend to whoever arrived. Helena had to make a quick run to the store for more cleaning supplies, and I told her I would take care of things here until she returned.

"Welcome to Beyond Broken—Nathan? What are you doing here?"

Nathan stands by the front counter in white sneakers, light denim jeans, a dark-green button-up Henley tee with his Carolina-blue and white letterman jacket over it. God, how could I have been so stupid to ignore this man all these years? Maybe I need to have my eyes checked …

"Well, I'm not sure if you're allowed to eye-fuck potential clients, but I'm here for my consultation with Helena."

At the mention of Helena, I come back to reality. "I'm sorry, did you say you have a consultation with Helena?"

"I did. I think it's time I got some help to work through my grief over the loss of my brother. Figured I would look into this place first, see if it suits me. And if it doesn't, I have pamphlets of other therapists to look into."

I rush over and embrace him in a hug, squeezing him tightly. "I'm so proud of you for wanting to get help, baby."

"Did you just call me baby?"

"Mmm … maybe." I smile up at him before he leans down to kiss me gently. "Is that okay?"

"I'm okay with anything you want to call me. Except manwhore. I'd actually have to sleep with a bunch of girls in order to be considered one like Chad."

I pull away from him. "You mean to tell me all those girls I've seen you around, you never slept with them?"

"You've been watching me?" He wiggles his eyebrows and smiles.

I smack him hard across his chest, and revel in the muscle underneath my palm.

*Daaammmmnn … what is Nathan working with under these clothes?*

"Ahem."

*Focus Jenna!*

"To answer your question, no. Did those girls want to get with me? Sure. But I was raised to be respectful, and I would let them down gently, letting them know I wasn't interested. None of them caught my attention the way you always managed to."

"I find that hard to believe, Shop Boy." I smirk before turning and heading back to the spare room. "Helena's out for the moment, by the way, but you're more than welcome to hang around until she gets back," I say over my shoulder.

"What's this?" Nathan asks from the doorway.

"This is the spare room where Helena keeps her extra canvases and easels. She's letting me use it to work on my piece for the art competition. It's why I've been coming in right after school this week. I'm on a deadline."

Nathan tilts his head from side to side. "What exactly are you painting?"

"It's still a work in progress, but the idea is to place a woman in the center." I point to where the woman will be placed. "She'll be covering one side of her face with her hand, like she's kind of screaming in pain while the other is outstretched, breaking free from what looks like glass, but the glass will be an array of colors. It looks crazy right now, but once I add in all the layers, it will be more prominent."

"So, kind of like a woman breaking free from her darkness and pain and fighting her way to the light of healing?"

"Light of healing ..." I whisper. "Nathan, that's actually a really beautiful way of putting it." I turn to face him, seeing the pride radiate from him. "I wanted to ask Helena if she would be okay if I called this piece Beyond Broken Colors because it felt fitting, ya know? But maybe I should change it to something like, Breaking Toward Light of Healing? Or is that a mouthful?"

Nathan chuckles softly as he grabs my hand and pulls me toward him. "I think whatever you call it will be perfect. Besides, you got some time to figure that out. It'll come to you." We lean in to kiss each other, only for my cell phone to ring, disrupting the moment.

"It's Helena," I say before answering her call. "Helena, hey!"

"I'm so sorry to disturb you. I know you're in the middle of working on your art."

"No, it's okay. I actually took a small break." I assure her.

"Guess now I don't feel so bad." Helena chuckles. "Listen, Jenna, can you get in touch with my appointments for today and let them know I will reschedule with them. My brother called and said they admitted my mother."

"Oh, no. I'm so sorry to hear that. Are you sure you don't want me to take over?"

"Well, two of my appointments are consultations and then I have a one on one with Mrs. Garrison. She's not comfortable with new people."

"Okay, I will get in touch with your appointments and lock up the studio for you."

"Jenna, you're a goddess! Thank you so much. I'll keep you posted in regard to the rest of the week."

"Sounds good, Helena. I really hope your mom is okay. I'll talk to you later. Bye!"

I get off the phone and face Nathan, who's leaning against the wall. "So, it looks like that consultation of yours is going to need to be rescheduled. Helena had a family emergency come up."

"Soooo ... what happens now?"

"Well, I will need to book your consultation for another time. Then I have to call her two other appointments to reschedule theirs before I clean the studio and lock up."

"Want some help?" Nathan asks.

"Sure, if you want to." I shrug.

He moves away from the wall and tilts my chin up so I'm looking into his eyes. "What I want is to be with you every single minute I can get. If there's one thing I've learned after losing my mother and brother, it's to never take for granted the time you get with the people who matter to you the most."

I feel my cheeks warm, and for a moment, I get lost in his green eyes. Standing on my toes, I press my lips to his. "Let's go reschedule those appointments so we can get out of here."

I flip the sign on the front door to closed and go over the cleaning process with Nathan. He offered to get a head start on the cleaning while I rescheduled the appointments to help make the closing process go faster. Once I have handled the appointments, I help him finish cleaning the studio before I handle the money and safe, making sure the front door is locked and all the lights are off.

When I enter the room where my art piece is to clean up my materials, Nathan places a blank canvas onto another easel.

"What are you doing?" I hesitantly ask.

"I was thinking since we locked the doors and handled everything, we could have a little fun."

I lift an eyebrow. "Fun?"

"Yeah. Fun," Nathan says as he removes his Henley and tosses it with my things, leaving his firm pectorals and chiseled six-pack on full display. "Messy fun."

My mouth salivates looking at a shirtless, tanned Nathan. From those well-defined biceps to his chest, down those ridged abdominals to that delicious V that leads to something I wouldn't mind taking for a ride, this man takes his workouts seriously.

I swallow deeply, trying to gather my thoughts, but all I can think is how much I want to see the rest of this gorgeous man without clothes.

*You dirty, pervy girl.*

Wetness splashes my face, making me come to my senses. Nathan smirks back at me, a paintbrush in his hand coated in white paint.

I raise my index finger. "You did not just splatter paint across my face."

Nathan dips the brush into the white paint before flicking the bristles at me again. This time, paint droplets splatter across my long-sleeve top, chest, and face. "Oops. I did it again."

"Oh. You're going to regret getting paint on one of my favorite shirts." I reach for the nearest brush and dip it in some vibrant blue paint. I make an attempt to smear the paint across his face, but he dodges my brush, and I end up painting his chest instead. Damn him and his reflexes.

I go for more paint and make another attempt to smear his face when he reaches out and grabs my wrist gently. He pulls me flush with his body, my arm still raised above my head, and takes the brush out of my hand and runs it over my lips, painting them a deep-sky blue.

"What are you—" Nathan shushes me.

"I want you to mark me, Spitfire."

I'm not sure what he means, and my face must give it away, so he clarifies.

"I want you to press those perfect, pillowy soft lips of yours onto my skin and kiss me anywhere you want but *only* if you want to. Remember, you hold all the power here with your words. If you say no, we stop. I will throw my shirt back on, clean up this mess, and we can go do whatever it is you want to do."

I let his words sink in. The way he is reassuring I control the situation and determine how things unfold ... it's like a defibrillator. I control the narrative, and no one has the right to take that from me the way my manipulative, narcissistic demon of an ex did.

Nathan is reminding me of my power, and damn if that doesn't turn me on.

Leaning forward, I press a kiss to Nathan's heart, ensuring I leave the perfect smoochy mark. Pulling away, I smile, loving how my lips mark his skin. I press more kisses along his stomach, slowly working my way toward the top of his jeans before dropping to my knees.

As I begin to unbutton Nathan's pants, he reaches out, placing a hand over mine.

"Jenna, are you sure?"

I don't say a word, keeping my eyes focused on his face, and giving him my most devilish smile while pulling his jeans and boxer briefs down. His cock springs forward, smacking me in my face, and a soft moan escapes me.

I glide my hands slowly up his inner thighs, and goose bumps break out along Nathan's skin. With one hand, I cup his balls while lifting my other hand up.

"Paint my hand, Shop Boy."

As Nathan goes to dip the brush into the paint, I wrap my lips around his hardened cock and take him as far back into my throat as I can. I bob my head slowly, swirling my tongue around his shaft. The moment he groans, I pick up the pace.

"Fuck, Jenna. That feels so good," Nathan rasps.

Once I feel like there is enough paint on my palm, I pull my mouth off Nathan's dick and wrap my painted hand around it, slowly stroking him up and down while my other hand massages his balls.

"Spitfire, I don't want you to stop, but if you keep going, I'm not going to last very long," Nathan grits out. "It's ... been a while ... for me."

"Don't worry. I'll take care of you." I stand up and walk over to my backpack to retrieve a condom from an interior pocket.

"You keep condoms in your backpack?"

"Yes. You never know when you might need one or when the occasion may ... rise." I quirk my eyebrow. "You said it's been a few years for you, so I'm going to assume you're clean."

"We get tested for physicals before football season starts."

"I always use condoms. But after Saturday ... Not knowing entirely what happened, I would much rather use one of these with you."

I make my way over to Nathan and hold the foil up to his mouth. "Tear it open for me, Shop Boy."

Nathan's teeth clamp down on the top of the gold condom wrapper, and he tears it open, his eyes never leaving mine. The move is so sexy it sends a tremble through my body.

"Such a good boy," I coo as I reach down and sheath Nathan's cock.

Nathan's nostrils flare, his eyes filling with lust. "You going to ride my cock, beautiful?"

"I'm a little overdressed for that, don't you think?" I tease.

Grabbing the bottom of my shirt, I slowly lift it over my head before tossing it where my backpack sits. I turn around, giving Nathan my backside as I taunt him with a little strip tease, dragging my jeans and underwear down my legs. As I look over my shoulder at Nathan, he groans like a starved man ready to feast.

"Do you even know how stunning you are?"

Turning around, I give him a full view of my naked body, and his heated gaze roams over every inch of me as he strokes his cock.

I grab a clean paintbrush from nearby, dip it into some deep-purple paint, then hand the brush to Nathan.

"I want you to paint my breasts, top to bottom," I command.

"With pleasure."

As the bristles brush over my hardened brown nipples, I gasp. Tingles move through my body, heading directly to my core. My clit throbs with each stroke of the brush, and by the time Nathan has covered my boobs completely, I'm in need of relief only he can give me.

I take the blank canvas off the easel and set it on the floor, and Nathan tilts his head.

Pressing my painted breasts onto the canvas, I arch my back, putting my ass on display just for him. He grabs another brush and adds some red paint before he walks behind me.

"Don't move," he commands before he smothers my whole ass in paint. The cold, wet paint soothes my heated skin that is craving more, wanting a release. As soon as Nathan pulls back, I flip around and plant my ass onto the canvas.

Sitting in this position, I slowly spread my legs, giving Nathan a full view of my glistening pussy.

"Nathan ..."

His Adam's apple bobs. "Yeah, Spitfire?"

"I need you to fuck me. Right. Now!"

"As you wish, my queen," Nathan says before dropping down and crawling over me. Slowly, oh so slowly, he lowers until his hardened body presses with mine, and he takes my lips with his. Our lips part, allowing our tongues to enter, tasting each other before he gently bites my bottom lip, and I moan into his mouth.

His dick prods at my core, teasing me, driving me crazy. I wrap my legs around his waist, pulling him to me.

"Nathan, I need more. I need you inside me," I say as he presses featherlight kisses down my neck to that sweet spot where the neck and shoulder connect. With Nathan nibbling on my neck, my pussy gets wetter. The moment he releases me, he thrusts his cock inside of me, and we groan at the delicious sensation.

He takes a moment to adjust before he glides his dick in and out ever so slowly, ensuring I feel every inch of his delectable appendage.

"God, Jenna. You feel amazing." Nathan groans. He picks up the pace, skin slapping skin, his balls smacking against my ass while fucking me into the canvas, and the beginnings of my orgasm build before he pulls out, making me whimper.

"Ride me, Spitfire. Take what you need from me."

*You ain't gotta tell me twice.*

Flipping us over so he's on the ground, I straddle his body and gradually glide my pussy over his thick dick, savoring every sensation as I go down. This man was blessed in the male appendage department. I roll my hips, grinding to feel the friction I've been yearning for to soothe the throbbing in my clit.

Nathan takes his thumb to my clit, rubbing in gentle circles, adding to my need. I bounce on him, gaining momentum as the tightening in my belly builds again. He thrusts up as I come down, and I'm so close to my release.

"Oh ... god ... yes!"

"Come for me, baby. Let me feel you squeeze my cock." Nathan grunts, pumping into me faster. Harder.

My orgasm hits, consuming my body with the aftershocks only a good orgasm brings. I let out a satiated sigh as Nathan's release follows shortly after mine. We take a few moments to dwell in our postorgasmic bliss, catching our breaths before we get off the floor.

"I'm going to go take care of this," he says, pointing to his cum-filled condom.

"Bathroom is across the hall, door to your right."

He leans in, pressing a kiss to my lips before darting out of the room.

I pick up the canvas that we just fucked on and place it back on the easel.

"Here, spread your legs," Nathan says as he comes back from the bathroom, dropping down to clean me up with a warm, wet paper towel.

"I've never had anyone do that for me before," I whisper.

"That's because they didn't know how to treat a queen." He stands up and tosses the paper towel in the trash can in the corner before wrapping his hands around my waist.

"What are we going to do about all of this?" I point between us at the paint all over our skin.

"I'll take you home and you can shower there, but your parents may have some questions."

"What? Why?"

Nathan pulls his phone from the pile of clothes in the corner, snapping a picture before showing me how I look. There are paint splatters across my face, in my hair. Paint is smudged on our necks from when our bodies were rubbing against each other. Truthfully, I look like a hot mess.

"I can tell them there were some ... paint mishaps with one of the sessions. It's believable."

He chuckles. "If you say so ..."

"I do say so."

He passes me my clothes, and we get dressed quickly before we take in the mess we made.

"I'll get the cleaning supplies," Nathan says, and heads out to the main part of the studio to get what we need.

Looking at the canvas we literally just fucked on, my creativity takes over. I grab a brush and some paint and get to work, adding some lines and a few strokes in various places until I've got a beautiful art piece featuring my breasts and ass.

"So, is this how art therapy works?" Nathan asks from behind me.

"Oh, God. No! Definitely not." I laugh. "Well … maybe in a … sex therapy way? But this is definitely not what goes on here."

"Bummer. I would sign up for every session if it involved you." He wraps his strong arms around my waist as we look at the painting we created. "Can I keep this piece, then?"

"What else am I going to do with it? I sure as hell ain't taking it to my house or leaving it here. Helena would have some questions, ones I do not plan to answer."

"I think I'll hang this in my room. A Jenna Altwood original." Nathan winks, and I just roll my eyes. The two of us get to work cleaning up the room, the supplies, and putting everything away before we head out to Nathan's car after locking up.

"Are you seriously going to put that up in your bedroom?"

"Very serious. I have the perfect spot in my room in mind where I can look at it everyday and know that your boobs and ass made this."

"You're unbelievable," I retort.

"Yeah, well, I think you're incredible. Plus, I think you've opened my eyes to something."

"Oh yeah? What's that?"

Nathan's lips curve up, with the cockiest smile I think I have ever seen grace his handsome face. "I really like art therapy."

# Chapter 21

## Jenna

It's been a week since Nathan and I *created art* in the spare room of Helena's studio, and true to his word, he hung that painting in his bedroom. He even took a picture and sent it to me that night as proof. I honestly thought he was joking, but I guess I got the last laugh. What can I say, though? The guy is clearly enamored with me.

Over the past week, we've only gotten closer. Sometimes I question if we are moving rather fast, but he reminds me that tomorrow is never promised. As someone who has harbored strong feelings for me over the years, despite my prickly personality toward him, Nathan never lets me forget my worth. He always goes out of his way to show me just how he feels about me, always telling me how beautiful

I am and he's the luckiest guy in the world. The way this man cares about me speaks volumes.

Whenever I'm with him, I feel like I can be myself, the way he wants me to always be. A strong, outspoken, independent woman. Most importantly, I know that in Nathan's arms, I am safe and protected too. He would never bring harm my way. My fearless protector.

We have spent any and every free moment we could get in each other's presence. When I'm not working and he doesn't have football practice, I'm at the garage watching him work or helping him maintain the front desk when there's a small influx of customers. Nathan worries I'm bored when I'm at the garage, but there is nothing boring about watching him work. In nothing but his mechanic overalls hanging at the waist and a white muscle tank on, sweat glistening off his sun-kissed skin with spots of dirt and grease splattered about, seeing his muscles flex while he works. It's like foreplay and I always leave there wet and wanting.

I never thought I would be so turned on watching someone change oil and rotate tires.

Over the past weekend, he took me on our first date to this fancy restaurant in the town where he grew up. We feasted on the most delicious Italian food, topped of with a heavenly slice of tiramisu for dessert. After dinner, he drove me around, showing me all the places he went as a child and even where he had lived before his father and him moved to Bellwood.

He told me stories of his mother, of what he could remember. The ones friends and family have shared with him. He even took me to the elementary school where she used to teach kindergarten. She seemed like an incredible woman who would be so proud of the young man he is becoming. I just wish she was here to see it herself.

To brighten the evening, we went to the movie theater and picked a popular rom-com that recently came out. We laughed, we swooned, and then it was time to head home. It was the perfect evening, or it was until I got home. As I walked into the kitchen to get a drink of water, I spotted a bouquet of flowers sitting on the island. I assumed the flowers were for my mom as a surprise from my dad, but when I stepped closer, I saw my name written on the card, tucked in the center of a dozen pink and white lilies.

I opened the envelope, thinking maybe Nathan sent me flowers while we were away and this was just a sweet surprise, until I read the message inside.

*If you think blocking me will keep me away, you got another thing coming, sweetheart. I'll be in touch soon.*
XoXo
*Felix*

My heart instantly dropped to my stomach knowing who these flowers were really from. I thought Felix had taken the hint and was moving on with someone new. But I was wrong to make such assumptions. I grabbed the flowers and stormed into the garage, throwing them into the trash bin. Fuck him. Fuck him all the way to hell, because I'll be damned if he thinks he can just reappear and disrupt my life, my happiness.

I had hoped the flowers were just his way to shake things up, a one time occurrence but it appears to have just been the beginning. Ever since that Saturday evening, he has only gotten worse.

Sunday, another bouquet was delivered to me. A dozen red roses in the most gorgeous mosaic vase. I was hoping they were from Nathan this time, but somehow I knew in my gut they were from Felix.  Instead of an open-ended threat, he was telling me he loved me and how much he missed me, wanting me to give him another chance. Not in a million years was that going to happen. Once again, I chucked those flowers into the garage trash bin, in disbelief he thought I would ever take him back.

Monday, there was an Amazon package sitting at my house full of random art supplies I never ordered. I thought it was strange, considering how everyone knows I prefer to get my art supplies from the local craft store.  A gift receipt was included with a note attached:

*Miss me yet? Xoxo Felix*

He's becoming relentless. Instead of tossing the materials in the same fashion as the flowers, I decided to ask Nathan if he could drop the box of supplies off to the local elementary school as a donation in honor of his mother. Why waste perfectly good art supplies when they can be put to use?

On Tuesday, I was called to the front office as I was heading to lunch. The school secretary said a sushi order was delivered just for me, already paid for, tip included. As I looked inside the bag, any appetite I had dissipated. The very same order, the same food I ate that night was in the bag. My stomach churns, bile slowly rising up as I'm overcome with nausea. I'm not sure if Felix is being cruel or this is an attempt to win me over, which he isn't. I'm not ever going back to him, but I can't help feeling perturbed. How did he know when I went to lunch?

I took the bag with me to the cafeteria and gave it to a fellow classmate who was short on lunch money. With no appetite, I didn't want it to go to waste, and my classmate was more than thrilled to take it off my hands.

I hadn't told Nathan about Felix's love bombing gifts. In my opinion, it was best to keep him in the dark. As long as he had no idea, there wasn't anything for him to worry about. Besides, as long as I ignore Felix, he will eventually take the message and move on, forgetting I exist. I thought I had it all handled and everything would work itself out. Until I didn't.

Nathan beams at me as we head to Bellwood High. "I have a surprise for you when we get to school."

"Really? What kind of surprise?"

"The kind that you're just going to have to wait and see when we get there."

"You're no fun." I pout.

"What good would it be if I told you the surprise beforehand? It wouldn't really be a surprise, now would it?"

A few moments later, we pull into the school parking lot and into Nathan's designated spot.

"Don't get out just yet." He grabs his backpack and quickly exits his car to come to my side, opening the car door and taking my backpack from me. Nathan grabs my hand and pulls me out of his car and into him. I drape my arms around his neck and lean in to give him quick small kisses. We've been a bit more open in the PDA department as of late, and honestly, I don't care anymore. Nathan makes me happy, and I want it to be known he's mine.

"Okay, okay." He chuckles. "We need to stop before I drag your cute ass somewhere and have my way with you. I can't exactly walk into school with a hard-on."

"Fine, I'll stop. But I'm holding you to having your way with me."

"Oh, it's happening. *Later.*" Nathan gives me his devilish grin as he turns me so my back is pressed against his front. I smirk at the bulge in his pants, knowing it's all because of me. He places his hands over my eyes as he leans and whispers, "Are you ready for your surprise?"

"Yes!" I exclaim, full of anticipation to whatever it could be.

"Alright, but you got to promise. No peeking!"

"I pinky promise!"

Nathan guides me along the parking lot or what I'm assuming is the student parking lot. We don't go too far, though, before he counts down to one and lifts his masculine hands away from my eyes.

"Oh ... my ... God ... Nathan!" Before me, parked in my designated parking space, is my beautiful white Beetle! I walk up to look at her closely, running my hand along her smooth curves. "It looks like it did before the accident. This is incredible! But how did you manage to get it here?"

*When did he find the time?*

"I asked my uncle to tow it over for me this morning. I gave him your spot number so he knew where to park it. Figured you would want it so you have a means of driving around this weekend."

My heart sinks a little. This weekend our football team is heading to the South Carolina Championship game out in Hillsboro. It's between Georgetown and Myrtle Beach, a little over two-hours drive away. The team and cheerleaders are boarding charter buses tomorrow night to get to their hotels later in the evening. The game isn't until four in the afternoon on Saturday, but the teams want to arrive ahead so they can warm up and practice before game time. I'm bummed I won't be going, as the art competition is Sunday afternoon. I have to get the finishing touches done before then so it has time to dry.

"I'm sorry I can't be there to cheer you on," I say, somberly.

"It's okay, Spitfire. You can still watch me on the tv screen."

"Ugh, it's not the same!" I jut out my bottom lip, giving my best pouty face which makes him smile.

"The weekend will fly by, and before you know it, we'll be stuck together to the point you will get sick of me."

"I would never!" I swat at his chest before he grabs my waist and pulls me close.

"I can't wait to see your art piece take out the competition when they announce you the winner."

"Oh no. You better go knock on some wood! Don't you dare jinx this for me, Shop Boy!"

"It's not a jinx. Think of it as me just speaking it into existence."

Well, when he puts it like that ...

"C'mon, Spitfire. Let me walk you to class so you're not late."

We kiss once more before lacing our fingers in each others hands and head toward the front doors to another school day. Something in my peripheral vision catches my attention, and when I glance over my shoulder, my stomach drops as I spot Felix in his blue truck parked near the entrance of the student parking lot.

And he looks pissed.

*Fuck.*

The truck rumbles to life, and Felix peels out, driving off down the road like a bat out of hell.

"Was that who I think it was?" Nathan asks, tension in his voice.

"Yeah, it was, and it looks like he knows about us now."

"Good." He takes my hand, brings it to his lips before pressing them against my knuckles. "I want him to know, and I hope it hurt like hell seeing that you moved on. He didn't deserve you."

I shove down the fear that's riddling me and force a fake, soft smile, as I allow Nathan to feel like he was the victor in some imaginary conquest for my heart. Felix knowing I'm with Nathan now only makes me fearful that I just put a bullseye on Nathan's back.

# Chapter 22

## Jenna

Sadie and I are sitting at our table having a conversation when someone calls my name.

"Jenna! Jenna!"

I look around the cafeteria before I spot Marcus jogging toward our lunch table, panting and out of breath.

"Whoa, whoa, Marcus. What's the rush?"

He holds up a finger, taking a few moments to catch his breath so he can speak.

"I'm. To give. You this," he says between trying to get oxygen into his lungs. He hands me a white envelope with nothing on the front. "It's from Kasey. She said Felix gave it to her at school and basically threatened her."

"What do you mean he threatened her?" I growl out.

"Kasey called me last night crying and panicking, so I rushed to meet her at the bowling alley where we have had a few date nights. She said if she doesn't give it to me to give to you as soon as possible, he'll hunt me down and beat me until I'm unrecognizable."

Marcus plops down into the seat next to mine so I'm sitting between him and Sadie. Their eyes are on me as I carefully open the envelope and pull out the folded piece of paper to find a typed letter.

*Oh, you dirty little whore. You told me that pretty boy wasn't a problem. He was a nobody to you. Clearly I was mistaken. I should have known better. Now he's going to pay for stealing you away from me & I'm going to make sure you pay too. For lying to me. Breaking my heart. Using me.*

*You lied. You lied like a rug. A dirty, slutty rug. I mean, I guess that was the way I took you that night. Right? On my floor. In my house.*

*I'll be watching you and when you least expect it, I'm coming for you. Especially since your new boy toy won't be around town this weekend to protect you.*

*See you soon, sweetheart.*

*xoxo*

"J-Jen, you need to-to do something about him. Okay? We-we need to go to the police and report this." Sadie's voice shakes as she speaks. Her eyes are wide, glistening with the tears she's fighting back.

"Sadie's right. We should take this to Principal King or maybe Nathan's dad—"

"We can't," I state, void of any emotion as I stare at the disturbing letter before me.

"What?" Marcus whisper-shouts. "Have you lost your ever-loving, beautiful mind!?"

"Jen, this guy nearly ran you over last week and now he's making threats? He's clearly a dangerous person."

"I get what you're both saying, I really do, but don't you two get it? He typed this out and didn't leave any names. Not mine. Not Nathan's, and he sure as hell didn't sign his name for a reason. Which means there isn't anything the cops can do to put this on him."

Marcus snaps his finger. "What about fingerprints? He typed it up and had to print it out, right? Which means he touched it. Got to use your hands to fold up a letter and put it inside an envelope."

"That would be the logical thing, but who says he didn't have a friend type it up and give it to some jersey chasing bimbo to touch. Or use gloves to keep their prints off the paper."

"Kasey said he personally handed it to her, so his DNA would be on there too."

"Along with Kasey's and yours," I point out.

"Oh ..."

I have not a doubt in the world Felix would go to  great lengths to ensure he never goes down for any of his wrong doings, especially when you come from money like he does. He has an image to maintain after all.

"Well, I'm not going to the game."

"Excuse me?" I stare at Sadie, shocked my bestie would even say those words. "Uh, no bitch. You're going to that game. You have to be there, you're the cheer captain."

"And Stacey is who I put in charge if I am unable to go to a game. She knows the routine and can easily manage the squad. Plus, Marcus will be there too, and he can help her."

"Hell no! Nope! I can't allow you to do that, Sadie. I refuse!"

"Refuse what?" Payson asks. Her and Nathan just arrived from the lunch lines. Marcus moves to the next available chair so Nathan can take the seat next to me.

"Tell your girlfriend she needs to go cheer you on at tomorrow's game. It's a huge deal, and I refuse to have her missing out."

"Cherry Pop! You don't want to watch me slaughter this team and take the trophy?"

"Of course I do, QB!" Sadie coos as she leans in and kisses Payson while stroking a finger along her cheek before she directs her steely blue eyes at Nathan. "Nathan, why don't *you* tell your girlfriend that it would be a better idea for me to stay back so I am with her at all times so Felix can't get to her."

"What?" Nathan grinds out, turning his attention to me. "What's she talking about?"

*Gee. Thanks, best friend. I guess this is karma for telling Brady that Sadie caught him with Lydia in the parking lot when she was too chicken shit to dump his sorry ass.*

All eyes are now on me, but I don't say anything. The last thing I want or need is to burden them with my problems. I don't need them worrying over me when they should be focusing on this weekend's game.

"Oh, for Christ's sake," Marcus says, and snatches the letter off the table, passing it to Nathan.

"Marcus Consuelos! I will disown you as a friend," I sneer.

Marcus glowers back my way. "I know you don't mean that, but I want it to be clear. Your safety and Nathan's are in jeopardy here. He has the right to know so we can formulate a plan on how to keep you protected. This is a serious matter—"

"Spitfire …" I hear the angry timber behind Nathan's nickname for me as he crumbles the paper into a ball with his fists.

"And ya'll wonder why I didn't want him to see it." I drop my head into my hands, rubbing my temples to massage the slight headache that's forming.

I hear the paper bounce off the table before Nathan cups my face, forcing me to look up at him. "I'm sorry for getting angry. My anger is not directed at you, okay?"

"I know," I whisper. I stare into his eyes. The way this man is looking back at me, with warmth and adoration, I question why I never made more of an effort to get to know him. The *real* him. I judged him solely out of my own distaste for someone he simply just hung out with, making me miss out on time with this incredible man before me.

"I'm so relieved to hear you say that because I need you to understand something. My rage? It all stems from fear. Fear for you and your safety. You already know my history. How much pain I've been through." I nod to acknowledge him. "Then you should also know that the mere thought of anything bad happening to you, the possibility that someone could take you from me? That scares me the most."

The moisture in my eyes builds up, and my lips tremble. Nathan leans forward to press a soft kiss to my forehead, down my nose, and one more to my lips.

"I'm going to stay back," Nathan announces to the table.

"What!?" we all say out loud, causing some tables to turn and look at us.

"Dude, I need you out there for this game!" Payson states.

I scowl at my boyfriend. "Are you crazy? You can't miss this game. What about your uncle and your grandmother? They paid for those tickets to go see you play."

"I know ... but how can I play when I'm going to be worried *he's* going to come for you?"

Sadie clears her throat. "I'm still standing on the whole 'me staying back' so I can be with Jenna at all times. I think I have pepper spray somewhere in my room if I need to use it."

"Actually, I may have something better than pepper spray," Nathan says. "I have been reaching out to Cassidy—"

"Cassidy? Who is Cassidy?" I'm not trying to sound like a jealous girlfriend, but after the shit Brady pulled over on Sadie, it catches me off guard to hear another girl's name cross Nathan's lips.

"She's a police officer who works with my dad. Ever since the Halloween party, I've been trying to get her to find anything on Felix for me. I'm talking assault charges, time in juvie ... concrete proof that he's a violent person so I could get you away from him, no matter how much you despised me."

I stare into his green eyes, looking for the lie, but I don't find one. "You swear to me she means nothing to you?"

"On Ryan's grave, I do."

"Ryan? Who's Ryan?" Marcus asks.

"Spitfire, you're the only woman I want. The *only* woman I need," Nathan confesses. "I'm crazy about you, and if going to a cop that I trust to get intel on someone behind the police chief's back in order to protect you doesn't prove that, I don't know what will."

I lean in to this sexy, godlike man and press my lips to his, kissing him with every ounce of emotion in me.

"Okay. That's enough. Let's keep it PG-13, kids," Dom says as he takes a seat with us. Everyone laughs, breaking the tension hanging over the table.

"Alright, so we need to come up with a plan," Payson says. "Nathan, reach out to your cop friend and see if maybe she can play bodyguard while we are out of town. Cherry Pop?" Payson turns to my gorgeous friend. "As much as I want to see you shaking your pom poms and rocking my number on your beautiful face, cheering me on from the sidelines, I agree you should stay back with Jenna. I'll be honest, I'm don't like it but I know how important she is to you and if it makes you feel better, I'll go with it. I'll make sure you guys have pepper spray and both of you are well protected."

"Thanks, babe," Sadie coos. "I'll let Stacey know now. I'll have her inform the cheer coach that I've come down with the stomach bug or food poisoning."

"Okay. What in the world did I miss?" Dom looks around at all of us, no clue as to what he just walked into.

Nathan pats his friend's shoulder. "I'll explain everything to you later."

# Chapter 23

## Nathan

I contacted Cassidy, and we got a plan in place for her to keep an eye on Jenna while I'm out of town this weekend. It's her weekend off, so it couldn't have aligned more perfectly. Now we won't have to find a way to do this behind my father's back and raise any suspicions. I would much rather stay behind, but Payson and Jenna are right. My team needs me, and my family already made plans to be in attendance to see me play. I can't let them down.

Jenna got the night off so we could spend as much time together before I have to board the bus this evening. She followed me to my house in her car so when it's time to go, she can drop me off at the school where the charter buses will meet. From there, Sadie will ride home with her, and Cassidy will follow them from within watching distance.

I'm hoping like hell Felix is just making empty threats to get a rise out of Jenna for some sick pleasure he has. I just wish the dude would move on already so we can all live our lives without Jenna having to look over her shoulder.

Jenna and I head upstairs to my bedroom to pack my bags. The team is leaving Bellwood around seven thirty to make it to the hotel between nine and ten. Saturday, we will all get up for breakfast before we head to the stadium where the game will be played. We will do our warm-ups, then run through drills during our scheduled practice time before we have to head to the locker rooms to get in game gear. Since kickoff is late in the afternoon, that means the game will go well into the evening, so we will be staying Saturday night too. If all goes well, I should be back in time to be here for Jenna at the art competition.

"Are you going to be okay this weekend?" I ask as I hand her my things to pack in my suitcase.

"As good as I'll ever be," she shrugs. "I do have to finish my piece, so that will keep me distracted for as long as possible. Plus, Helena and Sadie will be there with me." She's trying to put on a front, but I can see past it. She's scared, and she has every right to be. He almost ran us over in public, what would he do when no one is around?

"Keep the pepper spray on you at all times, and just remember, Cass is keeping an eye out from a distance. She has a taser she is not afraid to use if need be and can radio in if she needs backup." I move my bags to the floor to sit on the edge of my bed before gripping Jenna's hips and pulling her closer to me. "I want to say something to you, something I've been wanting to say for a few days now. I know we just started dating, and I want to preface this by saying it's okay if you don't feel the same way. But I need to get this off my chest before I leave tonight."

Jenna's eyes bounce back and forth between mine, her forehead scrunched. "Ookayy ..."

I lick my lips and clear my throat, feeling the nerves seeping in. Staring into her beautiful chocolate-brown eyes, I see my whole future in them. All the things I want in this life, I want them to be with her. This woman, this beautiful woman before me? She's it. She's my endgame. This is the one I want to spend the rest of my life waking up to. The woman I want to start a family with, if it's what she wants. The only woman I want to grow old and gray with and kick it in the nursing home until the day we take our last breaths, hopefully together because I cannot imagine living in this world where she isn't in it.

Before I chicken out, I say the words I've been longing to say. "I love you, Jenna."

I give her a moment as she processes those three little words.

"You ... you ... love me?"

"I do. I love you so damn much that the mere thought of not being with you makes my heart ache in a way one grieves the loss of someone close to them. I love you so much, I just envisioned my whole future while looking in your eyes, Jenna. You are the only one for me, the only woman I will ever want. I know that's crazy to say at just eighteen years old, but I want what I want. And I know without a shadow of doubt I want you. I want a whole future with you by my side. Nobody else. Just you. I'm not saying let's run off to Vegas and elope right after graduation. Unless, I mean, if you want to—"

She shoves a delicate finger against my lips to shush me. "Nathan?"

"Yeah," I mumble against her finger.

"Shut the hell up and make love to me." She slowly pulls her sweatshirt over her head and unhooks her black bra, letting it fall onto my bedroom floor.

"As you wish, my queen."

Placing my hand onto her midsection, I give her a slight push to take a step back so I can drop onto my knees before her. With my eyes locked onto hers, I slowly glide my fingertips along the insides of her legs, moving them up toward the top of her leggings. My fingers latch onto the waistband, and I gently pull her leggings down, ensuring she doesn't fall over.

"I'm going to worship every inch of you," I tell her as she steps out of her bottoms, and I chuck them to some part of my bedroom.

I groan inwardly at the sight of her black thong hiding the sweet treasure I'm after. Leaning forward, I press a kiss to the top of Jenna's toes, placing a kiss every few inches as I work my way up the inside of her leg. Once I pass her knee, I open up my mouth, kissing and sucking as I go, making my way up to where her thigh and hip meet.

I kiss her panty-covered pussy, eliciting a moan from her. "Mmm ... Nathan. I need more."

"Patience, my queen."

I move my mouth to the top of her thong, using my teeth to clamp onto the waistband and tugging her thong down her long legs. After stepping out of her panties, I grab one of Jenna's thighs and place it over my shoulder, catching her off guard.

"Nathan, what—"

"Just hold onto my hair while I feast on your cunt. Don't be afraid to pull either." Before she can say another word, I swipe my tongue through her slit, nice and slow as I taste her, the sexiest moan escaping from the beautiful woman before me. I suck her clit into my mouth, swirling my tongue around the little bud before releasing it.

"Oh ... god ... Nathan ..."

Hearing her say my name all breathy like that makes my dick hard, tenting the front of my sweatpants. It's not my turn for pleasure, not until I have fulfilled my duty of pleasuring this woman first.

As I plunge my tongue in and out of her pussy, I slowly work in one finger, moving it in the same rhythm as my tongue. Before long, she is squirming and panting, tugging on my hair as her cunt clenches around me as I continue my ministrations.

"I'm going to come soon if you keep that up, Shop Boy."

"I want you to come all over my face, beautiful."

Adding a second finger, plunging into her over and over again, I can feel Jenna's release is close. Swirling my tongue on her clit, I pull it into my mouth once again, only this time I suck a little harder while I pump my fingers in and out of her faster. Her breathing gets heavier as she inches closer to her climax.

"Oh, Nathan!" she shouts as her release takes over her body. I wait patiently for her to come down from her orgasmic high, in awe of how gorgeous she looks when she does.

I gently place her leg back onto the floor, ensuring she doesn't fall over before I pick her up as if she were my bride and lay her on my bed. I quickly pull my shirt over my head and waste no time removing my sweats and briefs before reaching into my nightstand for a condom.

I rip the wrapper open with my teeth and sheath my dick before crawling onto the bed and over her. My eyes roam her body, from her raven-black hair to her white painted toes before landing back on her face.

"I am so crazy in love with you," I confess.

"Show me," she whispers back.

Leaning down, I pull her lips, soft and warm, into my mouth and we kiss slowly, savoring each other as if we have forever to do this.

Her lips wrap around my tongue as if it were my dick, bobbing up and down as if she was giving it a blow job. Instantly, I groan, feeling the pre-cum leak out of the tip as my cock swells, ready to sink into her. Not yet though. I pull away, moving my lips to her neck, kissing and licking as I move down her body.

Finding her sweet spot on her neck, I gently bite down, ensuring I don't leave a mark on her flesh. Jenna gasps, and her back arches off my bed, nails digging into my bare back. My spitfire seems to like a little pain with her pleasure.

Continuing down her body, I make my way to her beautiful breasts, her nipples hard and at attention, ready for my mouth to devour them. Pulling her nipple into my mouth, I gently bite down before massaging the pain away with my tongue while my hand tends to her other breast, rolling her nipple between two fingers.

"Mmm ... Nathan. I need more ... baby ... I need you ..."

Adjusting so I'm back over her, my face even with hers and my cock lined up with her entrance, I gradually enter her body, enjoying every inch as I push myself inside.

"Ohhh …" I moan out. "God, you feel like heaven."

After pulling out to the tip, I sink back inside, continuing to go slow as we consume each other's mouths.

Gradually, I thrust harder, deeper, feeling my orgasm build, ready for a release, but I won't blow my load until Jenna comes for me.

Switching positions, I adjust myself into a kneeling position, moving her legs to rest beside mine as I hold her close to me, her breasts pressed against my naked chest.

"Ride my cock, Spitfire. Take what you need from me," I rasp out.

Jenna's pace quickens, her inner walls squeezing me as she chases her release. I grab the globes of her ass, helping her to bounce harder.

"Oh, I'm so close, Nathan."

"I think I know what you need," I grit out.

Reaching down between us, I press my thumb against her clit, massaging it in gentle circles, and it doesn't take long for her orgasm to hit.

"Yes … oh yes …"

Shortly after Jenna's orgasm, mine hits, cum spilling into the condom.

The both of us drop down onto my bed, breathing heavily as we come back down from our post-orgasmic high.

"I'll be right back." I press a kiss on Jenna's forehead before getting off my bed to dispose of the condom. After washing my hands, I grab a clean washcloth and return to my bedroom to clean her up before tossing the rag into my hamper.

Jenna and I snuggle under my blankets, her head resting on my chest while I stroke her back. Neither one of us says anything, but we don't have to. Lying here in each other's arms, holding one another close is simply enough.

# Chapter 24

## Jenna

After making sure Nathan's bags are packed with everything he needs, the both of us back in our own clothes, we head downstairs to the living room. He places his bags near the front door so they are ready to grab on our way out when we must leave to head to the school for drop off.

A somber feeling overwhelms me. Between Nathan professing his love to the way he claimed my heart while making love to me, proving his feelings for me, I'm just not sure how I'll be able to be away from him for an entire weekend. I'm doing my best to not let the sadness ruin what time we have together before he leaves. The last thing I want is for him to worry about me more than he already is.

*God, how am I going to get through these next few days without him beside me?*

"Pick whatever movie you want to watch," Nathan says as he hands me the remote, dragging me out of my somber thoughts. "I'm going to get us some snacks."

I give him a light hearted smile, hoping like hell it's convincing enough.

Plopping down on the couch, I scroll through the movie selections, trying to find something that could lift our spirits from the looming countdown. Settling on a *Fast and the Furious* movie, knowing how much Nathan enjoys cars, it was the best option.

Moments later, Nathan returns with a plate of pizza rolls, some popcorn, and two bottles of water.

He takes a seat on the couch beside me, his legs sprawled out like any typical guy. I move to snuggle into his side, resting my head on his chest as he drapes an arm around me, and I breathe in his cologne, wishing I could just bathe in it.

Why did the art competition and football game have to be on the same weekend?

*Did you really foresee yourself being in this predicament?*
My brain makes a valid point.

We are halfway through the movie when the front door swings open and Police Chief Ward steps through.

"Nathan—oh. Hello. I didn't know you had company over, son." Mr. Ward's face flushes a slight shade of pink. "You must be the Altwoods' daughter?"

"That would be me, sir. I'm Jenna. Nice to meet you." I lean away from Nathan to shake his dad's hand. He's not a bad looking guy for someone in his forties, and if Nathan looks like *that* when he's his father's age, then I'm going to be a very lucky woman. Go me!

"Pleasure is mine," he smiles back before his eyes look past me to his son. "Uh, Nathan, may I have a word with you in the kitchen, please?"

"Sure, Dad."

"Excuse us, Jenna," Mr. Ward says as he makes his way into the kitchen.

"I'll be right back." Nathan presses a kiss to the top of my head before following his father into the kitchen.

# Nathan

I walk in on my dad pacing in the kitchen. His mouth is tight, and he looks like he's fighting to keep from blowing his lid. I recognize the emotion. He's angry. About what? I don't know, but I'm guessing I'm about to find out.

"I got the results of your exam today, and I'll have you know I was shocked to see this!" He slams my exam down on the kitchen table. "You failed!?"

Honestly, I'm not surprised. I didn't really put forth the effort. For starters, it was just a practice test, not the real deal. Plus, I was trying to get to the studio in time for my consultation with Helena. Granted, we had to reschedule the appointment for after Thanksgiving. With her mom being touch and go and my football-work schedule plus the holiday, it was the best time we could squeeze me in.

"Dad, look, I know you're upset—"

"Upset? Upset!? I'm more than upset here, Nathan. I'm disappointed in you!"

*Ouch.*

"I thought you were studying, going over the handbook. Not to mention all those tests I brought home for you. I mean, you have an advantage here, son. I thought since you agreed to quit the garage, you were taking this seriously." Dad shakes his head side to side. "If your mother was here, she would be just as disappoint—"

"Bullshit!" I yell at my father, catching him off guard as its something I have never done before.

"What did you say to me, boy?" There's a warning in his tone, telling me I'm on thin ice.

My heart is racing, clashing against my ribs. I usually don't argue with my dad, but I'm so furious he would even go there, to mention my mother in our dispute.

"You do not get to bring Mom into this, because if she were still here, the only person she would be disappointed with is you!"

My father scoffs. "Is that so?"

"Mom would have let me make the choice to choose what I wanted to do with my life, what made me happy. Not try to control it, forcing my hand to follow in your footsteps. Did you ever, for once, consider asking me what I wanted to do?"

My dad simply stares at me, having nothing to say.

"No, Dad. You didn't. Not once." Now I'm the one pacing in the kitchen, fighting back tears. "You know what I don't get, Dad? How come you let Ryan do what he wanted? Hmm? How come Ryan got to fix cars, work in the shop, and do what he wanted, but God forbid Nathan wants to do the same thing. Tell me that!"

"I let Ryan choose cars and look where that got him! So pardon me for wanting to not chance a repeat happening to my other son!"

"Ryan's death had nothing to do with working on cars or at the garage! If the blame needs to be placed, then blame me for his death because I'm the reason he's gone. His death is *my* fault!"

Dad sucks in a deep breath. "That's not true ... how can you say that?"

I swipe at my eyes. "Ryan and I got into an argument right before he sped off. Looking back on it now, I can't even remember what the fight was about, but I'd give anything to go back. If he hadn't been angry with me ... if I hadn't upset him ... Ryan ... Ryan would still be here."

"Nathan ... you cannot blame yourself for your brother's death. It was an accident."

"Yeah, so you say. Yet here you are, still blaming Ryan's love of cars for his death."

"Because I thought he was drag racing!" My dad places his hands on his hips, taking a moment for himself. "I never told you this because I didn't want you to find out, but your brother got into some trouble with the local street gang, racing cars for bets. The night of the accident ... I thought

... I thought it was him racing again. It wasn't until much later that I found out the truth."

"Why did you hide that from me?"

"So you could follow your brother like you did with fixing cars? Huh? I couldn't allow that to happen because, Nathan, you are all I have left! I've lost your mother ... your brother. My parents have long been gone. So I'm not sorry for wanting you to follow in my footsteps where I can look over you—"

"News flash, Dad. That's you trying to control my life and not giving me an option. I don't want to be a cop. It doesn't make me happy or feel accomplished. You want to know what does? Huh? It's the pride of fixing someone's vehicle while not charging them an arm and a leg. It's the conversations with Uncle Dean where we talk about Mom, and he helps me to keep her memory alive because I can barely hold onto the memories I do have with her. He helps me see the kind of woman she was, the woman I missed out on. It's my one connection to Ryan that I still have today because we bonded over cars, it was our thing since you were barely home as it was. It's keeping Grandpa Wesley's legacy going in this family, one I hope I can pass on to my own children someday, if they choose. What's being a cop ever done for me?"

My dad says nothing and swipes a hand over his face, his brown eyes glistening with unshed tears. "Nathan, I—"

"No, Dad. Just ... stop. Okay? I'm done with this conversation." My eyes flash to the microwave, noting the time. "I need to get to school if I'm going to catch the bus with my teammates. In case you forgot, the championship game is tomorrow."

With nothing else to say, I turn and walk away from my father. Guess my rant rendered him speechless. *Good.*

Walking through the living room, I make my way to the only bright light in my life, the one currently pacing by the front door, knowing she overheard everything.

"Let's go," I softly say as I grab my bags off the floor, and guide Jenna out of the house, making our way to her car.

# Chapter 25

## Jenna

The drive from Nathan's house to the school is silent. After hearing that conversation between Nathan and his dad, I have no doubt my man needs time to gather his thoughts. A lot of words were said, and it seemed like they needed to be spoken. I had no idea how much Nathan was being pulled in two directions.

His father believed he would follow in his shoes into law enforcement. I think all of Bellwood did too. Or I at least thought so until I saw the way he worked in the garage. You could see how happy he was getting his hands dirty under the hood of a car, changing the oil, or fixing God only knows what was wrong with a car. Hearing what he said with how the garage resonates with him, I can only hope his father heard what I heard.

Shouldn't his son's happiness matter more than forcing his hand into a career he doesn't have the heart for? Especially one that places other people's safety before his own?

I pull into the parking spaces, near where the charter buses are lined up in the drop-off lane as we wait for everyone to show up. We're about ten minutes early, but I know Nathan needed to get out of the house away from his father.

"I'm sorry you had to overhear that, Jenna." He sounds so distant, so broken that it's hurting my own heart.

"No. Don't do that. Don't you dare apologize to me, Shop Boy." This earns me a small smile, but my man is still hurting, and I need to find a way to lift him up.

Looking around to ensure I don't see anyone, I unfasten my seatbelt and crawl over the center console to straddle his lap.

"What ... what are you doing?"

"I'm comforting you because you shared some powerful words back there going head-to-head with your dad. Sounded like words that needed to be said for a while, words you've held back for some time. Am I right?"

I lean down and press a chaste kiss on the bridge of his nose before resting my forehead against his, wanting him to know that I'm here for him, the way he has been there for me.

Nathan nods. "My dad has been shoving practice exams down my throat every chance he could get this year. But I could never tell him how much I didn't want to do it. I was too afraid ..."

I grip his chin, the way he tends to do to me, only I'm not as gentle as he is, and I lift his handsome face so we are looking into each other's eyes. "You were afraid if you upset your father, got into an argument like tonight, that something bad would happen to him?"

Nathan swallows deeply. "Yeah ..."

"Babe, it is perfectly normal to have that fear. Especially for someone who has loss as much as you have. But you were denying yourself your own happiness by trying to appease the two most important male figures in your life. How were you going to deal with both your dad and uncle after graduation? Huh? Are you going to manage a double life as a police mechanic?"

Nathan laughs, breaking the tension, and the sound is music to my ears. "You really know how to make a man feel better."

"You mean my man?"

Nathan flashes his big white smile, both dimples making an appearance, and God, I swear I could melt into a puddle at the sight.

"I'm proud of you for finally standing up for yourself and coming clean with your dad. He needed to know." Nathan nods in agreement, wrapping his arms around my waist, squeezing me in a hug.

I pull back, cupping his face in both of my hands. "Take this weekend to focus on the game. Okay? All those emotions you have dealt with today? Pull all of it out of your mind and into your playing. Leave it all on the field. Strip the ball, force fumbles, whatever. Tackle the shit out of the other team because I want to hear about my man taking some offensive players out of the game."

"Damn, you really know how to give a pep talk."

"Of course I do." I lean in and kiss him softly. "Don't worry about me, okay? I'll be safe, and we are taking all the necessary precautions. Just focus on kicking ass tomorrow night and bring that title home to us."

"Yes, my queen."

"Mmm ... keep up with the *my queen* stuff and I'll make you kneel before me."

"Oh, Spitfire. Did I not prove to you earlier how much I enjoy kneeling for you?"

*Lord ... this man.*

After seeing Nathan onto the bus and kissing him goodbye, I make the drive home alone. I told Sadie she should probably not tag along since she told her coach she has the stomach bug and that if she showed up, it would defeat the purpose of the lie.

Driving home, I make sure to keep to the main roads since they are lit up the most. Cass is keeping a good distance back as she follows me just in case Felix decides to make an appearance. If he spots the patrol car, there is no telling what he would do or how that could set him off.

After I pull into my driveway, I send off a quick text to Nathan before heading inside.

As I approach my front porch, the sound of a diesel truck revving its engine echoes in the night. I quickly turn around, desperately trying to find the source of the noise when I spot the truck down the street. How the hell did I miss him?

I make a dash for my porch as Felix drives by, taunting me. "Your ass is mine, sweetheart!"

My heart rate speeds up, and all of a sudden, I can't catch my breath as I run inside my house and slam the door behind me.

"Jen?" Sadie calls out. "Oh my God, Jen! Are you okay?"

"Can't … catch … my breath," I pant out.

"Put your head between your legs and take deep breaths 'til you calm down. It will help with the panic attack," Sadie instructs me.

I do as my best friend says, steadying my breathing until my heart slows down and I can breathe normally.

"Good. Nice and easy," Sadie says, her voice soft and soothing.

Once I feel like I'm not having a heart attack, I tell her what set it off. "Felix drove by the house just a few moments ago."

"Oh my gosh, are you serious?"

"Wouldn't be almost dying if I wasn't."

"Awe … there's that insensitive sense of humor I love," Sadie says, rolling her eyes. "Wait … Is he still out there?"

"I don't think so. He sped off after he caught my attention. Haven't heard him come back."

"Hopefully, if he knows what's good for him, he will stay away."

I don't bother to tell my best friend to not get her hopes up. Felix has done nothing but prove he won't give up on me yet.

My phone goes off, alerting me to a text. I unlock my screen to open the message from Nathan.

SHOP BOY

Glad you made it home. Miss you already too. Will you think of me tonight?

"Aww," Sadie coos. "You two are the cutest! I knew you guys had feelings for each other underneath all of that heated tension, if you know what I mean." She wiggles her brows.

"Shut up," I laugh. "And stop reading my stuff over my shoulder."

I give her a slight shove, making us both laugh, our bantering calming my nerves. I don't know how I would get through life without our friendship.

"C'mon. Let's go devour chick flicks and rom-coms while we eat our weight in sweets and weep about being away from our lovers." Sadie pulls me off the floor, and that's what we do for the rest of our Friday night.

Hours later, I toss and turn in my bed, unable to fall asleep. Every time I attempt to shut my eyes, memories of

Felix grabbing me and holding me down replay on a mental reel. I try to shut it off, but nothing seems to work.

"Ugh, this is useless!" I whisper-shout into my room.

Grabbing my cell phone from my nightstand, I pull it off the charger to see what time it is.

11:49 p.m.

Ugh. I'd give anything to call and talk to Nathan, but he's probably sound asleep, and I don't want to wake him up. He needs his rest for the big game tomorrow.

Too bad I didn't have my competition piece to work on right now. It's currently locked inside the studio, and I won't dare try to go there in the middle of the night.

What I would give to put my air pods on, blast some 2000s hip-hop, and get lost in a painting.

*Wait a minute!*

I shoot up in my bed as I remember the exchange I made with Nathan.

*The mural for the Chevelle!*

How could I have forgotten!? Especially since Nathan held up his end of the deal. Now, I need to do the same on my end. But ... how do I go about this?

I think it over, pondering all my options.

*I could go to the garage and work on it tomorrow?*

No, that won't work. His uncle closed the shop so they could attend the game. Not to mention, I need to finish up my painting at the studio if it's going to be ready in time for Sunday.

Can't go on Sunday. I have to stop by Helena's to get my art piece to take it to the hotel and get it setup for judging.

*Think, Jenna, think!*

I massage my temples, thinking how in the world I could get into the shop to paint the mural before Nathan returns on Sunday. It would be the best surprise for him, especially if the team wins, and if they—nope! Not putting that negative juju out into the universe. They *will* win tomorrow. I know it!

Thinking back to the night I wrecked my car, an idea forms as I recall the spare key and alarm code Nathan used to get in. What's a little breaking and entering? I mean, can it even be breaking and entering if I know how to shut off the alarm so it doesn't alert the police?

Before I talk myself out of it, I'm out of my bed, heading straight for my closet. I throw on a pair of black leggings and the darkest hoodie I can find.

*I can do this. I can do this. I. Can. Do. This!* I silently hype myself up while breathing through my nose as I calm my nerves.

All I gotta do is sneak down to my car and drive over to the garage, repeating everything Nathan did that night of my accident.

After grabbing my phone and whatever else I need, I make my way quietly down the stairs and out the door to my car.

Twenty minutes later, with no sign of Felix, I pull behind Wesley's garage where the employees always park. Checking my surroundings, I make my way to the cinder block at the back door, lifting it and hoping like hell the spare key is still—it's here!

I unlock the back door and dart toward the alarm system, punching in the code before it has the chance to go off and alert the authorities of a break-in. The last thing I want or need is Nathan's dad showing up to arrest his son's girlfriend.

After locking the door so no one attempts to sneak in, I make my way to the small garage on the end of the building, using the flashlight on my phone to see.

As soon as I enter the room where the Chevelle sits in all her reincarnated beauty, a sense of peace washes over me. If I breathe in just a little harder, I can almost make out the hints of vanilla, amber and mahogany of Nathan's cologne in here.

It's calming, almost as if Nathan were here himself. Who would have thought a garage could provide solace for my anxious soul?

Pulling my sketchbook out of my bag, I set it up on the countertop so I can see the design I have planned for this mural, hoping Nathan will love the finished result.

God, do I miss him and his strong arms.

After I gather all the paints I will need, I set them out in a system to make the process flow flawlessly. It makes all the difference to have a well thought out process, especially when you are on a time crunch. Once I've found my air pods, I pop those suckers in, press play on my playlist, and get to painting.

# Chapter 26

## Jenna

I may be exhausted, but my mind and soul feel at ease. I spent about five hours in the early Saturday morning working on the mural for the Chevelle, only to turn around and do it all over again late Saturday night.

Not to mention the several hours I put in at the art studio with Sadie, adding the finishing touches on my art piece for the competition. I'm so happy it's officially finished! And I'm in love with it! Now, it's a matter of letting it dry overnight before I return tomorrow to pick it up on the way to Bellwood Hotel, the location for this year's competition.

I thank Helena for letting me use the studio today. Most of Bellwood traveled to go watch our high school play in the big game. So many businesses closed, Beyond Broken

Colors included, but Helena was kind enough to open the door to Sadie and me.

Sadie and I rushed back home, so we could watch our footballers play it out on national TV. After a nail-biting close game, our team came out with the victory! Sadie and I jump around the living room, screaming out in excitement as the confetti drops and the TV crews rush the field towards our players and coaches for the post-game interviews.

The biggest highlight for me was when Nathan made an interception and ran it in for a touchdown. The moment he made it to the end zone, he dropped to one knee and pointed a finger toward the sky. My eyes welled up seeing that beautiful moment, knowing he dedicated that touchdown to his mom and brother. I grabbed my cell phone to snap the shot, relishing how monumental it was for him. With a few quick edits, I sent the picture to him so when he checks his phone later, he would know I had seen him and was cheering for him all the way from home.

Our team did it! Bellwood High's football team are South Carolina State Champs!

"Does this look okay? Or should I go with the dress?"

"It's a bit chilly for a dress. Definitely go with the black pantsuit and purple top. It's warm and looks professional."

"You're not wrong." I'm so nervous. My palms won't stop sweating. Or my pits. I feel like maybe I should bring my spray deodorant with me. Competition day is officially here, and I am so ready for it to be over.

"Jen, stop stressing! You're the most talented artist I know, they would be crazy not to select your piece. You got this in the bag." My bestie reassures me.

"We will see after today, won't we."

God, I wish Nathan was here right now. I wouldn't be such a mess if he was.

"Girls!" my mother yells from the bottom of the stairs. "We are heading over now to get good parking. We will see you both there. Love you!"

"Okay! Love you too!" Sadie and I shout back in unison.

After we finish getting ready, we make our way over to Main Street to grab my painting from the studio. I park out front since I'm just grabbing my canvas and don't plan on being here long.

"Jenna, this piece is absolutely breathtaking! You are going to knock them dead when they see this!"

"You think so?"

"Honey, I know so—who is that?" Helena's brows furrow as she looks out the window of her studio.

"Fucking hell," I whisper. "Helena, I need you to contact the police."

I rush outside to find Felix double parked his truck beside my Beetle, preventing me from leaving. He's leaning against the passenger side of my car, arms crossed over his chest, wearing a smug expression.

"Well, if it ain't the artist of the hour," Felix says.

"What do you want, Felix?" I glance up and down the road, trying to spot Cassidy's patrol car. She's supposed to be nearby in case he shows up. Where the hell is she?

"Well, sweetheart, you should know what I want by now. Haven't you received all of my gifts?"

I'm so over this lunatic and his crazy obsessive need to want to own me.

"Felix, you need to get it through your thick-headed skull that I don't want you. I've moved on, and you need to do the same." I stand tall, my back straight and my voice firm and strong, needing Felix to understand that there will never be an *us*.

Apparently, that's the wrong thing to say, because the smugness is quickly replaced with anger.

"What the hell does that pretty boy got over me?"

"For starters, he understands the word consent!"

Felix moves toward me. "I'm so sick of you crying rape when you were the one to initiate sex with me!"

I walk backward into the big bay window of the studio, as Felix pulls a fist back and slams it next to my head. Turning away, I scream as fear courses through my body.

"Stop it!" I yell as loud as I can.

This time, Felix tightly grips my cheeks, forcing me to look him in his face and stare into his cold, dead hazel-blue eyes.

"Tell me again how I raped you when you were so willing to put out for me." Felix presses his mouth to my neck, where he glides his big, wet tongue over me and up the side of my face. "Mmm ... So sweet."

Thinking back to the night Nathan confronted his dad, and the courage it took him to finally speak his truth, I decided it was time I did the same.

"You're a disgusting pig who can't accept it when a woman doesn't want to be with your ugly ass!" I spit at him.

His hand moves from my face to my throat, and he squeezes, slowly cutting off my oxygen. As I begin to feel lightheaded and Felix's face becomes hazy, a sound comes from my right.

"Let her go!" someone yells. It sounds like Helena. "The cops are on their way, and I've got you on camera for assaulting this young woman. With this video evidence, it will be the proof they'll need to lock you up. You're going to go away for some time. Maybe your future prison pimp could show you some manners."

Felix turns to face Helena. "Fuck you, you bitch, and mind your dam business."

His grip loosens, and I use the distraction to kick him in his groin. Felix hunches over, holding onto his balls as he groans out in pain. I go to run, but he manages to snatch my ponytail, yanking it with the strength of ten men. I'm pulled back with full force and slammed into the sidewalk, forcing me to drop the canvas.

"Oww ..." That's going to leave a bruise. Or a few.

"You're going to regret that, you whore!" Felix grunts out, heading for me again until his eyes find my painting on the ground, a few inches away from me. The most devilish smile crosses his face and I hope like hell he isn't thinking what I fear he is thinking.

"You know ..." Felix huffs. "I don't get art, honestly. I mean, what's so great about it?"

I watch in horror as Felix picks up my painting, raises a leg up and snaps my canvas right in half.

"Noo!" A shrill scream escapes me.

"Let's see you win your pretty little competition now."

Sirens can be heard in the distance, and when they get closer, he darts toward his truck in to make a getaway.

"Freeze! Put your hands in the air where I can see them and turn around slowly!" A brunette, Alexandra Daddario look-alike in a police uniform, shouts.

*Cassidy! Thank God she's here.*

"Damn, since when did they let hot chicks enforce the law?" Felix gets flirtatious with Cassidy before his body drops to the ground and he flops like a fish. Don't flirt with cops, otherwise you may get tased.

Another two patrol cars pull up, and the officers quickly make an exit, their guns at the ready as they approach him. Cassidy backs up, allowing two of the guys to arrest Felix.

"You have the right to remain silent. Anything you say can and will be used against you in the court of law."

The officers lift Felix off the ground and place him into the back of one of the cars as they continue to read him his rights.

With Felix placed in a patrol car, Sadie and Helena rush toward me, helping me up off the ground.

"Oh my God, Jenna. Are you okay? I was so fucking scared," Sadie says as a few tears escape her eyes.

"You should get checked out at the hospital to make sure nothing's broken and get pictures of those marks," Helena says.

Cassidy approaches us with hesitation. "Are you okay, Jenna? Do you need a ride to the hospital?"

"Where were you?" I bluntly ask her.

"I'm sorry. I got caught up by that slow-ass train over by Elderberry Street. Had it not been going at a snail's pace, I would have been here. I would have been able to protect you. God, Nathan's going to chew me out for this. I'm so sorry, Jenna."

"Yeah, that train and I are mortal enemies." I chuckle, lightening the mood.

Relief floods Cassidy's face, washing away her guilt. I can't be mad at her for something out of her control, when I've been caught by that damn train far too many times myself. She showed up before Felix could get away and didn't let him go until backup arrived. She did her duty.

"I've recorded the whole incident on my phone. Do you think it will be enough to charge him?" Helena asks.

"Bring it down to the precinct and ask specifically for the chief. We are actually building a case against Mr. Martin. A few girls have recently come forward with assault and rape claims. I think your video may just help put the nail in the coffin."

"I'd also like to press charges against Felix. Not just about this, but for rape and prior assault incidents."

Cassidy gives me a grim smile. "I'm sorry, Jenna. No young woman should have endured what you have. I personally have been where you've been. Same crime, different monster. Mine got away with a slap on the wrist and it was enough to light a fire in my ass to go law enforcement. It's why I wear the uniform."

"I'm sorry you went through that, and they got away with what they did. I hope Karma finds her way to them and you get the justice you deserve."

A moment later, a yellow Jeep pulls up onto the sidewalk nearby. "Hey! You two need to hop in. We got an art show to get to."

"It's a competition, QB."

"Show. Competition. What's the difference?"

"There's scholarship money on the line in competition," I sass Payson. "Honestly, what's the point of even going? Felix destroyed my artwork and now I have nothing to showcase."

Fuck that asshole. I hope his ass rots in prison after all the bullshit he caused today.

"You just leave that up to your man," Payson says.

Sadie and I look at each other with furrowed brows.

"Come on! Not going to get there any faster if you're going to just stand there. Just ... trust us. Him. Us?"

Sadie hops into the passenger seat of her girlfriend's Jeep as I gather my things from my car since it's still barricaded in.

"Jenna ..." Helena starts. "Please make sure you get checked out afterward. For my sanity. I'd like to know you're physically okay."

"Yes, ma'am ... and thank you for recording. You probably got the first physical evidence showcasing the real monster he is."

"No problem." Helena pulls me into a hug before going back into her studio, probably to immerse herself in some art after the events that unfolded.

"Thank you for being my security detail over the weekend, and for making sure Felix didn't get away. I appreciate what you did for me. And ... don't worry about Nathan. I'll make sure he knows better than to give you a hard time." I give Cassidy a hug and tell her bye before I get into the Jeep, headed to the hotel for a competition I had set out on winning ... with no entry piece. Bye, bye college dreams.

# Chapter 27

## Nathan

Our buses were almost to the school when Payson received a call from Sadie. Payson urgently flagged me over to trade seats with Colton so she could put the phone between our ears as we listened to Sadie.

She was screaming, pure terror in her voice recounting what was being played out before her. Sadie wanted to get out of the car, but Payson assured her girlfriend she was better staying where she was. She knew Sadie was terrified for Jenna, wanting to go to her best friend's aide, but Payson, feeling as helpless as I did at the very moment, needed Sadie to understand how it was unsafe. She informed us that Helena was outside with her phone out, making sure she was recording this as physical evidence, so charges could be brought against Felix.

Pure, unadulterated rage consumed me that I wasn't there to protect my girl. I should have been there; I should have stopped it. Stopped him.

"Sadie, listen to me, baby. We are about to pull into the school. My parents already dropped off my Jeep and then we are coming your way. Okay? …. I love you too, Cherry Pop. Muah!" She gets off the phone, and I see the same anger in her eyes.

"The cops showed up and arrested Felix." She takes a deep breath, as do I. "His ass better fucking go to jail, or I'm going to ask my father how we can personally deal with the likes of him."

"If Helena got the it all on her phone, we have enough to charge him with assault. Plus, Cassidy told me early this morning that some girls have come forward wanting to charge him with rape. They definitely got a solid case against him."

"Why Jenna?" Payson asks. "Why was it Jenna? I mean, yeah she's beautiful, smart … talented. I mean, she worked her ass off on that painting and he fucking smashed it. The girl just wants to pay for her own education so her parents don't have to. That's the heart of a good woman. If anyone deserves to win, it's her."

"I agree."

"It's a shame she didn't have a backup piece," Payson mutters as she looks out the window as our buses approach the school.

"Wait … what if she does?" I perk up.

"What do you mean?"

"I'll explain it on the way. Can you do me a favor?"

"Yeah, anything," Payson replies.

"Can you drop me off at Wesley's before you pick up Jenna and Sadie and get them to the hotel for the competition? I'll handle the rest."

A playful smile forms on her face. "I don't know what you have in mind, but I'll take your word for it. Let's do this." Payson and I slap hands and get ready to depart the bus.

If my plan goes through, I may just be able to give my girl her chance at that prize money she's had her heart set on winning. Her work deserves to be seen by those judges and I'm going to make sure that they do.

I could never be more grateful for my uncle than I am at this moment. He called me when he got into the shop early this morning to let me know that my girl did a beautiful job on the mural for the Chevelle. I called him as soon as I got off the bus, asking if he could make sure it was ready for me, and explained my plan to him, as well as ensuring Payson was listening so they both knew what was going to happen. He had just finished attaching the hood onto the car when Payson dropped me off.

"You've got yourself one extremely talented woman, kiddo."

"I sure as hell do, Uncle," I tell him, in awe of the artwork Jenna did to my car.

A male figure, kneeling on a darkened ground in the center, his hands covering his face. From one hand, blue and black streams pour towards the ground, forming one path, whereas green and silver streams, the same colors as Wesley's shop colors, pour from the other hand to form a second path. Above the man, the black ombrés into baby blue with white swirls that resemble whispy clouds. Two angels—one woman and young man—rest their hands on top of the shadowed man's shoulders, as if they are comforting him, loving him from above.

I tilt my head back and forth, wondering if I'm seeing things as I inch closer to get a better look. It … it can't be. It couldn't …

"She really nailed them, didn't she? They look … they look just as I remember them," Uncle Dean's voice cracks.

I feel the tears well up, brushing them away before they get the chance to fall. I don't think Jenna knows the magnitude of her skills because he's right.

It's my mom … and Ryan. The detailing in their faces, the coloring of their eyes and their hair … she captured them just as they were, as if she's met them in person and retained every single feature, right down to the the little mole on my mother's right cheek, and Ryan's crooked grin.

"I'm trying to understand the rest of it, though. I know art is supposed to express emotion but … I'm just not sure what the rest of it is supposed to be."

"I do, Uncle," I tell him, smiling like a crazy fool. A crazy fool who is madly and deeply in love with the most incredible woman to bless this planet. God, how I've missed her this weekend, wishing she was there in person to cheer me on. When I finally got back to the locker rooms after the game and could check my phone, I saw that picture she sent me. Her excitement, and her happiness for me, even from miles away solidified how much I love that woman.

"You care to share?"

"I would, but I really need to get this car to the hotel if I'm going to help Jenna."

"Well, then, you're going to need these." He reaches into his pocket and pulls out a set of keys before tossing them to me. "Tell her I said, congratulations when you see her. I know in my heart she's going to win it."

"Will do," I nod.

I climb into the Chevelle, putting the key in the ignition and start her up, listening as she rumbles to life, loving that classic old muscle car roar.

I wave to my uncle and set out towards Bellwood Hotel, sending a little prayer in hopes the judges will accept this as Jenna's replacement entry.

After sitting for ten minutes, waiting for what could possibly be the slowest train ever to pass on Elderberry Street, I finally make it to the hotel in town. I'm so grateful the competition is being held in Bellwood, otherwise I wouldn't be able to help my girl out in her time of need. I pull up to the front entryway and lay on the horn, hoping it will draw all the judges and spectators outside.

# Chapter 28

**Jenna**

As soon as we make it to the hotel, Sadie rushes me into the ladies room to help me freshen up and make it look like I wasn't just viciously attacked by a psychotic ex-boyfriend.

"And ... there ... you go. All done! No one would ever know what a mess you were when we got here," Sadie says after doing a quick touch up on my makeup. We managed to brush off the dirt on my pantsuit but not much can be done as far as the scuffs on my heels go.

"Are you ready to go out there?" Sadie asks me.

"As ready as one can be in my situation." Truth is, I rather just go back home, put on my sweats and curl up in my bed to sleep the rest of today away. Preferably, while Nathan cuddles me in his arms.

Speaking of Nathan ... where is he? Payson said he was coming here after she dropped him off and I haven't seen him yet. I hope he's okay.

We make our way into the ballroom where there are easels and tables with so many amazing art pieces on display. I would be in heaven right now if I had my own piece to display among all these masterpieces.

As Sadie and I make our way around the ballroom, we cross paths with Mrs. Wailing, my art teacher.

"Jenna! There you are! I have been looking all over for you. I haven't been able to find your piece yet and was wondering if you could show me where it is?"

"Actually, Mrs. Wailing ... you see ..."

The screech of a microphone being turned on cuts off all conversations and a handsome older gentleman graces the stage.

"Ladies and gentleman, if I could have your attention please. It seems one of our participants has gone outside the box with her entry piece. If you could all kindly step outside, we would like for you to view Miss Jenna Altwood's artwork to ensure you have viewed every participant's presentation. Thank you."

"Did he just say my name?" I look at my best friend, who shrugs, seemingly as confused as I am.

"Did he say outside?" Mrs. Wailing asks.

"I believe he did," Sadie responds.

Mrs. Wailing, Sadie, and I follow the crowd moving toward the front doors of the hotel. Payson meets us in the lobby with one of the biggest guys I've ever seen, decked out in a tuxedo and looking every bit like the security detail for the President. "Sadie, Jenna. Meet Otis, one of my best linemen. He's going to help escort us through all of these people."

"How is he ..."

"Excuse me, ladies and gentlemen. The artist, Jenna Altwood, coming through. Pardon us, thank you. Excuse us ... Sir, if you could kindly step aside, the artist is coming through. Thank you."

"Just stay right behind him. He will make sure they move for him. Think of it like Moses parting the Red Sea."

Sadie and I do as Payson says and follow behind Otis as he clears a path through the crowd until the crisp fall air greets us. Once the last of the people have cleared out of the way, I spot him. Standing before me, in his Bellwood High football hoodie and distressed jeans, is my handsome boyfriend. My eyes glance past him, spotting the baby-blue Chevelle he worked so hard to put together, glistening in the November sunshine.

"What is this?" I ask Nathan as I approach him, my heart fluttering slightly faster, trying to piece what is going on.

Before he even utters a word, Nathan pulls me into his arms, placing a hand at the middle of my back, and dips me, kissing me like his life depends on it, the world disappearing all around us. The crowd of spectators, artists and their families whistle and hoot, breaking our heated kiss.

I feel my cheeks warm, feeling a tinge of embarrassment at the many people witnessing such an intimate moment between us.

"You have no idea how badly I've waited to do that," Nathan confesses. "God, I've missed you this weekend."

"I missed you to—"

"Excuse me. Miss Altwood?" A photographer with a press badge approaches us. "Can I get a photo of you with your design for the article?"

"Of course, as long as it's okay for my boyfriend to be in it with me? It is his car after all."

"Of course."

Nathan and I stand next to his car, embraced in each other's arms as the photographer directs us, taking several photos to get the perfect angle of us along with my painting.

"I think we got the shot," the photographer says, looking at the display screen on his camera. "Thank you!" He gives a slight bow before disappearing into the crowd to take more photos of the event.

Nathan grabs my hand, gently moving us out out of the way as people brush by us to get a better look at my design. "Uncle Dean called me early this morning and informed me that someone was sneaking into the garage over the weekend." He gives me a pointed look.

"Hmm. Sounds like maybe you should install a better security system," I tease back. "You going to arrest me for breaking and entering? Get me for vandalism?"

"You know I don't want to be a police officer."

"I don't know, babe. Maybe you should reconsider it. I mean, think about all the fun we would have with a pair of handcuffs ... you in a uniform ..." I pull my bottom lip into my mouth and bat my lashes, just for added measure. It's all an act though. I know how much being a mechanic matters to him and I want him to pursue that dream.

Nathan shakes his head, and just smiles, making those adorable dimples appear. "When my uncle saw what you painted, he called me right away, trying to explain it to me but I'm not entirely sure he knew how. I think your work rendered him speechless." Nathan chuckles. "I asked him to just send a picture of it, but all he could say was how much better it would be for me to see it in person. Pretty sure it was his way of teasing me about it. But when I finally did see it after Payson dropped me off ... wow ... was he right."

I tilt my head, gazing at him, wondering if Nathan understands the meaning behind the art. "You get the mural, don't you?"

"It's me... the kneeling person in the middle is me. And the angels are ... they're my mother and brother."

Sensing his sadness over his lost loved ones, I wrap my arms around Nathan, hugging him close to me.

"I painted them touching your shoulders, to show that they're always with you, even when you can't see them. They are always looking over you. I knew when I started sketching out the design, how important it was to incorporate them into the mural because they were so important to you. Plus, I thought you would want them with you as you drive the Chevelle, like you were taking them with you on your travels. The darkness, represents all the pain and grief you've suffered through in your life and where the dark paint blends up into the baby blue? That represents your healing journey you're embarking on. Now, as for the colors flowing from your hands into the two different paths? That came to me over the weekend."

We stand there, my head resting on Nathan's chest as we hold each other, watching people admire my hard work. No words could possibly explain the feeling of having something you poured your heart and soul into being judged by others. No matter what they may say or think about it, there is only one person's opinion on it matters to me most.

His.

"I couldn't sleep this weekend, between you being away and Felix on his revenge path. Art calms my mind and I needed that release. Since my original piece was locked up in Helena's studio, I remembered I needed to work on the mural for your car. You held up your end of our deal, I needed to do the same. Not to mention it felt like the best way to surprise you when you got back into town."

Nathan kisses the top of my head as I take a moment to gather my thoughts, bracing for his reaction with what I'm about to tell him next. "I remembered your confrontation with your dad in the kitchen, about your future and felt how important it was to include it into the mural, a reminder that you should be the one who decides your future. No one else."

"Baby ... ," His voice cracking. "You embodied so much of me into this piece. I-I literally don't know what to say other than you are incredibly gifted."

"You like it?"

"No, baby. I *love* it!"

My heart swells with pride, hearing his confession.

Nathan's eyes move across the hood, taking in every detail of the mural, a smile lighting up his face before it quickly disappears and I sense the change in his mood.

Nathan shifts us, leaning his back against the car door and pulling me so I'm standing between his legs.

"When I heard that ass clown destroyed your original piece, snuffing your opportunity to be a part of this, I wanted nothing more than to head straight to the precinct and ask my dad to give me five minutes alone with him. But Payson made a comment about you not having a backup piece, and well ... baby, I had to try. I had to bring the Chevelle down here and see if you could enter it. I know how much this prize money means to you, Spitfire."

I shake my head, so in awe of this man who has gone to great lengths to prove how much my future matters, a chance to give me back what Felix destroyed.

Nathan reaches for my hands, his eyes glossing over me. "I also heard what happened earlier, Jenna. Sadie called Payson. I don't think I can ever get her terrified screams out of my head, giving us a play by play of what was happening. I'm so ... I'm so sorry I wasn't able to protect you. I should have been there for you, but instead, I-I failed you and for that I am sorry."

A tear falls down Nathan's face, and I brush it away with my thumb as I caress his cheek. "Oh, baby boy. Please don't beat yourself up. You couldn't have known anymore than I did. I'm still standing here, aren't I? I'm still breathing. My heart is still beating." I place his hand over my chest, letting him feel my warm skin as my heart beats in a steady rhythm under the palm of his hand. "I'm here another day to touch you. To kiss you. But more importantly, to love you."

Green eyes dart to mine. "Did ... did you just say you love me?"

I give him my best smile. "I did. I do. If there is anything the past few days has shown me, it's how much I hate not having you around. Missing your hugs. The way butterflies take flight every time you look at me with love and adoration. But above all else, you make me feel protected and safe. I'm sorry I held you at arms length for so long because how much I dislike Chad and Brady, and I will regret the time I've wasted never giving you a chance. But I can't dwell on that too much because we are together now and I see you for who you truly are. I love you so damn much, Nathan Ward, and I don't want to waste another second of time where I don't get to tell you."

"What happens when you leave for college next year? Are we still going to be together or are we taking a hiatus until you graduate?"

The mere idea of Nathan being with anyone else sets the jealous bitch off in me like an atomic bomb. Hell would have to freeze over before I were ever to consider us taking a break, giving any girl a chance to steal away the one person I have ever felt so strongly about.

I grab the front of Nathan's hoodie and drag him so he's on my eye level. "Listen up, Shop Boy, because I'm only going to say this once. You. Are. Mine. Got it?"

The smirk with the dimples in his cheeks reappears. "I only ever want to be yours, Spitfire."

# Epilogue

## Seven Months Later

## Nathan

A few weeks ago, Jenna and I, along with the rest of the senior class, walked the stage to receive our diplomas. We are now free to explore the real world and make something of our lives. No more schoolwork. No more homework. No more school dances and high school drama. Well, at least for most of us. Can't say the same for Brady since he's stuck with Bellwood's drama queen.

Life changed for the better after the weekend of the championship game. My dad and I finally got to sit down and talk about all the shit we said that night in the kitchen. He even came by the shop one day to just watch me in action, and I think it was the verification he needed to be okay with me not going into law enforcement. He apologized for putting that pressure on me, for not being there when I needed him. Of course, I forgave him but on the condition we both took up therapy to help us work through our grief. The both of us see Dr. Hamilton twice a month, and it's definitely helped us on our healing journey. Dad has even cut back on his hours so he can be around more. Our relationship has never been better and will hopefully continue to get better, especially since I'm staying in South Carolina.

I'll be attending a local college to get my certifications as a mechanic as well as my business degree so I can one day take over my grandfather's business, like I envisioned. Classes don't begin until late August, so I'll be busy working with my uncle at the garage, getting all the experience I can get while making money to pay for school.

Right now, though, I'm enjoying a weeklong vacation with Jenna in Key West, Florida. A full week, just the two of us as we enjoy the Florida sun, taking in the sights and spending quality time together. I want to soak up every minute and every second with her this summer before she leaves me for California. Jenna not only got accepted into her dream school, but the mural she painted on my Chevelle helped cover all the costs of her tuition when she won the grand prize in the art competition. Now, Jenna can attend the school she always wanted without the worry of adding debt to her parents finances.

I have one very special moment planned for the woman I love while we are down here, and tonight is that night. I reserved us a table for two on the veranda of the Hot Tin Roof. With their floral centerpieces, low lighting, and a gorgeous view of the ocean, it sets the tone for a romantic evening.

After the host directs us to our table, I help Jenna into her seat before taking my place across from her, giving her chair with the view of the ocean. I don't need any other view than her.

She thinks we are here to celebrate the good news my father shared with us yesterday. He informed us that Felix Martin was sentenced to forty years behind bars without parole. Not only did Jenna face her fears and testify before a jury of what happened to her, but the video footage Helena captured, along with the many testimonies of the brave girls who came forward as victims of Felix, the judge and jury were able to put Felix where he rightfully belongs, unable to harm or terrorize another young lady again.

After the waiter comes to take our drink order, I stare at the beautiful woman across from me, feeling like the luckiest man in the world to be hers.

"This place is beautiful, Nathan," Jenna says in awe, her eyes dancing around the room and taking it all in. "This seems a bit much for a celebration though."

I reach across the table, taking her hand in mine. "I might have fibbed a little about this dinner."

"What do you mean?"

"Jenna ... this is more than a dinner celebration for that monster getting the punishment he deserves. Tonight is solely about you and me ... the love we have for each other." I squeeze her hand gently before reaching into my pocket and pulling out the little black box. Jenna's eyes widen when she sees it, a gasp coming from her pretty mouth.

"Nathan ..."

"Relax, Spitfire. Just let me say what I want to say before you freak out."

"I'm not freaking out." She glowers, but I give her a pointed look in return. Rolling her eyes, she relents from our little stare down before saying, "Whatever," and I chuckle at her fiery persona I love so much.

"Jenna, the main point of this trip is for the two of us to spend as much time together as possible. With the minutes ticking by, I know the summer is going to go by so fast and I'm going to have to let you go off to Cali without me."

"It's not too late for me to switch somewhere closer—"

I hold my hand up, stopping her spiel of changing schools. "You're going to California to your dream school, and you are going to kick ass while you're there. I will not allow you to ditch your dreams for us."

Jenna's eyes well with tears, knowing the toll a long-distance relationship will have on us. Which is why I have the box.

"I don't want to be away from you anymore than you want to be away from me. But I couldn't live with myself if you didn't follow your dreams and one day wake up to resent me for choosing us over that school you've had your heart set on long before us. That is why I got you this."

Grabbing the box, I open it up so she can see the ring sitting inside. It's a white gold double infinity-style band with a perfect round white diamond in the center. Accent gems line the infinity band on each side, adding a little extra sparkle, because my girl deserves the extra sparkle. I remove the ring from the box, holding it in one hand as I hold hers in my other.

"This is a promise ring. A symbol of the love I have for you and *only you*. Let it be a reminder of our love and that no matter how far apart we are, our hearts will always beat for each other. This is my way of saying, I'm all yours. The day you graduate from that college with your degree is the day I will replace this ring with an engagement one, because I plan on asking you for your hand in marriage, Spitfire. Now, before I can place this ring on your finger … do you accept my promise and in return promise to be all mine until graduation day?"

Tears start streaming down her beautiful face as she smiles and nods.

"I need your words, beautiful."

"A thousand times yes, Nathan!" She pulls me toward her, kissing me with all the love she can put into a single kiss. A few couples close to us who must have overheard my little speech clap and cheer, causing Jenna and I to break apart.

With her hand outstretched, I slide the ring onto her ring finger and admire how it sits beautifully on her hand.

"Nathan, this ring is so beautiful … you outdid yourself."

"Did you see the inside?"

"What?"

"I had it engraved. Take a look." I smile at her as she removes the ring to read the interior of it.

"*Forever Your Shop Boy*," Jenna reads aloud. Her eyes raise to look at me, all the love and joy reflecting back in those chocolate pools. "I love you. So, so much."

"I love you infinitely."

Jenna slides the ring back onto her finger before reaching for her phone. Her fingers quickly move across the keyboard before she sets her phone down. A moment later, my phone vibrates in my pocket.

I raise an eyebrow as Jenna stares at me with the sexiest smirk, her delicate chin resting on top of her hands as she eyes me.

Taking out my phone, I open our text thread and read the message she just sent.



> **I brought some of my art supplies with me.**
> **What do you say to a little "therapy" session?**

My eyes shoot up from the message to the sinful woman across from me winking at me. She stands from her chair and walks over to me, leaning in to press a soft kiss.

"I'm going to the ladies room. Why don't you take care of the check so we can go back to our room to create some ... art."

I glance around the room 'til I spot our waiter, waving him over the moment we make eye contact.

"Yes, sir. How may I help you?"

"We're ready for our check now."

# Acknowledgements

First and foremost, I must thank my wonderful husband. Ever since the idea of becoming an author touched my heart and this opportunity came about, he ensured I saw this through every step of the way. Always providing me with love, support and being my rock when I need him to be. Whenever I'm questioning myself, wondering if this dream is really worth it all, he is *always* there telling me it's going to pay off, and to not let life allow me to give up. Having a supportive partner is everything and I'm grateful I have someone like him by my side.

To my four, beautiful children ~ I hope I'm showing you that anything is possible when you put in the work and effort to make it possible. I hope watching me as I achieve this dream motivates you to find your passions and follow through with them. To give it all you have and not let fear stand in your way of achieving what it is your heart truly desires. Chase your dreams and know that your mother is going to be behind you, cheering you on every step of the way.

To my family and friends ~ Thank you for all the love and support you have shown me on this newfound journey of mine. I hope I make you all so proud and give you the bragging rights to say *I'm related/know an author*. Whether you read my work or just buying my work to support me, I am so appreciative that you are just showing your love for me and it does not go unnoticed. But if you do happen to read my books, all I ask is that you try not to look at me differently after reading my work. K? Thanks! Love you!

To Maria ~ Thank you for the All Write Well program and your always positive feedback as I stepped foot into the writing world. I would not be turning this dream into reality if it wasn't for you and the program you have created. I hope I make you proud with my book and all future books to come. I will continue to use what I learned from AWW to help me build this author dream of mine.

To Tracey ~ Thank you for all the advice and help I needed to make sure I showcased Jenna and my POC characters in a way that was respectful and accurate as I never want to offend anyone; just inclusion and diversity.

To my sister, Lex ~ Thank you for not just being there for me throughout our lives, but also for helping me hash out the ideas of Nathan's side of the story, for bouncing all that creativity and helping me find a direction for his part in my story. It was a huge help and Nathan's journey would not have been possible without your ideas. I love you and appreciate your beautiful mind!

Finally, to the readers who took the time to read this book. Thank you for taking a chance on a new indie author. It means the world to me that you chose to read my story. Whether you loved it or felt it could have been better, I appreciate you and thank you! If you could leave an honest review on Amazon and any other social platform, I would greatly appreciate it! Reviews help indie authors such as myself get our books out to more readers.

# About the Author

Dev Hahn is a new indie author who is ready to bring her notebook of story ideas to life and share them with the world. Reading has always been an escape for Dev when her depression became too much or when she just needed to escape reality for a few chapters. She hopes she can do the same for anyone willing to take a chance on her books. Besides reading romance and falling for fictional characters, Dev enjoys watching American football, singing karaoke with her family, iced coffee all year round, and spending quality time with the people she loves most. She's a stay-at-home mother who writes around her children's schedules. She resides in Maryland with her husband, two fur babies and their four children who make life fun, chaotic and entertaining.

# Connect With Me

Be sure to follow me on my socials for updates and new releases!

**Bookbub:** bookbub.com/profile/dev-hahn
**Facebook:** facebook.com/authordevhahn
**Goodreads:**
goodreads.com/author/show/47750634.Dev_Hahn
**Instagram:** instagram.com/authordevhahn/
**Pinterest:** pinterest.com/authordevhahn
**TikTok:** tiktok.com/@author.dev.hahn

# Also By Dev Hahn

**<u>Standalones</u>**
Beyond Broken Colors


**<u>Bellwood Lady Baller Series</u>**
Coming Out on the Sidelines
Catching Feelings in the End Zone, *Coming November 2024*